Praise for Th̶

"… a compelling novel that weaves together fantasy elements with the dark, absurd, and sweet aspects of a family's ordinary life. Alcoholism, divorce, and sibling relationships are touched on realistically and often hilariously; everything is seen through a young teen's point-of-view, and her relative innocence keeps the story from veering too far into adult territory for young readers (although adults will be moved too)."
—Miriam Angress, author of *How Water Speaks to Rock*, and other plays

"Gretchen Wing has a natural talent—a very distinctive voice, great timing and a good punch, creative imagery, and a super sense of humor. I absolutely loved the story…a sensitive and imaginative tale of one girl's struggle to deal with the junk she's been handed by life."
—Michelle Isenhoff, author of the *Divided Decade* trilogy, and the *Song of the Mountain* and *Taylor Davis* series

"Bought this book for my 13-year-old daughter, but both my husband and I gulped it down in a few days…Well written in a convincing teen's voice, and fun, despite the background of serious topics."
—Abigail Porter

"So great! The characters are quickly likable, not syrupy, and very relatable. The author authentically addresses topics all preteens, teens; and even adults can relate to. I loved the genuine relationship interactions between the characters in the book in the midst of the "fantasy" parts…Deals with topics of love, relationship hardship, friendship, and family dynamics in an authentic but PG-rated way. ..A definite recommend."
—Lindsey Webster

THE FLYING BURGOWSKI

Gretchen K. Wing

To Will -- fly high !

MADRONA
BRANCH
PRESS

THE FLYING BURGOWSKI

www.GretchenWing.com
info@GretchenWing.com

Book cover and interior design by
Robert Lanphear
www.lanpheardesign.com

Library of Congress Cataloging-in-Publication Data
Wing, Gretchen K.,

The Flying Burgowski
Gretchen K. Wing

ISBN: 978-0-9991421305

Printed in the USA

To my "boys,"
Ken, McKenzie and Casey.
And to my niece Jocelyn,
for loaning me her name.

ACKNOWLEDGEMENTS

My Tacoma Writers, Leslie Birnbaum, Allen Cox, Deborah McKesson, Matt Rizzo, Tom Wright: you guys got Joss off the ground.

Craig Tenney at Harold Ober and Associates, you gave me the confidence to push on.

My Lopez Writers, Suzanne Berry, Iris Graville, Kathy Holliday, Rita Larom, Ann Norman, Lorna Reese, Helen Sanders: y'all got Joss flying and kept her in the air. She would have crashed a long time ago without you.

Bonny Becker and her YA Fiction Workshop at the Northwest Institute for Literary Arts Residencies: thank you, thank you.

Anah-Kate Drahn: thanks for loaning me your hands.

Virginia Herrick, editor: you've been a joy to work with.

Bob Lanphear, book designer: since I don't have your talents, I'm so grateful I got to use yours.

CONTENTS

FOREWORD

My mom only packed one suitcase, which is how come my dad didn't realize she was leaving.

It wasn't even a suitcase, just a big canvas tote, so he thought she was going to Dalby Thrift Shop to make a donation, like she'd always done with my clothes as soon as I outgrew them. "But Beth, what if you decide to have another baby?" one of the thrift shop ladies asked her once. "Not happening," she shot back, and no one ever asked her again.

That part of the memory's not mine; my brother Michael told me that one. Only recently, actually. And he also admitted it made him cry when she said it, like, is having kids that awful? But I do remember the blue-and-red tote. And Mom and Dad's voices in the kitchen. I don't remember their expressions, because I was staring hard into my cereal, thinking I could make the voices stop. So I remember the cereal: it was a mixture of Kellogg's Corn Flakes and Rice Krispies, which I still love.

Dad's voice, sounding thinner and more fragile than I thought his voice could sound: "Bethany. You can't."

Mom's, more crackly and harsh than ever: "Oh, I know that's usually true. But not this time, for once."

Dad: "What are we supposed to do?"

Mom: "What you always do, Ron. Get along. You guys're way better at it than I am." I remember her scratchy little laugh. "Who isn't?"

You know how memories are, like a CD with a scratch: some things get skipped right over, some things get sped up and connected where they shouldn't be. So I'm sure there was more to the conversation, but I was watching my cereal. So all I have left of that day is this:

Dad: "What do you mean, tired? Haven't I taken care of you? Haven't I lightened your load with the kids so you don't have to worry about anything except what's for dinner? What exactly are you so tired of, Beth?"

Mom: (almost whispering) "I just can't do it anymore."

Across the table from me, Michael started to cry, so I did too.

Dad: "Beth, please. Don't do this. I'll try harder."

She must have picked up her bag then. I think I closed my eyes for that part because the cereal wasn't working. "I have to catch the ferry," she said.

Dad, with a voice like a brick: "Just tell us one thing. Here we are, we're all listening. What is it, huh? Why is it so hard for you to stay with us?"

Mom: "Ron. You have no. IDEA. What I've sacrificed for you."

The door closed. Michael says I sat at the table with my eyes shut until I fell asleep. I was five.

CHAPTER ONE

PRETTY BASIC GHOST

If you think Harry Potter's lame, you might want to stop reading right now.

I know. But some people think that. When this kid in Language Arts told Mrs. Mac, "Harry Potter's lame, I watched the first movie," I couldn't believe it.

"*You're* lame," I told the kid—it was Tyler Howe, total jerk. Mrs. Mac told me not to be rude, but she was smiling so I know she agreed with me.

But my point is, some people can't handle that kind of wildness in a story. And if you're one of them, you won't like mine.

You have been warned.

My name is Jocelyn Olivia Burgowski. I used to sign my name JOB, but I have a way better signature now: The Flying Burgowski. Too bad I don't get to use it.

That's why I'm writing this now. Some things you just have to tell; some secrets eat away at you like rust until you get all weak and crumbly. But already, half a page in, I'm feeling kind of fortified, like someone's giving me a thick new coat of paint. When you're a Flyer you have to find a way to deal with the biggest secret ever. Because you're—I mean, I am—the only one. I know I am. That video we found, back in June? That's just a hoax. Duh.

Harry Potter didn't have to worry about keeping his magic

1

secret; everybody around him was magic too. I'm really more like Spider-Man, but without the tights and the mask and stuff. That *would* be lame. Plus I don't need to grab on to buildings. But I'll share some inside info, so you know I'm not making this up. Number One: When you're flying, the sky smells like lilies. No kidding. And Number Two: Flying doesn't come with instructions, like a new video game. So if it cuts out on you, too bad—no customer support. You're on your own.

The whole flying thing started with dreams, way last spring. Flying dreams. I usually had one after falling asleep re-reading Harry. Next day I'd tell my best friend Savannah about zooming over the clouds or whatever, and she'd go, "Whoa, sounds like the one I had where…" I mean, she could relate. But then the dreams changed and I quit telling about them.

On the last Saturday before the end of middle school, I woke up grabbing my bed frame for dear life. *Whoa. Flying in spirals! Never knew a dream could make you dizzy.* I shuffled into the kitchen wishing Dad still did Saturday pancakes like he did for a couple of years after Mom left. All I found was a note: "M & J, pnck. batter in frig. Do yr. chores. J check vac bag. Back @ 9:30 w/ special present." Well hey, pancake batter. And "special present"? The man was trying. My birthday always seems to wake up his guilt about us not being a Real Family.

Summer Solstice, June Twenty-one: turning fourteen. Finally. When Michael joined me in the kitchen I started planning out loud.

"Hey, so I was thinking of doing a Fortune theme for my party. Like getting someone to do our fortunes with cards and stuff." I turned the stove on, tossed some margarine into a pan and watched it slide around. "'Cause 'fortune' sounds like 'fourteen,' right?"

My brother poured himself a bowl of Cheerios without saying anything. I hate when people don't answer you. Michael does it on purpose.

"Oh, and I can have fortune cookies. Remember those joke ones Mom had once? Think Dad would get me some from the mainland?"

He dumped half the sugar bowl onto his cereal.

"Or we could make 'em! Wonder how they get the little papers in there."

Michael opened the milk carton and sniffed. "This better be better than yesterday's. It was stamped the sixteenth and it was already off." Dad brings us stuff that's too near its expiration date to sell at our store, so we have to watch it. Right then I hoped Michael would get a whole snootful of sour milk.

"Whaddya think?" I asked him right out.

"'Bout what."

That did it. "You know, you sound just like Mom when you do that." That usually gets his attention.

"What the hell is that supposed to mean?" Finally I saw his eyes as he swept the hair away.

"At least she's got an excuse for not listening. At least when you're taking a bunch of pills or something it's not really your fault if your brain's out taking a walk or…or riding a trapeze, or…"

"Shut up, Joss."

"No, you shut up! You're the one who doesn't want to say anything! Fine. I can plan my party without you *or* Mom, or anybody!" *Great, now I sound like a ten-year-old.* The pan started smoking so I dumped the whole bowl of batter in.

"Hah!" Michael sat up straight. "You think Mom wants to have anything to do with your party? Dude, you're delusional. Remember last year? Your ultra-original Harry Potter theme and you tried to get her to dress up like a witch? Oh, *that* worked out great, huh?"

"That wasn't my fault!" The giant pancake bubbled like crazy. "She was all into the idea, I thought she'd love it…"

I'd thought she would. A month before my party, last year, she'd sounded enthusiastic. "Harry Potter, huh? You know I haven't read 'em, but I think I'm the only person on earth who hasn't. So go for it, babe." Yeah, that must have been the beer talking.

"Can you dress up too, Mom?" I'd asked on the phone. "All the guys are wizards and all the girls are witches, so you're a witch."

She had laughed her funny, scratchy laugh. "Always wondered when my daughter would start calling me that. Sure, babe, I'll be a witch. What time does your thing start?"

She'd come all the way from McClenton, nice and sober, dressed as a witch. Long, fake nose and warts and scraggly wig. Too bad I hadn't told her the Harry Potter witches don't look like that. How was she supposed to know? So the third girl who pointed this out to her, Molly, got an earful.

"Well, *you're* witchy enough," Mom had snapped at Molly, and her warty nose and the wig went sailing across the living room. "What *do* these Harry Potter witches do, then? Fly on broomsticks?"

"Oh, yes!" Poor old Molly had thought Mom had finally figured it out. "Here, you can use mine if you want."

I absolutely hate it when people bring up bad memories. Like you really need help with that.

"Oh, loved it, she did," Michael said in his snottiest Yoda voice. He drank a mouthful of Cheerios and talked right through them. "Threw the broomstick right through the window, she did. Good one, Joss. Way to make your loving mom look like a psycho in front of all your friends."

"Dad said it wasn't my fault," I insisted. Pancakezilla sent up a scorchy smell—hopeless. I turned off the burner . "He said it was a tough time for her. So that's how I know he still loves her."

All our fights ended up here sooner or later.

"Oh, grow up, Joss," my brother snorted. "You said it yourself—you think Mom's a mess, and so does Dad. Shee-it. Why would Mr. Perfect want to re-hitch himself to a druggie alky?"

"She's not a druggie, she just has issues with self-control sometimes, Dad knows that..."

"Yeah he does. Which is how come he likes Lorraine now. That lady's never had an 'issue' in her life."

"They're just friends! Dad said so."

"Keep dreaming, babycakes," Michael smirked. "You saw how he touched her shoulder last week when she came in for flour. Mr. and Mrs. Perfect, that's what they'd be, and Mom—"

"No way. You didn't hear him on the phone with Mom yesterday. He sounded..." I looked for the right word. "...tender. He asked if she was coming for my birthday, said he'd pick her up from the ferry. Why'd he say that if he was interested in Lorraine?"

"So is she?" Michael asked nastily. "Coming for your birthday?"

"She—she said she'd try," I said, "but Dad said she really meant it 'cause—"

Michael cut me off. "Whatever, babycakes. Enjoy your happy-rainbow life. I gotta go clean out the shed or Mr. Perfect will go ballistic on me. And you better vacuum." He slammed out.

"Dad!" I'm not a snitch, but Michael was asking for it. I crossed the kitchen to pull back the quilted curtain that separates us from the back of the store. Dad calls it our front door since so many people come in that way, sticking their heads in to say hi while they stop off for milk or fishing lures.

There sat the empty cash register stool, guarding the darkened aisles.

Shoot. Dad's note. I had forgotten.

Well, I wasn't about to vacuum since Michael told me to, so I stomped back into the kitchen. Dumped the nasty pancake. Called Savannah—her cell phone rang twice and quit. We get a crappy signal out here on Dalby Island.

5

"Fine," I said aloud. "I'll just bike over to Louis's." Louis doesn't have a phone, but he does have a built-in easygoing streak. Just the distraction I needed.

It was hot and dusty in the shed where Michael was lugging out piles of old fishing net. *Hah.*

"Where'd you put the bikes?" I asked him. He pointed with his chin, not bothering to answer.

Sure enough, my bike was around the back of the shed. With two flat tires.

"Whyn't you *tell* me?" I yelled, spoiling for another fight. But Michael only shrugged, dumped his load, and went back in for another. I stood there in the sunny yard feeling as flat as my tires. *Fine, I'll vacuum. Maybe that'll help.*

When I was little I pretended the vacuum was a rampaging hungry alligator, but now I'm turning fourteen, it's just another chore. Jabbing the machine around, I thought, *What's the matter with me?* Half the kids in my class have stepparents or parent-boyfriends or -girlfriends. Louis's mom seems like she lives with a new boyfriend every week. Why shouldn't my dad like Lorraine if he wanted to?

Because she's the librarian. *She thinks she's the smartest person on the island,* my brain tried. *She just wants Dad because he's all buff and manly and she's tired of people making librarian jokes.*

Even I knew that was ridiculous.

If Michael's right, Dad's not going to try to get back together with Mom. Ouch. Yeah. But Michael was just being snarky. Even he didn't believe ex-fisherman Ron Burgowski could trade someone as wild and fun as Mom for a whispery mouse like Lorraine.

Yeah, that wildness and fun-ness of hers…which will it lead to first, getting fired, or a wreck on I-Five?

All of a sudden the vacuum wouldn't suck up anything, not even a stupid dust bunny, and I realized I'd forgotten to check the bag even after Dad's note, so now it was all stuck with gunk and

I was going to have to unplug it and poke all the crud out with a chopstick. I shouted, "Damnit!" and yanked the top open and the bag detached and all the stuff I'd fed to the alligator last week got regurgitated all over the living room rug.

"Screw you," I hissed. I left the vacuum sitting in its own mess and slammed into my room to re-read Harry Potter Book Three. Reading helps a horrible day pass by. And Book Three's my favorite, the last one with a really happy ending. Kills me that Book Seven is a whole year away. It better end happy too…

"Whoa, check out this video!" Michael was calling from the living room. I hadn't heard him come in—Harry was meeting the hypogriffs. I wanted to remind Michael that he's been banned from web-surfing for, like, ever. But a new video…? I joined him.

"Says it was filmed here!" Michael's hair was so sweaty it stuck where he'd pushed it back. He hit the "play" arrow and a pale, fuzzy image started moving up a dark incline while a voice whispered something too low to hear. Then: "There she goes!" the voice said distinctly, and the image seemed to leap and disappear. The rest of the video was plain darkness, with the voice repeating, "Did you see that? Did you see that?"

"Did you see that?" Michael echoed.

"What is it? One of those ghost videos? We watched a ton of 'em at Savannah's birthday party."

"No, dude, she flies. I mean she takes off. One second she's walking and the next, *vroom*. Ghosts don't *take off*."

"Show me again." We watched it about five more times. It was pretty lame, just this slightly-lighter shape moving sort of upward, and then: step, step, boom. Gone. "The guy just moved the camera," I said. "Anybody could do that." But there was something about that last move…step, step, boom. "One more time," I demanded.

"Yeah, I know, pretty fakey," Michael admitted. "But dude, it's Dalby." He pointed to the video title: *Dalby Island Ghost?* "Wonder who made this?"

"Zoom in," I demanded. "I wanna see her feet."

"Can't zoom a video," Michael grunted. "But it's her face I want to see. Don't you think she looks kinda like…"

"Mom, yeah. The way she, like, bounces when she steps… Show it again."

"Ha, Mom in a nightgown! Let's send it to her."

We looked at each other. I know, it was idiotic. What would Mom want with a grainy fake-ghost video? But it felt like back when we used to stick together.

"Yeah, okay," I said, and watched Michael hit "forward" and type in Mom's email address. "But then you better go finish the shed. Dad's gonna kill you if he sees you online."

"Not if nobody tells him." Michael gave me his dangerous look. I'm not scared of him, but it was pretty nice of him to show me the video, so I nodded. "Nothin' wrong with a little surfing," he added.

"Is that how you found the thing? Wonder why we didn't find it at Savannah's when we were looking for stuff like that."

"Duh, Joss. Someone must've just posted it." He got up, stretched, and slouched himself back outside.

I was too distracted to snap back at him for saying "duh." What was it about that last second of the video, the step, step…? I plopped myself down, went to "History" and found it again. Even with the volume turned way up, you still couldn't hear anything the filmer said until "There she goes!" *How does he know it's a she?* I wondered. *Looks like a pretty basic ghost to me. Really, nothing like Mom except for that bouncy step-step.* That felt…familiar. My brain couldn't place it, but my stomach seemed to recognize it, a kind of lurch…

Whatever! I switched over to my Harry Potter fan site to read about the delays in the latest movie. Might be a crappy day, but I, at least, was not banned from the internet. And Harry made me forget about vacuums and messed-up parents and girlfriends for a whole hour. Till Dad came home with my special present.

CHAPTER TWO

IRONY

B y the way, if you think I write kind of mature for a four-teen-year-old, I accept the compliment. Mrs. Mac thinks I'm a terrific writer. Too bad no one else respects me.

"Sweet Little Fourteen," Mom called me on our last phone call. She must've heard me scowling, 'cause she followed up, "What? Is someone already getting sensitive about her age?"

Damn, I hate when people talk about you like a narrator and a psychiatrist and a kindergarten teacher all rolled together. I've never been to a psychiatrist, but Mom's been to plenty—like that's helped. But when I go, "Mommm!" she acts hurt, like, *What did I do?* And that makes my stomach feel like I swallowed a rock. Which is the main reason it didn't work out for Michael and me to stay with her in McClenton.

There were other reasons, but I'll get to that.

Before the last visit (if you call that disaster we just crawled home from a "visit") we used to go to Mom's every few months, unless she "can't handle us right now"—that's how Dad put it. In my opinion, she said something way worse and he was covering for her.

Mrs. Mac says if you're writing something, you don't need to say In My Opinion, because you're writing it, so who else's opinion could it be? She says it makes our writing sound immature, and if we absolutely can't stop ourselves from writing it, at least we should go back and erase it before our final draft. So I might do that.

At that McClenton school I went to, the kids had never heard of Dalby Island. When I explained it was one of the Santa Inez

Islands, they said, "Santa Inez? You're from Mexico?" Yeah, it does sound pretty Spanish-y for Washington State, but it's only a couple hours from McClenton! Still, I found out that the only people who have heard of our little island are the tourists who come for weekends and ride their bikes around.

Mom had never heard of Dalby Island either, till she met Dad at a bar in Seattle. She lived here with us till I was five. But now she's "Rentin' in McClenton," as she likes to say. In my opinion, Mom makes a lot of jokes that aren't funny. She works for the Boeing Company, which makes airplanes, but my mom doesn't do that. She cleans the bathrooms. "Yeah," she'll say, "I really thought Boeing would help my career 'take off,' but instead it's gone right into the toilet. Irony, huh?"

Mrs. Mac told us "irony" is one of those terms that's easier to give examples of than it is to define. So she showed us some *Far Side* cartoons: a wrecking ball swinging back and crushing the crane it's attached to. An astronaut waving his arms to celebrate a successful moon-walk and accidentally smashing his partner's face mask. And we made up our own examples: a fire station burning down, or a police station getting robbed. Then she said, if we have to define "irony," we should write this down: Irony = one part "ha ha" + one part "ouch."

Dad thought that marrying my mom and bringing her to nice, quiet Dalby would settle her down some. He thought having Michael would free her locked-up maternal instincts, and they'd come dribbling out with her breast milk.

Ha ha. Ouch.

So I was happily *not* thinking about parents, deep into a web interview with Alan Rickman, that spooky actor who plays Professor Snape, when the kitchen door crashed open, jolting me out of Hogwarts.

"G'mornin'!" called Dad. I hurried into the kitchen to find him hovering on the doorsill, smiling so wide his whole face looked like it was on vacation. He was wearing that silky blue shirt we got him for Christmas. Michael appeared from his room.

"Hey," we chorused. Michael sounded suspicious, but my heart leapt up in that birthday way. *Where's my surprise?*

"You guys make pancakes?" Dad asked. Still he stayed in the doorway.

"Um, yeah." Remembering my trashed breakfast, I realized I was starving. "Where've you been? How come you left the store closed? Why're you dressed up?"

"Oh, I've been out…taking care of something." His eyes can really sparkle. "Are you ready for an early birthday present, Joss? Well, it's more for me, really…well, no, it's for all of us…"

"You got the boat!" Michael actually gasped.

"Boat?" Dad looked confused, then laughed. "Oh! Hah! The trawler? No, son, sorry—that *would* be a surprise, if someone had left that kind of money in my bank account."

Michael and I looked at each other. Who knows how long this would have kept up, Dad leaning in the doorway like an immature Santa, if a voice hadn't spoken from behind him: "For goodness' sake, Ron, quit teasing them and let me come inside."

A quiet voice. Calm. A librarian's voice.

Which is exactly who walked into our kitchen: Lorraine the Librarian. Smiling a smile as calm as her voice. Wearing a very un-librariany green Chinese sheath dress, her long hair pinned back with something sparkly.

"We got married," Dad said. "Surprise!"

Things didn't go too well after that.

My friend Greta's mom makes plates, not the kind you eat off of, but the kind you set up on a special display stand and put on a shelf. In my opinion, people who have to set themselves up like one of those fancy dishes are sending you a message: Number One: I'm more special than you. And Number Two: Don't even think I'm ever going to match with your plain old patterns.

That's how I felt about Lorraine the Librarian.

I didn't always. Mom used to take me to Saturday Story Time back when I was little, and I remember liking how Lorraine's hair would drip over her arm as she held the picture book out to us, how she'd have to swoop it away.

That was a long time ago. These days she just shushes me and Savannah when we whisper over the library computers. And her hair's hardly red anymore; in the light from the doorway it looked more gray than anything. She'd probably call it *silver*, in that soft, shushy voice.

She's old. Her voice is way too soft. This can't be happening.

Here's how the rest of the morning went: Dad received our congratulations in the same way they were meant, meaning by the time we were done his happy-Santa face had closed into something hard and sharp. Lorraine started making tea in our kitchen without even asking where we kept anything, like she'd been doing it all along. I turned for comfort to my natural ally, following my beloved brother into the living room. He responded, "What the hell's the matter with you? Shee-it. You telling me you didn't see this coming?" So much for alliance.

Dad bribed us back into the kitchen with cocoa, but it didn't sweeten the atmosphere any. And I sure wasn't hungry anymore. Luckily even marriage wasn't enough to keep the store closed on a Saturday in June, so after some awkward sitting and watching our new stepmother drink tea, Dad noticed the vacuum cleaner gunk and sent everyone back to work. Lorraine went too; I guess Saturday Story Hour didn't quit after I grew out of it. "'Bye, guys," she murmured as she left, and we kind of grunted at her.

"Well, wasn't that special," Michael snorted as soon as we were alone. "Guess I don't have to get you a birthday present now that you've had such a great surprise, huh."

"That wasn't for me—"

"Damn straight it wasn't. But I told you so."

"Why do you think that makes it better?"

"Why do you think you're such a moron?"

"Why am I hearing this crap in my store?" Dad was standing at the curtain, and his smile and twinkle were long gone. "I got folks in here waiting on me to ring 'em up," he added. "Michael, shake a leg, the shed's not done. Joss, finish that dusty mess and feed the cat, she's driving me nuts in here."

"But Michael said…"

You'd think a guy who everybody says is The Nicest Guy wouldn't be able to hunker his eyebrows down on his nose like that, but you'd be wrong.

"Do you mind? Or is the prospect of domestic bliss just too much for you two to handle?" Then he disappeared back behind the curtain.

"Jerk," I hissed at Michael.

"Moron," he muttered back. But he headed for the shed, and I cleaned up the vacuum-vomit in slow motion, my stomach oozing downward.

When I finished, I sat down at the kitchen table, resting my head on my arms. Tried to think about my birthday party. But my thoughts kept getting stuck. *He got married. Without telling you. He thought it was a special surprise.*

After a while, the cat climbed up my shoulders and lay on my neck. Her name's Tion 'cause I wanted to name her Toyger since she looks like a miniature jungle cat, but Michael wanted to call her Liger, which is totally unoriginal, so Mom said what about Tion. That's right—a compromise from Mom. It happened two years after she left, when I was seven, when she still felt kind of responsible for us. *And now, with Lorraine around, she won't have to.*

Tion's weight pressed my thoughts into another rut.

Call her, my brain said. *It's Saturday morning.*

Yeah, but what if she's out?

Leave a message, stupid, like you always do.

What am I gonna say? *"Hi, Mom, just thought you'd want to know your cat's on my head. Oh, and by the way, Dad got married."*

...Like that's not exactly what she's been waiting to hear. No more stupid ferry boats. No more need to pretend to be all better...

There's still me, I thought fiercely. She'll still want to make herself better so she can come back to be with me.

Yeah, right, said my brain, and it didn't even need to use Michael's voice to say so. It was my own brain, after all. So I retreated back to Harry and read till my eyes got heavy.

"There she goes! There she goes!" But the voice meant me, as I rocketed out of the dark trees and into a sky still glowing with the leftovers of sunset. And Harry right beside me, but no brooms—just our bodies sliding through air that flowed without ripples or wind. Harry reached his hand out and grasped mine, green eyes shining in the early starlight, and I smelled the rich, sour mud of low tide...

Tion woke me, meowing cat-breath in my face just as we were wheeling to fly into a huge half-moon. It was past noon and I had forgotten to feed her. What a jerk. What an idiot. *Harry's a guy in a book. You can't smell in dreams. And you can't fly.*

I was groggily eating cereal for lunch when the phone rang.

"Hey babe."

"Mom?" *Wait—I hadn't called her, had I? Oh jeez—so she still didn't know about Dad.* "Hey," I said, weakly.

"Joo sen' me anemail?" she slurred.

Uh-oh. I knew that sound. "Email?" I repeated.

"Jooguys senme avideo? Tha' was so thofful of you. Thoughtful. Really really really.

Muss've watched it twenny times." She laughed like a hysterical horse.

"Mom, you're..." I've never been able to talk about her "issues," okay? Even when I'm not already depressed. "Did Dad call you?"

"No, swee'ie. 'Mm callin' you, notcher dad. So thofful of you, muss've watched it thirty times."

Oh, that stupid ghost video! I'd forgotten all about it. "We thought you'd get a kick out of it, Mom. But it's dumb, I know." No way was I telling her about Dad and Lorraine right now, if she was already...this way...by lunchtime.

"Wanna tell your brother how thoff...thought-ful. Michael there?"

"No, Mom," I lied. I had no idea where Michael was, but he didn't need this any more than I did. I managed to get off the phone by telling her I had to feed Tion, even though I already had.

So, my brother and I had shared a bonding moment over that ghost video and sent it to Mom for a laugh. She was laughing all right, with the help of her favorite substance. Ha ha. Ouch. And I could fly away from this crappy pre-birthday Saturday in awesome dreams, but when I woke up, I had a drunk mom who didn't need me and a sober new stepmom I didn't need. Ha ha...

You get the idea.

CHAPTER THREE

WHAT ARE FRIENDS FOR?

This was the start of my Week From Hell.

Mom says "Week From Hell" a lot. Whenever we talk on the phone, she goes, "Oh, well, babe, this is the Week From Hell, I'm just trying to make it till Friday." That used to reassure me, like, *if Hell's that common, what's the big deal?*

Turns out, Hell has lots of weeks. But last June, it was my first one. And it brought out my...let's say hidden talents. But if you think magical power fixes everything—sorry. It didn't fix Harry Potter's problems and it didn't fix mine.

Oh, I *saved* Mom all right, and it was a total rush. I just don't think I *fixed* her. I still have no clue why she's such a mess. Or what to do about it.

Mrs. Mac has a satellite picture-map of Washington in her room, everything tiny but perfectly laid out. Dalby Island is this little green squiggle, surrounded by the bluest ocean that looks fake until you focus on the tiny white flecks and realize they are real ferryboats, lumbering along, crammed with people.

But I could never find McClenton on that map. It sort of fuzzes into this grayish mass that must be buildings and freeways and Boeing, but I can't tell where it begins or ends.

That's what Mom wanted, maybe. Something fuzzy to disappear into, after ditching Dalby Island, and us.

Dad grew up here, so everyone knows him and he couldn't disappear if he wanted to. He runs the Quik-Stop Convenience Store in the village, which is not like a 7-Eleven even though it sounds like one. Dalby has so few stores that "convenience" has to mean more than a hot dog and a Big Gulp like in McClenton. It means twelve different kinds of herb tea, and a whole aisle of fishing lures.

Dad hates it. He doesn't complain, but I can tell. When the fishermen come in, the few who are left, he leans on the cash register and gabs away about the weather and the catch, and he asks about their boats by name like they were wives or something. Dad used to be a fisherman, but he lost his boat when my Grandpa Al died—just when Dad was supposed to take it over from Grandpa and be captain. He didn't lose it in a wreck or a giant tsunami, like I used to think. He lost it to Fidelity National Bank. In my opinion, Dad never got over having his destiny scribbled out like that.

But I thought he was happy enough with me and Michael. Or plotting how to get back to our little family of four. The real one.

That's what my brain was stuck on that morning in the kitchen, and would have stayed stuck all day, if Louis hadn't saved me by barging through the curtain. Most people stick their heads through first, but Louis Cleary isn't most people.

"Got any milk?" He opened the fridge without waiting for an answer.

"Sure," I said. He could drink the whole gallon, I was so glad to see him. "Guess what?"

Louis didn't answer me right away, but not in a jerky way like Michael; he was just too busy glugging milk straight from the jug. He and his mom have goats, and wow, their milk tastes just like they smell. So Louis loves our milk to death. Watching him, I felt my stomach lightening up.

"What?" he said finally, wiping his mouth with his arm and

putting the jug back in the fridge. Then he poured some corn flakes into his hand and started munching them like a horse with a feed bucket. Louis's mom, Shasta, is the original Dalby Hippie Health Food Lady type, so he never gets to eat regular stuff. Last time I was over there for lunch, Shasta made Seven Grain Cereal sandwiches from the glop of their leftover breakfast. Kids at school don't even bother to tease Louis anymore. About his lunches, anyway.

"My dad got married to Lorraine," I told him. My stomach sank again, hearing that.

"Oh," said Louis. He didn't ask me how I felt; if he had I probably would've started crying and totally embarrassed us both. Instead he licked his hands and asked me, "Wanna go to the Toad?"

I looked at him in surprise. The Toad had been our best buddy, Louis and me, since we were old enough to ride bikes together. Hidden by scruffy woods from the tourists' sight, the Toad rose granite-y, lichen-covered, and majestic, offering itself to any kid with an urge to climb and a good imagination. The Toad had been a castle, Narnia, Middle Earth, back to a castle again (Hogwarts), and always, always, just a benevolent Toad. But we hadn't visited our lumpy old friend for a couple of years.

"Yeah." Suddenly, I did want to go. "I have some homework, though."

"Who gives homework the last week of school?" Louis demanded, reaching for another go-round of corn flakes. "Oh. Right."

Louis is a year behind me, so back last June he was still in seventh grade while I was finishing eighth. His writing looks like worm-wriggles, though, so we'd talked about how much trouble he was going to have with Mrs. Mac—the only teacher who assigns homework the last week of school.

"But I can do it later," I decided. "Yeah, let's go. I just have to tell Dad." *Yeah…and while you're at it, want to mention that little phone call from Mom?*

The familiar smell of dusty cans hit me when I thrust my head through the curtain into the store. Dad was sitting on his stool behind the register holding a newspaper in front of his face. The usual bike-tourists were wandering around the aisles.

"Me and Louis are going biking."

He nodded without looking up. I use that move all the time when I'm at Mom's.

"By the way…" What was I going to say? *Mom's drunk again. She hasn't even heard about your marriage yet, but it's still your fault.* My stomach hurt.

"Oh, never mind," I said, and let the curtain fall back in place. Then: "Oh shoot, my tires!" But I was in no mood to deal with patching and pumping. "Never mind, I'll just take Michael's." It's way too big for me and he would kill me if he found out, but I didn't care.

We heard Michael cussing out back where he couldn't see us, so I guess Working On The Shed wasn't going too well. *Serves you right,* I thought. But next moment I was swinging my leg over and reaching for the pedal, and the sun felt gorgeous. Someone's fresh-cut hay was scenting up the air, and my heaviness seemed to slide away behind me. There were zero clouds anywhere and the wind in our faces was soft as baby animals. We hit the big downhill on the way to the Toad's woods and I stood tippy-toe on the pedals. *Almost as good as that last flying dream!* I was in a decent mood by the time we reached the Toad.

Something wasn't right, though. Louis and I looked at each other as we leaned our bikes against the biggest tree. We pushed through the brush to where the great swelling of rock ballooned out, green-gray and furry with reindeer lichen still wet from dew.

Voices! Low but unmistakable, coming from the back of the Toad. No other bikes in sight. *Did someone walk here from the other side? Who?* This was our special place.

Up we climbed. Each foothold reminded me of past fantasies:

in that crevice we had decorated a tiny palace for Louis's collection of miniature unicorns, complete with chandelier made from lichen and huckleberries. That mossy hummock was sacred to the Goddess Shannarabistra, to whom we brought offerings of Cheetos. All the way up the memories followed me, like the Toad was flipping through my childhood album. Then someone laughed, up and down like a piano scale, and I recognized the sound.

So did Louis. "What's she doing here?" he demanded.

Savannah and Louis aren't enemies, but they sure aren't friends. She's never been in the group that teases him, but she's friends with people who are—like Nate Cowper and Tyler Howe. Dalby School is so small you can actually be friends with boys without everyone thinking you *like* them, but Nate and Tyler started acting different last year and messed everything up. They actually started keeping a Top Ten Titty List—I know because Mrs. Mac took it away from them in Language Arts and they got in trouble because they tried to steal it back from her desk. How can you be friends with someone who's listed you as "Itty Bitty?" "They're just being idiots," Savannah had said, rolling her eyes. "They listed me as 'Luscious Lemon,' how dumb is that?" But she didn't quit talking to them.

Louis was still looking at me, poised in midcrawl three-quarters up the Toad. "How's she know the way here?"

I felt myself blush. When I said it was our special place...I lied, okay? I did take Savannah here—once.

It had been last winter break and we were totally bored. We'd walked over to the Angstroms' farm to ride their donkey until it started raining, so we came back and started messing around with Michael's Legos till finally Savannah said she couldn't believe I was still into this baby stuff. Instead of telling her off, like, *Oh, you mean I should get all excited about your new cell phone that barely works half the time?* I said, "Fine. Let's go somewhere."

We went on foot and took the shortcut, which is through the woods and kind of brambly, so Savannah was scratched and wet and grumpy by the time we got there. Not me; I was revved up from being outside again, even in the rain, and excited to finally introduce my best friend to the Toad.

What an idiot. I forgot there was a reason I'd never introduced her to it in the first place.

"That's it? You just climb up on here and…play Let's Pretend?" It didn't help that the top of the Toad is out in the open, so we were getting totally rained on.

"We don't *play*," I lied. "We just talk and stuff. You know. Like you and me do."

"Why here?" Savannah snorted. "This is so immature. I can't believe you just hang out on a rock all day with Louis. Jeez, Joss. No wonder…"

"No wonder what?" I asked, even though I already knew I wasn't going to like the answer.

My best friend, hair flattened wetly on her face, looked at me with pity. "Don't take this the wrong way, 'kay?" she said. "It's just, everyone says Louis is so weird, and if you hang out with him, well, it's no wonder they think…"

"I'm weird? Maybe I like being weird," I told her defiantly. But I wasn't ready for the next part.

"No, you've always been weird," Savannah said. "That's why I like you, girlfriend. But Joss, you're just so immature sometimes. Hanging out on a rock, just making up stuff… Sometimes I think you're the same exact person you've always been."

I was so flabbergasted my mouth hung open. The same person? Who else was I supposed to be?

Savannah took my silence for something else. "Don't be mad at me, I'm just telling you what other people think, okay? Hey, you're still my Bestie. But I am so frickin' wet. Your rock is cool. Really. But can we go home now?"

Now here she was again, and Louis wanted to know why.

"I dunno," I lied. Explanation was only going to mess things up worse. I concentrated on trying not to rip the lichen with my shoe.

I guess Savannah thought my rock *was* cool—cool enough for mature people like Nate and Tyler. That's who was up there.

As we crawled up the haunches of the Toad, we could hear their voices clearly, even though we couldn't see them. They were sitting behind one of the Toad's eye-lumps, where a thick pad of moss makes a natural cushion.

Savannah has such a musical laugh, Mrs. Mac calls her Miss Mozart. Lately I've heard her drawing the notes out on purpose, like she wants you to notice how pretty it is. She was laughing that way now.

"…and the dumbass actually thought *he* killed Kenny," I heard Tyler say.

Beside me, Louis looked stunned. "They're talking about *South Park*," I whispered, even though I knew that Louis had never watched that show for the simple reason that his mom doesn't own a TV and I, his only friend, have a dad who won't pay for cable. I'd watched *South Park* at Savannah's before; it's gross, but pretty funny. But that's not what was bothering Louis.

"Let's get out of here," he whispered back, and turned to scramble down.

I grabbed the end of his T-shirt. "No, wait. I wanna talk to them." Not true; I wanted to throw them off the Toad and into the blackberries, but talking seemed like a good start.

Louis stared at me, his little blue eyes all squinched up in his freckles like they were scared of getting punched. As far as I know no one's actually hit Louis since second grade, but in my opinion there are other ways to beat someone up. *Who does Savannah think she is, bringing those jerks here?*

"C'mon." I turned back to the top of the Toad, clutching Louis's shirt so he had to follow me. He yanked himself free, but he came.

The three of them sat enthroned on the moss-cushion, looking out over Dalby Harbor like they owned the view. I know because that's how it makes me feel when I sit there. You can see the whole sweep of it, from the far spit which encloses the harbor, to the little forest of masts which grows thicker when the Summer People come. Away to the right runs the skinny channel that connects our harbor to the Strait of Juan de Fuca and the Real Pacific Ocean, as Mrs. Mac told us, where Washington State is the Number One Asian Trade Partner of all the United States. It's what Dad looks at through the store window: the place where he should have been driving his boat every morning and evening instead of sitting on his stool.

"Hey, what's up," I said, striding around to block their view.

Savannah squealed. She was sitting cross-legged next to Tyler and wouldn't meet my eyes.

"Hey, Hamburger," Tyler said lazily. He and Nate have all these cute little nicknames based on people's last names. Mine's from Burgowski, isn't that clever? And of course Louis is Queery.

"Nice piece of real estate you got here," said Nate. In my opinion he could be Orlando Bloom's younger brother, but who cares since he's such a jerk, which I'm totally sure Orlando Bloom never was.

"It's not for sale," I said, narrowing my eyes.

Savannah was recovering fast. "Hope you don't mind I shared your spot," she said gaily. "It's hella better in the sunshine, huh?"

I could feel Louis looking at me.

"What're you guys doing here?" I snapped. Pretty stupid, but there wasn't much to start a confrontation with.

"What's it look like, duh," said Tyler of the Most High Intelligence.

"Chillin'," shrugged Nate.

"You don't own this place, Joss," said my best friend Savannah.

"Yeah, well," put in Louis's high voice, "at least we know better than to sit on wet moss."

Me and Louis don't mind getting our skinny butts damp to sit there enjoying our realm. It dries, doesn't it? But he was right to think our three buddies wouldn't feel that way. They leaped up like the moss was red-hot instead of just wet, and I was pleased to see that the Toad had left his mark on Savannah's white shorts. The guys cussed, but Savannah laughed again.

"Oh, well," she sang. "Guess I should've called you for advice before coming here, huh?"

Yes, you should, I wanted to tell her. *You should've used up some precious minutes on your little red phone so I could tell you, don't you dare take those jerks to hang out on my rock after telling me how immature it is!* I tried to send that message through my eyes, but she wouldn't look at me.

"Hey, I know what!" Savannah kept going. "You should have your party up here, Joss! Really! It's the solstice next week, right? We can make, like, a fire up here..."

"I'm—not—" I spluttered. *I'm not polluting the Toad with a stupid campfire. I'm not ever in a million years inviting Tyler and Nate to my birthday. I'm not ever speaking to you again if you don't shut up.* Too many words tried to force themselves out and got stuck.

"What's solstice?" Tyler wanted to know.

"Oh, you know..." Nate smiled slowly. "It's Midsummer Night, like that play Mrs. Mac made us read. Longest day of the year. When everyone's supposed to think about sex and stuff," except he didn't use the word "stuff." He elbowed Tyler. "Fertility rites, dude."

Savannah's laugh set some kind of record. "No, you idiot, I don't mean that! I just think it would be totally cool to have a fire. You're supposed to have a fire on the solstice, right, Louis? Don't you know about stuff like that?"

"Yeah, Queery, tell us what you know about fertility rites," said Tyler.

Louis took a step backward.

"You. Guys. Are. NOT. Invited." That's what my mouth said. My eyes kept telling Savannah, *Shut up, shut up, shut up.*

"Oh, wow, Burger, that hurts my feelings," said Nate. He has the absolutely longest eyelashes I've ever seen on a guy. "Guess we better have our own rites, Ty."

"Don't be such idiots," Savannah told them, which meant she was finally soaking up my telepathy. "You guys go on, okay? Me and Joss are going to hang out, we don't want you." She ignored Louis.

I said nothing.

"Well, thrilling as it's been, we gots to be gone," Nate said, and Tyler grunted, "Whatever," and the two of them ambled down the Toad's snout, joshing each other to show it was their idea.

"Joss-I'm-sorry-I-forgot-you-don't-like-them-please-don't-be-mad-at-me-'kay?" said Savannah all in one breath as soon as the boys had disappeared. "I know you don't want them at your party, I'm sorry, it just came out," she added before I could respond.

It's what Mrs. Mac taught us to do when we're writing a Persuasive Essay: pretend you're about to have a showdown at high noon with another cowboy, and you have to shoot the weapons out of his hands before he gets to take a shot at you.

My best friend Savannah is very smart.

"'S okay," I grumbled. What else could I say? "I just wish you hadn't brought 'em here," I added, seeing her brighten up so quickly.

"Oh, don't worry," Savannah said, nodding confidently. "They're *guys.* They won't come back, there's nothing here."

Louis stared at her with an expression I'd never seen on his face before, his eyes like arrows of ice. Savannah took no notice.

"So they're not coming to my party," I repeated, just to make it clear I'd won the battle.

My bestie said, "Oh, of course not," and no one talked about fires anymore. The three of us just stood there for a while in the sun, fiddling with the lichen on the Toad's eye-hump.

This is the part where I should've gone on home with Louis, maybe fed him some exotic food like a salami sandwich. But sometimes you spend all day thinking the world is being a jerk to you, only to find out you might be the meanest jerk of all.

Louis said he had to go, and I just said, "Okay, see ya." After he left, I got Michael's bike and followed Savannah through the brambles where hers was parked.

We went to her house. My excuse was, I wanted some sympathy. Savannah's got both parents, still married and everything, so she could understand how horrible my life was going to get with Lorraine as a stepmom.

It didn't work out that way. Savannah didn't see what the big deal was.

"Hey, think about it, Joss, your dad'll be in a good mood all the time, he'll let you spend the night on school nights prob'ly." She didn't see anything wrong with Lorraine either. "Don't you like the way her hair smells? Like apple blossom shampoo or something. I want to get some."

"Yeah, but now my mom..." The memory of her horrible phone call sucker-punched me. *Yeah, like I'm going to tell ANY-ONE about that—not Savannah, not Louis, not Michael, not even Dad.* It wasn't that I was afraid of crying if I did. I was afraid I might not be able to stop.

Savannah was looking at me. "What about her? She's happier where she is now, right? So why not let your dad be happy too? Hey, d'you think he'd let me take you shopping on the mainland for your birthday?"

Serves me right. By the time she started telling me that push-up bras were more comfortable than they looked, I decided I better ride home and do my homework. As I was leaving, Savannah's mom, Carolyn, asked me, "How *is* Bethany doing these days?" with this really sympathetic face, and that made me re-member what Mom said last week after I'd skipped a phone call: "Maybe you better start calling me Bethany like your dad does, since you seem to be having trouble with the concept of 'Mom,' huh?"

That's when two things occurred to me. Number One: Mom was right. My concept of "Mom" was more screwed up than ever now. Number Two: Lorraine would be there for dinner that night, screwing it up even more. And every other night from now on.

And a third thing. I couldn't have both Louis and Savannah at the same birthday party. And a fourth: I had zero clue what to do about that.

So I told Carolyn, "She's fine," and rode on back with my stomach feeling as draggy as ever. Clouds had covered up the brightness of the day and I had to fight the wind all the way home.

CHAPTER FOUR

DREAMS DON'T HURT

Turns out I was wrong about Stepmother Lorraine joining us for dinner. But turns out I was also wrong to feel good about that, since Dad and Michael used our last Burgowski-only dinner as a stage for their worst fight ever. Ha ha. Ouch.

When I got back I found another note on the table: "Just us 3 for dinner 2nite. Preheat oven 350 @ 5." Happily surprised, I checked the fridge, wondering what Dad had made—*gotta be something special, even without the bride! Maybe lasagna?* But no, Dad must have used up his store of special surprise. Tuna casserole again. So much for the wedding feast.

So I did my homework in a rotten mood, doing a really skimpy job answering Mrs. Mac's Reflection Questions. By the time Michael came in from the shed smelling like turpentine, I was feeling more rotten than ever.

He read Dad's note. "What's for dinner?"

"Guess."

That made him look up. "You gotta be kidding. Tuna?"

"Yup," I said, taking that mean delight people feel in making someone else feel as bad as they do.

"Shee-it," Michael growled. "He's turning us into frickin' Chickens of the Sea." But frickin' chickens sounded so funny we laughed, and the day might have improved right there if Michael hadn't started washing off all his shed gunk in the kitchen sink, which in my opinion is unsanitary, so instead of making up over our shared loathing of tuna, we got into another fight. So I forgot to preheat the oven.

"Honestly, Joss," Dad said when the three of us were sitting around the table, probably for the last time. Through the window the sun had come back high and golden, a mocking picture of a happy summer day. "You're turning fourteen. I thought by now I'd be able to quit leaving notes and just have you make dinner, but I guess that's too much to ask."

His bright face blurred up as the tears I'd been holding back all day finally decided to take charge. I clamped my mouth hard to hold them in.

Michael, of all people, came to my rescue.

"Well, we're not gonna have to worry about that anymore, right?" he said quietly. "Or doesn't Lorraine know how to cook?"

Dad put his fork down. Michael held his stare.

"Okay," Dad said finally. "Let's get something straight. You don't have to be in love with Lorraine. That's my job; I'm the one who married her. I understand this is going to be an adjustment for you guys. But I will not. Tolerate. Rudeness." He turned his glare to me, then back to Michael, eyebrows as low as they could get. "Is that clear?"

My bite of casserole turned to a lump of fishy steel in my mouth, and the clamped-down sob morphed into fury. *What's he looking at me for? I didn't say a thing!*

Michael chewed carelessly, but his eyes dropped to his plate.

"*Clear?*" Dad's skin was fading into an ugly pale.

"Sure, whatever," Michael muttered.

Dad's lips twitched like a fish about to snap the bait, but then he pulled them tight and forced in a bite of casserole. When I looked up again I saw him chewing as if dinner were tough steak instead of mushy noodles. It was hard to stay mad at him.

"So, when is…you know…Lorraine…going to move in with us?" In my opinion, if you have to talk about something you might as well talk about it.

"I don't know, hon," Dad said, his face relaxing. "She's been cozy in her place for so long, neither of us is in any hurry. We thought we'd see how you guys…see how things go, you know."

"Very sensitive of you," said Michael's voice, pitched below Dad's hearing.

"*Does* she cook?" I blurted. "I mean…will she want to, like, fix dinners for us and stuff, or will you keep on…you know."

"Keep on being the faithful Single Dad Cook?" He smiled. "I don't know if that's a vote of confidence or a plea for rescue. Yes, Lorraine can cook—she's from Indiana, for goodness' sake," he added, though I didn't see what that had to do with it.

I continued down the checklist of necessary questions. "Did you tell Mom yet?"

"Not yet," Dad said. I waited, but that was all.

"Do you…do you want me to tell her?"

"Well," Dad said slowly. "I guess that's up to you. I guess you'll probably want to say something about it, next time you talk to Beth."

"You guess," Michael snorted under his breath.

"Yeah," I said hastily. "I think I'll call her after dinner." *Oh, great idea. She'll probably be passed out by now.* But I blundered on, trying to keep Dad's attention from the icy waves radiating from my brother. "She prob'ly wants to know what I want for my birthday, right? So I'll call her and… tell her. Yeah."

"Why don't you invite her to your party?" Michael asked. The one eye visible through his hair looked blank and innocent.

I opened my mouth but Dad beat me to it. "Oh, maybe not, Joss honey. You need to give your mom more notice, she probably has to work."

"'Course she'll have to work," Michael smirked. "It's not like there's any reason she'd feel unwelcome around here all of a sudden."

Dad put his fork down again. "That was uncalled for."

"Sorry," Michael muttered.

And I thought, *Hah*. But also…*Really, Dad? Uncalled for?* Suddenly I didn't know whose side I was on.

We all sat there for a minute with our newest family member, Icy Silence.

"Is there any dessert?" I asked finally. I wasn't hungry, even in my dessert stomach. Half my casserole still sat there in a greasy pile.

"Some ice cream bars in the freezer," Dad said, and we fell over each other getting them.

"Well," I heard myself say through my Creamsicle, "I think Mom'll be fine with the whole Lorraine thing." *Liar, liar.* "She's really smart, and…um…good at her job, everyone says so…"

"Mom's good at her job too, you know," Michael said in a new, hard voice. "How come you never happen to mention that?"

"No one said she wasn't," Dad put in peaceably.

"I'm just saying," Michael went on, the old fierceness creeping in, "she never gets a break, does she? She has this crappy job and this crappy life, and here we are all happy on our little island paradise…"

"What?" I exploded. "You hate this place, you said so yours—"

Dad screeched his chair back. "Does this conversation really need to proceed?"

The ice cream bars sat and melted for a while on our plates.

If there's one thing I can't stand, it's unfairness. *Hey, I'm trying to make peace!* "But Dad, he said—"

"I repeat," my father responded, sounding like he had a toothache, "is this an essential topic of discussion? Is there some powerful need you two have to drive me crazy tonight?"

"What's that mean, 'need'?" Michael said. "According to you, all I have is 'wants,' dude."

Uh-oh. Michael said the d-word. Now Dad was on his feet, his face racing after Michael's bait. "I thought we were talking about my marriage," he said, which was unfair since he'd just banned the subject. "But if you want to go there, fine: No, I don't happen to think you *need* a PlayStation. No, I don't think you *need* a driver's license. No, I don't actually think you *need* anything right now except a better sense of perspective."

"Dude, that is so unfair. Just because you choose to live like a caveman or something, why's that mean *we* have to suffer?"

Dad turned his back and started piling up dishes, even though that was my job.

In my opinion, anger is like dye in water. Once it's in your system it swirls around and stains every little drop of you, till every topic that pours out of your mouth is the same color. Who knows which dye-drop had stained Michael first—Lorraine? Mom? Driver's license?

"Nobody's suffering," I pointed out. Ha—like you can stop a hose by putting your hand over the nozzle.

"I'm sick of it," Michael sprayed. "It's like nothing's mine around here. Everybody just helps themselves to your stuff."

Dad's back stiffened, but so did my temper; I abandoned my noble cause of peacemaker. "What're you talking about? I just used your stupid bike."

"Are you frickin' kiddin' me? What about last year with my Legos, and my Mariners shirt, huh?"

"You weren't even using those Legos anymore."

"That's not the frickin' point!" Michael blasted, except this time he switched from "frickin'" to the real thing. "You're driving me out of my frickin' mind—!" and this is where Dad slammed a plate on the counter.

He turned slowly, his face as jagged and pale as the half-plate still clutched in his hand.

"If I hear that gangster language in my house again, Michael,"

Dad said in a near-whisper, "so help me, I'm going to walk around this table and smack your little gangster behind so hard you won't be able to sit down for a week. Is that understood?"

The temperature in the kitchen seemed to drop and I hugged myself. You have to understand, Dad's never hit us. Oh, once or twice a swat on the butt in passing, but never a real threat carried out like an execution sentence. *Well, at least that'll finally make Michael stop and apologize for real.*

But I was wrong. Someone had just opened the pressure valve to the max, and Michael turned the hose of his rage full force on Dad.

"I'm not a frickin' gangster! I'm just frickin' cussing, all right? That's the problem with you people! You and your girlfriend live on this stupid frickin' island and you think the rest of the world is like this alien planet, and you feel so superior 'cause you don't do normal stuff like play video games, and everything that's normal and real-life is just a big frickin' threat to everybody! I'm sick of it! You won't let me drive, even though nobody here cares if you're sixteen or not and there's no frickin' place to go anyway, so I have to ride my frickin' bike like a frickin' first grader, and then my frickin' sister just goes and helps herself and all you do is tell me to watch my frickin' language 'cause, oh yeah, you married your frickin' girlfriend and now she's gonna be here every frickin' day cooking meals in Mom's frickin' kitchen…"

It was like watching someone vomit without stopping, like one of those nightmares where you're rooted to the ground and the bad thing, whatever it is, just keeps happening in front of you. Dad must have felt the same way, even though he was the one getting vomited on. He just stood there, leaning against the counter with that stupid broken plate in his hand. His face seemed to tighten, like every word of Michael's was pulling some invisible wire in his skin.

Finally he set the plate down, detached himself from the counter, and walked through the kitchen, straight past my screaming brother. The screen door slammed behind him.

Michael's voice slammed shut with the door. His face was red and his hair was crammed back behind his ears.

"What just happened?" he asked weakly.

My mouth was too dry to answer. The sad remains of casserole and Creamsicle on my plate made my stomach clench, so I stared out the window.

We both sat there for a while. The sun hit a small cloud and shot some dazzling rays at us like one of those religious cards.

Finally my brother muttered something.

"What?" I managed.

"Sorry," Michael repeated. "Didn't mean to get so mad at you. He's the ass—he's the jerk, not you."

I know—hardly a hug and an "Oh, honey," which is what I needed just then, but for Michael this was pretty much the same thing. Sympathy is the worst thing in the world when you're trying not to cry. A huge sob burbled up from my stomach, and I ran out of the kitchen like a stupid six-year-old.

It took me a long time to get the crying heaves to loosen their grip. *Worst Saturday in the history of the world!* When my pillow got soggy on both sides, I used my sheet for Kleenex.

But eventually even furious self-pity gets boring. I rolled over and started reading about Harry in Potions class. At one point I heard the screen door, then some footsteps and Dad's voice saying "Honey?" outside my room, but my head felt too full and wet for talking. So I kept reading.

Crying must be good exercise 'cause it always tires me out. I don't know what time I fell asleep, but the dreams began right away like a movie screened for my private delight.

This time it was just me—no Harry, no broom. I was flying like Superman, arms ahead. And it was no fantasy lake I flew over, it was pretty little Dalby Harbor, then the open ocean, ruffled with whitecaps. I flew so far out over the water I should have been terrified, but I wasn't: somehow I knew when it was time to turn around, so I did, angling my shoulder, letting my body follow.

You know how in dreams you're not supposed to feel things physically? So if you pinch yourself and it hurts, you know you're not dreaming? Well, in that dream I actually felt the Pacific breeze on my face, chilling first my right cheek, then my left as I wheeled. I felt the air part for my outstretched fingertips like some soft, yielding element that hadn't yet been invented.

And I saw things. I saw the lights of giant ships heading out to Asia, and the little fishing boats looking so alone in all that water. I saw the head of a seal, shining in the moonlight. Gliding low over the rocks, I saw pale clusters of goose barnacles exposed by the tide. I skirted Dalby's blobby eastern edge to fly across the strait to Owen Island, and the shapes of water and land formed beneath me like the satellite map in Mrs. Mac's room. Up I angled over Mt. Santa Inez, where they took us on the fourth-grade hike, and when I skimmed low over the old observation tower, a fir branch smacked me across the eye. *Ow!*

I woke up then with my hand pressed to my cheek. My room was bright with early summer sun. Wrapped in the bliss of my dream, I rolled out of bed and checked my mirror to see the branch's mark on my face.

All I saw was my own brown eyes looking back at me from behind the strands of dirty-blond hair fighting their way out of my ponytail. No scrapes. Not even the tiniest scratch. *Dreams don't hurt, stupid. None of that was real.*

What *was* real: Mom. Michael. Dad. Lorraine. Savannah. Louis. I glanced back at my bed. *If I went straight to sleep, maybe I could put myself back into that midnight sky, swooping over the tower...* "Yeah, right," I said aloud. I'd still have to wake up again and find myself facing what was starting to look like the Week From Hell.

CHAPTER FIVE

WEEK FROM HELL

Here's how we got through that week: nobody talked about anything. Nobody explained, apologized, or tried to smooth the sharp edges of our family time. And nobody called Mom.

Lorraine showed up for dinner—I mean *with* dinner—Sunday night, and I realized what Dad meant about Indiana. She pushed through the screen door, both arms loaded with baskets and platters like one of those *Little House on the Prairie* mega-meals. Yeah, Lorraine could cook all right: pork chops and greens and fruit salad and peach pie and jeez, even homemade rolls. *Who does she think she's impressing?*

But everyone stayed polite. Michael and I complimented Lorraine automatically after our first bite of each new dish. It *was* all pretty delicious. Michael used his new, hard voice, but at least he had the sense not to say "Dude," so he and Dad kept off each other.

But as the week went on, Lorraine was never there for breakfast. *What, she thinks we'll admire her sensitivity in not moving in?* Michael must have been thinking the same thing, because he muttered, "Aren't we the lucky ones? No evil stepmothers for us," too low for Dad to hear.

I nodded. That whole "Oh, don't let me intrude on your little family" thing—it was creepy. And still no one told Mom. *Well, don't look at me.*

At school, the last week before vacation, Savannah acted extra nice. I let her. She told me about putting Mentos in Diet Coke to make it explode, and she didn't mention Nate and Tyler. They left us alone. I never saw Louis, but I told myself that was normal; the only class we have together is P.E.. He knew he was invited to my party; I didn't need to talk to him about it.

By Tuesday my fun new family managed to discuss my party without getting into a fight. Dad said he'd get my favorite cake, this killer chocolate raspberry one, from Island Sweets, and birthday excitement flickered inside me. But no one called Mom.

On Wednesday right before closing, Dad got slammed with a big group from Oregon who wanted camping food, so he told us to go on and eat without him. This time Lorraine cooked right there in our kitchen: omelets, and she told us to choose what we wanted in ours. Michael chose sauerkraut and chili sauce, but Lorraine just smiled and cooked it, like a substitute teacher pretending she's in control. *Fine, might as well order what I like if she's playing that game.* Bacon and broccoli go great together. But then the three of us had to sit down and eat.

In that whispery voice, Lorraine asked us about our school year, our favorite desserts, our plans for the summer, and we answered in the shortest sentences possible. When Dad finally joined us, Michael excused himself.

Dad looked exhausted. "Now this is a family dinner," he sighed, tucking into his omelet.

Wow. Yeah. That's my sensitive dad for ya. I did some dishes while they murmured about things like gas prices. *Right, because that's way more important than discussing how to tell Mom about our new "family."* Then I went to my room and read until bedtime.

But my flying dreams kept getting better. I discovered I could guide myself: think about a certain part of the island while falling asleep, and sure enough, there I'd be in dreamland, swooping over the school, buzzing Nate's house out on the Spit. I even flew low enough to push in a loose shingle on Louis's cabin. Of course I didn't go check next day to see if it was fixed; I didn't want to keep reminding myself it wasn't real. Because the dream-nights almost made up for the crappy "family" days.

Almost.

By midweek, Dad and Michael stopped speaking to each other. Even with Stepmother Lorraine trying to keep the conversation going, talk just died on our kitchen table and lay there while we chewed. A new pattern started: everyone eats like they have a ferry to catch, then Dad and Lorraine go sit in the living room while Joss washes up and Michael shuts himself in his room with his guitar.

I could feel the buildup of unheld conversations like the air before a storm. Dad and Michael. Louis. Mom.

She's supposed to call about my birthday present, I told myself. And what kind of mom doesn't make contact with her kids when her ex-husband moves another woman into her kitchen? *The kind that doesn't know*, my brain reminded me. Yeah, the kind that walked out of her kitchen in the first place nine years ago, remember?

She still deserves to know.

But the last conversation we'd had…What if she was still…out of it? I couldn't handle that.

Louis, though—that was a problem I could handle. On Thursday, the day before my party, I knew I had to talk to him. I could explain about Savannah and the Toad, and we could laugh and everything would be great again.

Never assume, Mrs. Mac says. It makes an "ass" out of "u" and "me."

Thursday, school let out an hour early for some crazy relay races to celebrate summer. I bumped into Louis while they were setting up for the gigantic Tug o' War, half the middle school against the other half.

"You're coming to my party, aren't you?" I asked him straight out.

Louis was quiet for so long I thought he hadn't heard me. Finally he said, "What kind of cake are you having?"

In my opinion, people talk about the things they can talk about when there are other things they can't. Louis has never been picky about cake, as long as there's enough of it. So this was his way of saying "yes."

"Chocolate-raspberry," I told him. "And it's just gonna be Savannah and Heather and Greta and Molly." This was my way of telling him, *It's okay. No fertility rites. And by the way, I'm sorry about Tyler and Nate and Savannah and the Toad.*

Like I said, people talk about the things they can talk about.

Louis grinned at me. His whole face turns pink when he grins, and squinches till his eyes disappear. "I know what to get you," he said.

Before I could ask, we were being herded and shoved into teams along the tug-rope. Louis disappeared behind several bodies. "Grab hold, everyone! Wait for my signal!" yelled Mrs. Oyama, our P.E. teacher.

From behind me, I heard Louis's high voice continuing on as if there weren't ten kids jostling and shouting between us. *Oh, Louis, you are such a dodo.* "My mom talked to your mom on email at the library last night…"

"On your mark! Get set! GO!" shrieked Mrs. Oyama. Louis was still talking as the rope lurched.

The whole thing lasted about fifteen seconds. In the middle of the sudden quiet of grunting and straining, Louis's voice floated clearly. "Mom said Bethany told her what you want and I might as well get it for you 'cause Bethany doesn't know when she's gonna see you."

Louis's team let go and mine went staggering backward into a pile. Then my teammates began leaping and high-fiving around me. But I just lay there on the grass, feeling Louis's words drop down into my stomach, which had finally begun to feel normal for the first time in days.

Bethany doesn't know when she's gonna see you.

"Wow, I've never won at that!" Louis reappeared, grinning happily. Then he saw my face and his rosy glow faded. If he'd been Savannah, he would've asked, "What's wrong, Joss?" But since he was Louis and I was Jocelyn, we let ourselves be herded back inside to clean out our lockers.

It took me forever to fall asleep that night. I finished Harry Potter Three and couldn't find Book Four, so I stayed in bed, tossing around to find a cool spot and wishing I had an off-switch for my brain. *"Bethany doesn't know when she's gonna see you." "Why don't you invite her to your party?" "Hey babe, joo sen' me anemail?"*

But when I finally fell asleep, I got my reward. That night I dreamed about taking off. Somehow when you know the way something starts, it gets realer. I didn't have to run screaming down a flat surface like an airplane or paddling madly like a goose. I simply leaned into the wind, took two strong steps, hearing the crunch of dry lichen, and leaped.

Oh, it was glorious. From the earth to the air, and up and through...I knew how to do it now, and there was no fear, no doubt, nothing but lift and the softness of the evening.

I never dreamed about landing, but that was just as well. Waking up, as usual, was bad enough.

I lay there groggily, trying to will myself back into my dream. But instead, a memory ballooned like a Harry Potter shield charm. That ghost video of Michael's—now I knew why her takeoff steps felt so familiar! Step step boom! That was exactly what it felt like. *But wait...how could the video feel familiar if I hadn't had my taking-off dream yet?* I had no idea. *Who cares? It's my* birthday, *and last-day-of-middle-school!* Can there be a better combination?

Dad gave me a birthday hug like he always used to, and even Michael muttered "Birthday," when he shuffled in for breakfast. In Language Arts everyone sang to me, and Mrs. Mac let us play "Heads Up Seven Up" for our last day.

That was pretty much the high point.

My party was supposed to start at dinnertime. After school Dad let me pick out some soda and chips from the store, and he said we'd get fried chicken later on, and my cake. I felt like I was on a roller coaster, getting ready to swoop. But Michael managed to put the brakes on.

"Dad, can I use the truck to go over to Ned's?" He stuck his head in the store to ask as Dad was helping me bag up my loot.

Dad straightened up slowly. I could almost see him tightening his parenting muscles, like a weightlifter getting ready to tackle a really loaded barbell. "Son, we've talked about this," he said.

"I'll be back before dark," Michael assured him. *Big deal, it's solstice, it won't be dark until ten o'clock!* But I kept my mouth shut. My fluttery, happy-birthday feeling suddenly felt very fragile.

"You know that's not the issue. Just because Ned's dad lets him drive without a license doesn't mean I'm going to. We could get in real trouble if something happened."

My Dad was one smart showdown cowboy, shooting Michael's "but-everyone-else-does-it" gun right out of his hand.

"Nothing's gonna happen! Jeez, Dad, this isn't Seattle! No one cares! Gil will just wave at me as I go by, Ned said that's all he does."

Gil is our Dalby Island sheriff and an ex-Marine. He always looks bored to death.

Dad sighed and firmed his lips. "Ride your bike, son."

"I can't! I gotta carry my amp." Michael started to lose his teensy cover of cool. "How're we supposed to practice without amps? How'm I supposed to carry an amp on my frickin' bike?" But at least he did say "frickin'" this time.

"Why can't Ned come over here?" I put in, since Dad seemed to be done. My birthday feeling was calling, *Fix this! Make it go away!*

"He's grounded," Michael began enthusiastically, seizing a new argument, "and Battle of the Bands is in less than two weeks, Dad! We *gotta* practice."

Dad gave a small smile. "And why's he grounded?"

A teensy pause. One cowboy blinked. Michael's a good liar, but not a fast one. "He…"

A broad grin broke out on Dad's face. "Don't tell me, I already know. He was driving and Gil caught him, right? I heard all about it from his dad yesterday, son. Busted. Looks like the law is alive and well on Dalby after all. And *that* is a major reason—not the only one, but it'll do just fine—why I'm not letting you borrow my truck. End of discussion."

Amazingly, my defeated brother shrugged, kept his potty-mouth closed, and disappeared back into the house. My birthday-feeling flapped in triumph: *Saved! Let the party begin.*

In my opinion there's no better food than fried chicken. It gives you all those Sensory Details Mrs. Mac's always talking about. There's that eat-me-right-now! smell, and then you grab a piece, enjoying the rough, greasy flakiness. Bite in—crunch! Slup… Salty crust dissolves into silky juice…Then you wash it all down with a slug of soda and start over.

By six-thirty my party was in full swing at our backyard picnic table, with a nice pile of presents stacked up. Dad said Lorraine would come over later with the cake and he would take a picture. Savannah complimented Louis's haircut. Michael stayed in his room, playing his guitar just loud enough to send a message.

"So I brought the Mentos," Savannah said, reaching into her jeans pocket.

"Oh, cool! Great idea," Molly said.

Louis looked blank, so Savannah explained: "Diet Coke,

y'know? You put the Mentos in and it kinda explodes. There's all these videos." I was relieved that she didn't roll her eyes at him.

"I like explosions," said Louis cautiously. He hadn't been very talkative but I thought he was having a good time. Damn, that boy can eat potato chips.

"Okay, but let's finish the food first," I said. It's the birthday girl's job to stay in charge. "There's only two wings left, who wants one?"

"Forget wings, got any other white meat?" called an all-too-familiar voice. "How 'bout thighs?"

I whirled, and my birthday-feeling gave a squawk of alarm. Nate and Tyler were resting on their bikes at the edge of my yard. Tyler was wearing his usual smirk, but Nate looked sort of polite and mature. Something about his jaw. *But what are they doing here?*

"Thighs are dark meat," Louis said.

The newcomers cracked up. I never noticed before how Nate closes his eyes when he laughs. "Okay, you asked for it," he gasped. "Got any breasts?" *So much for mature.* Tyler laughed so hard he actually fell over, tangled in his bike.

Time to take control. "What the hell are you two doing here?" I asked.

"I dunno, Burger," Nate grinned as Tyler wrestled with his bike. "I *thought* we came over to say happy birthday, but it looks like we're having a discussion about body parts."

"Well, you can go home now. I'm having a happy birthday," I retorted, though this was becoming less true by the minute. I glanced at my friends. Louis looked glum, Molly, Heather and Greta were glaring at the boys just as they should, but Savannah...there was something wrong with her glare. It kept peeling off, giving me a look at something else underneath.

Nate smiled at me. "We're cool. We just wanted to see the Mentos thing."

I turned slowly to Savannah. "You *invited* them?"

Usually Savannah can bluff her way through anything; it's one of the things I admire about her. But that night she dropped her eyes and muttered like my brother does. "You weren't supposed to tell, you idiots."

"You got the Diet Coke? Gotta be diet," Tyler said eagerly. He had escaped his bike and now strode right up to my picnic table, the very core of my party.

"No!" I yelled.

"Oh, yes it does, Joss," Greta assured me, "I tried it with regular Coke and it—"

"Not the Coke, I mean the... the..." The whole evening, I meant. *My birthday's supposed to be special, even if everything else is crap.* Now it wasn't even mine anymore. I turned in fury to Savannah. "How could you invite them to *my* party?"

The old Savannah reappeared, tossing her head. "'Cause I thought it would be fun! *Day-ummm,* Joss! They're the ones who showed me the Mentos video, so I thought they should see it. What else we gonna do, just sit around?"

I didn't know where to start. I was gaping at her, my birthday-feeling wheezing its last breath, when Dad stuck his head out the screen door.

"Jocelyn. Seen your brother?"

My mind a total blank, I answered stupidly, "He's practicing in his room." The chords of some Red Hot Chili Peppers song whined from his window.

"No he isn't," Dad said in a funny low voice, and he barreled across the yard as though the eight kids staring at him were invisible. That's when I realized we'd been listening to the same song over and over for nearly an hour. Even Michael would get sick of that.

"What's going on?" whispered Savannah, and for a moment I reached for the concern in her voice like a saving hand. Then I realized she was just relieved at dodging my anger. For the first time I couldn't stand my best friend.

"*Damn* that kid!" Dad's voice came from behind the shed where he keeps his truck. I ran over to find him standing on a blank patch of gravel, his face hard and dark. Michael had really gone and done it this time. My friends and Nate and Tyler piled up behind me.

"Dude…" said Tyler.

"Oh no he *didn't* just take your truck!" Greta breathed, sounding appreciative.

"How could you not have noticed?" Dad rounded on me. "He must have walked right past you. You would've heard the engine. How come you didn't call me?"

In my opinion people who blame other people to make themselves feel better are the most immature of all. But I was too busy feeling horrible to say that.

"It wasn't her fault, Mr. Burgowski," came Louis's voice. "It's her birthday. She was distracted."

That's right. It's my birthday.

And my best friend just ruined my party, and my father was accusing me of helping my brother steal the car. I felt the first stupid tremble of tears in my lungs.

"Well, that doesn't matter now," Dad continued harshly. "Party's over. I'm calling Gil. Do you girls need a ride home? Oh, damn it, I can't—never mind. Stay here. Finish your party." He stalked back into the house.

With the Mentos experiment squashed, Nate and Tyler biked away. Too late. My party limped grimly on. Savannah tried to talk the situation back to normal, but for once I wasn't buying. *She knew how Louis would feel, and she still invited those jerks—to my party!*

We opened presents; Heather and Molly got me the exact same blank-book with a unicorn on the cover. I know, it's the thought that counts. My thought was: *Yeah. Perfect.*

After a while nobody could pretend we were doing anything besides waiting for the cake. Where was stupid Lorraine?

Heather said, "There's one more present here, Joss, don't you want to open it?" Wow—a set of seven gel-pens from Greta. Louis had just given me a set of three, so this was going to make him feel worse than ever. *Terrific.*

"I'm sure Michael's fine," Greta said. "He's just being an idiot, you know that."

Still no cake. Finally Savannah called her mom to take them all home. The sun lowered itself into the top branches of the fir by our driveway.

"Happy Birthday, Joss," they chorused from the car.

"Thanks for the presents, you guys. Sorry my cake never got here." Dad might be unfair, but he sure taught me manners.

As they pulled away, Savannah called out the window, "I'm sorry, Joss, okay? Call me later, okay?" and the promise of friendship in her voice pressed the sore spot in my heart that already hurt from Mom.

Louis kept me company, in a garden-furniture sort of way; we both just sat there for the longest time. Finally a police car pulled into the driveway, Sheriff Gil behind the wheel. The rear doors opened and Dad and Michael stepped out. No truck.

Now was the time for Dad to hug me tight and say, "Sorry, honey. Everything's okay now," and explain what had happened.

Or not. Dad walked right past me and into the house with Michael in tow, Sheriff Gil bringing up the rear. It took Stepmother Lorraine, who suddenly appeared with a white bakery box in her hands, to ask, "My goodness, Gil, what happened? Is Michael all right?"

"Fine," Gil snapped out, the way he says everything. "Truck isn't, though. Your boy thought he'd go visit his mom, looks like. Lost control coming down the hill to the ferry and put 'er in the ditch. But he's fine. Everything's okay now."

But everything wasn't; Gil's was the wrong voice to be saying that. And Lorraine, whose voice was much too soft, said, "Oh, my

goodness. Oh, Jocelyn, your poor dad. I better go talk to him."
Then she stopped. "Oh dear, and it's your birthday and everything. Your friends aren't here yet? Ron told me it was a slumber
party so you didn't need the cake right away…"

I wanted to burst out sobbing and tell her how messed-up everything was, but when I looked up, there was my stupid, skinny
stepmom, cake box in her arms, staring into the house as if she
wanted to give *it* a hug. So I said, "They're coming."

"Well, good," said Lorraine, gliding over, "because I picked
your cake up right before they closed, and oh, happy birthday.
But Jocelyn, I have to tell you. The bakery messed up, they accidentally sold the one they made for you, so I got this instead.
I sure hope you like carrot cake, it looks delicious…" Her voice
trailed off uncertainly.

"It's fine," I lied. What else was I going to say?

"Are you sure?" But grown-ups are good to go as soon as you
tell them what they want to hear. She nodded, set the cake on
the table, and headed in toward my wreck of a family.

Louis and I sat back down and did some more staring, although I could feel him itching to get at that cake. It wasn't
meanness that kept me from offering him some, I swear. I just
felt numb.

After a while Sheriff Gil came back out, the screen door
whacking behind him. "You kids gettin' a little chilly?" he inquired as he went past, but didn't wait for an answer. Dad stayed
inside with Lorraine. No sounds came from the house; someone
must have turned off the recording Michael had obviously made
of himself practicing "Californication" over and over. They had
forgotten all about me.

I *was* chilly. The evening was lowering itself into dusk, though
I didn't have the heart to turn around and watch the sun set into
the gap where the ferry glides past. I wanted to hug my arms,
goose-bumped in my tank top, but I couldn't move.

Finally I heard Louis's voice, a little rough from being silent so long. "Um, Joss? I should prob'ly go home."

My head nodded.

"I'll see you tomorrow, okay? I'm glad you liked your present," Louis said.

Nodding I could manage, so I kept doing it.

"Okay, then. Bye," and I heard his light footsteps on the gravel.

"Hey, Louis!" I croaked. The footsteps returned.

"Huh?"

"Take the cake with you."

"Wow, thanks!" he said, and disappeared into the evening with the last remnants of my birthday.

A big batch of starlings came swirling in like they do, and tucked themselves noisily into our fir tree. The Angstroms' donkey brayed a few times in the distance like a dying engine. A light went on inside my house, but no one came for me.

I sat there for a long, long time. And then I got up and walked the shortcut to the Toad.

I could follow that path in my sleep, which is how it felt that night: sleepwalking. I pushed through the wild rose scrub, their honey-smelling blossoms and their vicious scratches finally working on my numbness, but my mind stayed blank.

Until I got to the foot of the Toad and started to climb. Then I got the weirdest feeling, like I was back in one of my dreams. Everything felt really, really familiar. I stopped halfway up the bumpy slope, my breath returning the feeling to my body. I dug my fingers into the lichen and it crunched softly.

And that's when it hit me. Those weren't dreams I'd been having, about climbing the Toad and pushing off into the dusky sky: *step step boom*. Not dreams, planted by that ghost video—*"There she goes!"*—the pale image that leapt and disappeared. Not dreams at all. Those were *plans*.

Up I went, step for step from my dream the night before. A

light breeze was blowing at the top, and I leaned into it, took two strong, lichen-crunching strides—*step step*—and leaped. *Boom.* From the earth to the air, up and through…no fear, no doubt, nothing but the lifting caress of the sky.

CHAPTER SIX

THE SMELL OF THE SKY

I lied.

Dreams are crap, okay? I mean they do a great job planting an idea in your brain, but as a how-to manual, forget it.

First thing that happened was, I started to spin forward and down, just like the time I tried a flip turn in a swimming pool and got water so far up my nose I thought I'd die. That was the feeling, a kind of slow rush where the motion takes over and all you can do is flail around and try to follow. Only I was about to flail myself right back onto the Toad. Its rocky back seemed to arch like a cat's to meet me.

Hooray for instinct. I flapped my arms like a cartoon character and guess what, it worked—at least enough for me to clear the Toad, the brambles scratching my left foot as I reversed. Then I kicked like a swimmer and shot straight up into the sky.

Ohjeezohjeezohjeez. I flapped frantically, which only rocketed me higher. The treetops receded into a dark mass below me. My lungs felt sucked of breath. Flailing like a windmill, I tried to scream. Another slow roll through the limitless air.

At least that stopped the rocket jets. Flailing, as I've found out since then, can be your best friend when you've put on too much speed. Nothing a good flail can't handle. But at that moment all I knew was that I was way up high in the air all by myself, and this was definitely not a dream.

No kidding, I knew that from the get-go.

For one thing, I felt *everything*. Remember how my dreams kind of trickled the Sensory Details in, some visuals here, a little physical sensation there? This was the whole package, Sensory Deluxe. The wind played over my thrashing body exactly like water, only not cold—perfect, Hawaii-on-TV water. Now that stupid donkey sounded like a ferry foghorn; sure enough, I had flailed myself right over the Angstroms' farm.

I smelled the salty-sour tide—the real thing, not like when Tion woke me up with her stinky breath. I smelled manure, and cut grass, then the sharp scent of diesel. I even tasted the air! Up high, it tasted exactly like the smell of those pink-and-white lilies in the library's garden: drowsy-sweet and incredibly comforting.

And that's when I realized that I had stopped panicking. I was just...flying.

Slowly, slowly, my brain and heart and lungs started checking themselves out like survivors after a crash, and realized they could function just fine. Slowly, I moved my wavering arms from my sides—I must have looked like a little seahorse fluttering there—and extended them in front of me like a diver. Like Superman. It felt right. Then I waggled my knees a little, keeping them together like in swimming lessons, and...flew.

*Whssshhh...*the Hawaii-water air flowed over me, a whispery rush. *Whssshh...*I flew. Air. Flying. *Whssshh...*

Suddenly the rest of my brain awoke. *What if someone sees me?*

Well, duh, they'll see me! I'm going to fly right over someone's head, freak out some random camper getting into his tent... No, wait, I'll buzz Savannah! No, Nate! Imagine the shock of his upturned face, how big his eyes! They'll all be so amazed, I'll be the famous Flying Girl and go on Oprah, have my own reality show...Savannah will die of jealousy! And Mom! She'll be so proud of me, the Famous Flying Jocelyn! She'll straighten right up, move back to Dalby to be closer to her family, and Dad and Michael will forget all about their issues and focus on my amazingness…

Or not. Somehow, from that first flight, my buddy Instinct knew those fantasies were as dumb as they sounded. *Don't be seen*, it said, without bothering to give a reason. I decided to listen, and I've been listening ever since.

Turns out Dalby Island is a good place for flying without attracting attention, especially in the evening. There's no night life, unless you count bats and owls. The day-tourists are gone, the rest are lying in their rooms or tents or yacht cabins, exhausted from a day of biking or sailing or sitting around the bakery. Normal people are doing normal things, like dealing with their car-stealing kids. I had the whole island to myself, spreading beneath me in invitation.

I flew slowly, enjoying the *Whssshh.* At first I traced the edge of the harbor, following the road where I knew no one would think to look up. Flying low, I could make out the marina shop, now closed and quiet, where Savannah's mom works. There was that old yellow house with the porch draped in roses—I flew through a wave of their sweetness. There—

"Aughh!"

I swerved violently; something soft brushed my right hand and I was tumbling again, really falling this time, I hadn't realized how much speed I'd picked up and now I was heading straight for the jagged, broken-off top of an enormous fir tree, racing up like a big fat spear to impale me. I screamed again.

Dogs barked. I plunged. I closed my eyes. What an idiot.

Then I flailed, and that, of course, saved me.

Must have been an owl, I realized, when I had regained my altitude and my heart had stopped choking me, and I marveled to think how close the owl came, like I was just another night creature to share the sky with. *I guess I am!* The bats, on the other hand, must've been using their sonar to avoid me; I never met up with one of them. *They probably think I'm a giant owl.* That made me smile and then, for the first time in about a week, I laughed out loud. And just like that, laughing, tingling all over with joy, I veered right and headed across the harbor. *Hell with being seen—I'm a creature of the night, the sky is mine!*

From above, the water looked exactly like the silk of Mom's old bathrobe, Dad's last Christmas gift to her: glossy and smooth, with large crinkled patches where the wind blew. Sound carries amazingly over water, and for the first time as a Flyer I heard human voices, low murmurs coming from one of the anchored yachts. Carefully, I angled my arms up a few degrees and, sure enough, my body followed—more altitude. Cool! Then down again... easy...and back up. I tried banking, leaning my shoulder first one way, then another. And this was how I taught myself to fly.

I was experimenting with a slow three-sixty over that pointy house on the end of the Spit when its porch lights blazed on, and I suddenly realized how dark it was. What would Dad think? What if he was out right now looking for me? *Just what he needs, another missing kid—maybe he's called Sheriff Gil back!* I strained my ears, but all I heard were the sounds from the harbor. So I banked left and pointed for home.

As I crossed back over the road and headed for the dark mass that cloaked the Toad, a disturbing thought bubbled up in me: *what if this is it?* Maybe this was a special Birthday Flight, a reward for surviving my horrible week, a Summer Solstice gift. *What if I land and can never take off again?*

Or what if this was just one more dream?

I don't care. It was worth it. And anyway, it's not like I can keep flying forever, right?

That's when I realized how exhausted I was. In front of me my hands wobbled as if I was running out of whatever fuel was keeping me aloft. Maybe I was! Maybe I'd just had beginner's luck tonight, and happened to take off with my tanks fully loaded with *something*, which I was now out of. Panic bounded up through my limbs, sending my control haywire. I started to roll again, just in time for the pale back of the Toad to show itself through the veiling darkness. *Ohjeezohjeezohjeez*—I didn't know how to land!

Well, nobody taught you how to take off, either, my brain growled. *Quit freaking.*

I flailed back to horizontal. "Okay…" I said aloud. Here came the Toad. "You got this. Just…land."

Fifty more feet? Forty? Tyler's dad's yacht is forty-five feet long, he brags about it all the time… Is this longer? Maybe thirty-five? Too late—here it comes.

"*Oof!*" Landing, it turns out, is where you want to stop flailing. I hit the Toad with my feet pedaling an invisible bike and promptly flailed myself right onto my chest. One hand hit moss, but the other stung like fire, and the Toad knocked the breath right out of me. I lay there for a minute like I was part of the Toad itself.

Then my air came back on a heavy wave of nausea, so I lay there for another couple of moments trying to breathe without throwing up. Boy, if landing had stayed like that I don't think I would ever have wanted to fly again.

When I was finally able to sit up I listened carefully, but the breeze had picked up and I figured I was too far from home to hear them calling for me anyway. Down I scrambled, my hand throbbing, and raced for home. Good thing I know my way by feel, 'cause by now under the trees it was totally dark.

I could have used a little illumination in my brain, that's for sure. My thoughts were whirling and crashing into each other.

What just happened? How did I do that? That was so cool! Who can I tell? Who can I ask? Can I do that again? Did I almost just kill myself? But that was so cool!

In the end, that last thought was all I could hang onto. Nothing else seemed real: that I had flown. That anyone would believe me. That I would ever fly again. So by the time I reached the back of my yard and saw the comforting light of the kitchen windows, I was "landing" for the second time that night, my thoughts gliding back down to earth by their own weight. I had my cover story ready, and I knew that was all the sharing I was going to do.

Not that I needed to bother. From my first steps out of the woods onto our lawn it was clear that no one was out there calling my name. Not unless you counted owls; I heard one, maybe my same old pal still up there looking for me to run into again.

"I'm home!" I called, reaching for the screen door, and for a half-second I thought, *Maybe flying-time is like Narnia! Maybe you get to come back to the exact same moment when you'd left, no one the wiser!* But even before I saw the kitchen clock I knew that was bogus; it was *dark*, after all. There they were, Dad, Lorraine and Michael, sitting in a tight knot at the kitchen table.

"Hey, hon," Dad said, but he sounded distracted. *So much for being worried about me.* Michael didn't say anything, but I could see he had been crying. That was my welcome home.

"I went for a walk," I announced, daring someone to challenge me. Since when do fourteen-year-olds go for walks? "But I'm back now," I added, hiding my scraped palm behind my back.

They all just sat there, looking at the table.

"What're you guys doing?" I finally asked, hating the whininess in my voice. But hey, what do you expect? I'd just been gone who knows how long, experiencing the thrill of anyone's lifetime, almost killing myself, and here I was finally back and no one seemed to give a hoot but a stupid old owl. *And it's still my birthday!*

"We're, ah…," my father said, and I could hear that grown-up Truth Adjustment Monitor in his voice, the one that figures out how much reality the kids can handle. "We're just negotiating a little settlement with Michael here. About the future."

"What happened to your party, Jocelyn?" Lorraine inquired. "Mm, did someone give you perfume? You smell nice. But I didn't see anyone..." she added as I wondered, *Perfume?* "Did you meet your friends somewhere? Oh, and did the cake turn out all right?"

Maybe it was the fact that someone finally remembered my birthday, even if it was only Lorraine, even in such a pathetic way. Suddenly the whole evening came rolling back over me—Savannah, Louis, the Mentos—and I was so exhausted I had to lean against the door frame for support.

"Yeah, it was great," I lied again. "Thanks for, um, getting it for me. And letting me have the party. We ended up going over to Louis's." I didn't have to fake my yawn. "Think I'll go to bed now, though."

"Are the plates still outside?" Lorraine asked, and I was suddenly starving. I hadn't eaten anything since the fried chicken, and flying, it turns out, takes a lot of energy. But no way was I hanging out in that gloomy little kitchen with my new non-family.

"No, we threw everything in the outside trash."

Dad finally looked at me. "Jocelyn, your knees are bleeding."

So they were. They didn't hurt at all, compared to my hand. "Huh. Banged into the picnic table on my way in." This lying thing was getting too easy. "Well, g'night."

For the first time in a week, I didn't need to cry and I didn't need to read Harry Potter. I lay on my bed, letting my mind go flying back over the course I had traced that night. Eyes open in the dark, I saw the pale ribbon of road I had followed along the harbor, I saw the silken water once again, saw the gentle sway of the masts below me. I heard the sounds again: that first *Whssshh* as I leapt off the Toad, the dog replying to my scream, the voices drifting over the water.

"It happened," I whispered. *Yeah,* my brain argued, *but all those dreams you had felt awfully real too. You probably just fell asleep on the picnic table.*

I concentrated hard. Felt my left foot pushing off from the lichen, felt the liquid air on my skin.

You felt that in your dreams too!

The sky smelled like lilies...*but who says you can't smell in dreams?*

Then I let the terror zap through me again for a moment just to remember it. My hands rose of their own accord, flailing a little in the safety of my bedroom. And there was that Dalby-shaped scrape across my palm, still throbbing.

The scrape did it. "Dreams don't hurt," I said to myself. There was no argument.

"I can fly," I whispered.

I don't know how long I lay there, re-living the magic of my first flight, rolled up in a blanket of pure, little-kid joy.

I can fly, I can fly. No one knows but me.

That night I dreamed absolutely nothing.

CHAPTER SEVEN

AT LEAST HALF
FLYGIRL

I woke up next morning on a blaze of light coming through my window at eye level. It was way earlier than you'd expect a teenager to get up on the first day of summer vacation, but my waking thought was like one of those special messages that crawl along the bottom of your TV screen: *Breaking News: You can fly! All you have to do is get through the day and you can fly again tonight!* So I hopped right out of bed to get the day started.

Dad was doing dishes in the kitchen. "Hey, high schooler," he said, turning around to give me a soapy-handed hug. *Probably feeling guilty for ignoring me the night before,* but I couldn't help smiling.

"I'm starving," I said inside his hug. Dad offered to make me French toast—*wow, super-guilty!*—and while he fussed with the eggs, I pretended to be too sleepy to want to talk while figuring out what I wanted to talk about. And not talk about. *I can fly. I'm going to fly again. Let's not mess this magic up.*

"Your brother's still asleep," Dad told me. I resisted the urge to say, *You sure? Maybe he's just playing a loop of him snoring.*

"What's gonna happen?" I asked.

The frying pan sputtered and Dad plopped in two pieces of drippy bread. "Well, that's the question, isn't it," he finally replied, as though talking to a grown-up. I sat up straighter. "I know it's tough for both of you guys," Dad continued, "but I guess for Michael, well, his wings have sprouted a little sooner than yours."

I smirked to myself. Then stopped as the thought hit me: *I could tell him. I could.* Of course he wouldn't believe me, but if I showed him, he'd have to, right? And then— *Yeah. Then? He'd un-marry Lorraine to show you how impressed he is? You don't even know if you can still fly!*

"What is it?" Dad had turned around, spatula in hand.

"Ummm…" I rearranged my face. "Is Michael grounded?"

"Well, duh," Dad said, sounding like Michael himself. "Whaddya think?—here ya go—" I squirted syrup and lit into the toast as he continued, "—kid steals my truck, puts it in a ditch, he's not grounded for the rest of the summer? But that's nothing for you to worry about."

"Wherezhatruck?" I mumbled through my mouthful.

Dad frowned. "Still in the ditch. Till your brother figures out how he's gonna pay me back for the tow truck." He turned to finish the dishes, and we were back to our regular roles: busy parent, pesky kid. So for the next few minutes I focused on the spongy chunks of bread squooshing syrup around my mouth.

"Oh, your mom called last night." Dad turned around again, looking sheepish. "In the middle of everything. You were outside somewhere and didn't hear me calling you. Then we forgot. I'm sorry, honey, we should have told you, but we were all so…"

"'Sokay," I told him. *Mom remembered my birthday!* The sun seemed to blaze out over all my good fortune. *Dad made me breakfast, Michael's grounded, there's no more homework till September…and I can fly again tonight.* "I'll call her back later."

"We decided it'd be better if Michael's paycheck isn't coming from his 'jailer,' as he put it," Dad said with a sad smile. "So while we figure that one out, you want to take over the shed job?"

"Yeah!" After that horrible week, everything was coming together. Michael would get out of our faces and I'd make some money! The display window of Island Books popped into my head, full of delicious, brand-new covers. Harry Potter Book Seven was a whole year away, but there was the new *Eragon* book...

Dad was looking at me as if waiting for a response. "Okay," I agreed enthusiastically to whatever he must have said.

"That wasn't one of the choices," Dad smiled drily. "I asked what movie you wanted for tonight. It's third Saturday," he prompted.

Third Saturday at the Burgowskis' means Movie Night. We all sit around, eating expired junk food from the store and watching the latest DVD from Dalby Video. Movie Night used to be a weekly thing, but Michael started putting up a fuss about having to spend that much time with family.

Now Movie Night was my problem. Nighttime was when I planned to be leaping off the Toad again.

"Oh," I managed. "Do you think that's a good idea, Dad? I mean, Michael's still kind of—"

"That's exactly why it's a good idea," Dad said. "Nice and normal is what your brother needs—not to mention the rest of us."

Normal. Right.

"Okay...but..." I stalled. "Can we start a little later this time? 'Cause it's summer now. Like, nine or ten or something?" *Just give me enough time to zip on out there, do that leaping thing, fly around for*—what? Fifteen minutes? Twenty? I had no idea how long I'd flown last night.

On the other hand, I had no idea if it would work again tonight.

Dad laughed. "Hey, it's not your loss of sleep I'm worried about, kiddo, it's mine." But for once I didn't have to work my sincere-spaniel expression. He grinned. "Well, why not? Maybe Lorraine will think I'm being extra romantic."

"Oh, maybe she better choose then," I said politely. "And did you mean that about staying up?"

"Sure. Nine o'clock tip-off."

"Nine-thirty?"

"You're pushing it, my girl. But fine. I'll just nap on the couch if the movie gets boring."

Even with my scraped-up knees and hand, I cleared out more of that smelly old shed in two hours than Michael had in a week. My thoughts zoomed around and my body just seemed to follow. *Nice and normal—what this family needs.* I boxed up about a hundred old gears and bolts that Michael had ignored. *Your mom called last night.* I scrubbed out a disgusting corner which some animal had decided to use as an outhouse. Maybe my friend the owl. *Oh, the flying has to work again. Step step...* I was scraping the corners of the gummed-shut window—*oh, the whssshh!*—when I heard someone call my name from the back door. I stuck my head out of the shed.

"Jocelyn! Phone!" It was Lorraine. Had she been there the whole time? *Well, why not? Did you think she and Dad were going to keep on living in two houses forever?* No, I thought, it's just weird to have her calling me into my own house, like...Well, it's just weird.

"Thanks. Hi," I muttered as she held the screen door for me. She was wearing her hair down, and it smelled good, like...lilies. The flight-memory stabbed through me, this time an urgent longing. *It has to work again, it has to.*

But then I was picking up the receiver and Savannah's voice was saying something about puppies. I wasn't too thrilled with my best friend at the moment, but I had a whole day to get through before darkness arrived, and...puppies!!! I told her I'd be over as soon as I'd cleaned up.

Lorraine was making a cup of tea when I hung up. I smelled peppermint. "Heading out, then?" she said pleasantly. "Shall I pass that message on to your dad?"

I was already reaching for the curtain. "Oh, no problem, I'll just tell him—hey!" The stool by the cash register was empty. "Dad?" I called, stepping into the store.

Lorraine followed me, carrying her tea mug. She gave a deep sniff, like she was planning to drink it through her nose, but all she said was, "He's out right now, Jocelyn, I was just going to tell you."

"Out?" There isn't really any "out" on Dalby.

"Gil came by about an hour ago with...someone to talk to Ron about Michael," Lorraine smiled. "I told them to go talk at the café, I'd mind the store for a little while. Don't worry," she added, "I've done it before."

"You have? When?"

"Oh, on my lunch break sometimes, which your poor dad never gets. Weekdays, you know. That's why you've never seen me." She set her tea down by the cash register, gathered up her hair and somehow coiled it behind her head all in one movement.

"Huh." I fingered my sore hand, trying to absorb this information. No wonder Lorraine didn't have to ask me where we kept the teabags; she had already started moving in. "Wait—who's talking with Dad about Michael?"

"Um, I believe she's a social worker." *Never heard Lorraine say "um" before.* "Did you hurt your hand on the picnic table too, last night?"

"Oh." I jammed it into my jeans pocket. "No, just scraped it on some stuff in the shed."

She nodded, but her eyes narrowed as she sipped her tea. We stood there together in the empty store. *Social worker?* I wanted to ask, but that would mean a longer conversation instead of a polite escape.

"Well," I began.

But Lorraine was already saying, "So..." *Too late.* "So," she went on, "are you looking forward to having a little space for yourself this summer?"

I must have looked as blank as I felt, because she added, "Being the only child, I mean."

It felt like being in a play without a script. "I don't…"

"Oh, dear." Lorraine set her tea on the counter. "Ron hasn't talked about this with you, has he? Oh, shoot—I did not mean to be—I just figured by now you two had…oh, dear."

Her hair started coming down over one shoulder, and her normally pale, freckledy face flushed pink from the neck up. If she'd been Mom or Dad I would have yelled, "What are you talking about?" and that would've felt good even if it got me in trouble for being rude. But rudeness didn't seem to be an option here.

"He said Michael's grounded," I said. I was probably frowning. "He said I get to take over his job for now. That's all. Oh, except you get to pick the movie tonight."

"Movie?" She looked bewildered. The rest of her hair came back down. *Hah, I knew that wouldn't work without a barrette.*

"For Movie Night," I said impatiently. "Dad'll explain later. But what did you mean about only child?"

Lorraine sighed and sat down on Dad's stool. "Well, since I've put my foot in it, I'd better tell you, hadn't I." It wasn't a question. "Your dad was telling me he's decided that grounding Michael here on Dalby will only cause more trouble. So Michael's going to McClenton to spend the summer with your mother. He can get a better job there, pay for the truck damage. That's why the social worker came, to map out a strategy for Michael to stay with Beth and…have it work for everyone."

Most people, when they have to tell you something you're not going to like, find something else to look at. Lorraine wasn't like that. She kept her eyes on me the whole time. They're light blue, kind of watery. Kind of sad.

I said, "Oh."

Michael to Mom's? Why doesn't anyone tell me anything? What the hell is happening to my family?

There we stood. Lorraine sniffed again, then shook her head like she was arguing with someone. The shop door opened and a whole, touristy-looking family trooped in.

"So I'll tell Ron you're going over to your friend's, shall I?" Lorraine said quickly, and I just nodded like a little kid, then left her to deal with their questions about camping stove fuel, perched on Dad's stool with her mug of tea, looking like she owned the place.

Savannah thought it was a great idea. "How cool is that, Joss? You can totally breathe in your house if Michael's gone! No more 'How dare you use my bike,' right? No more—"

"He'll take his bike with him to McClenton." I pushed some Savannah-laundry under my butt for a cushion on her hard floor.

"Joss, work with me here. I don't see why you're so grouchy about getting the house to yourself for two months. Being the only child rocks."

She's only raving about Dad's plan because she's tired of apologizing for last night. Plus the puppies she'd promised were her neighbors' and they were napping. Leftover anger from my party, I had discovered, squooshed any desire to tell my bestie about my new magic…at least for now.

"It's like my family's totally disintegrating. Just me and Dad and Lorraine? What kind of a family's that? Plus Dad didn't even tell me." My stomach hurt, so I pushed a little, like with a sore tooth: "I had to find out from…her."

"So what?" Savannah breezed. She reached down from her bed and started scritching my scalp with her fingernails. "He prob'ly asked her to, like, float the idea with you, woman to woman. Men are like that."

"Quit." I pulled away. Savannah and I have given each other head rubs since we were in kindergarten. It's very comforting, like being part of a baboon pack. But I wasn't in the mood for comfort. "Plus it's not fair, Michael getting to go to McClenton after all."

"What's it matter to you?" Savannah demanded. "You don't want to go there, right? You don't even *like* your mom."

Ouch.

"Yeah I do," I said. But Savannah's smart, remember? She could easily have pushed on to win the argument— *"You told me she's a pillhead, Joss;" "You said she'd probably've sold you for drug money if your dad had let her"*—but instead she let it go.

"Well, never mind," she said. "Hey, I like your perfume, by the way."

"What're you talking about?"

"You, girlfriend. You smell good. What is it?"

Stupidly I smelled my own arm. It just smelled like me. "I'm not wearing any perfume."

She rolled her eyes. "Yeah, okay, whatever. C'mon, I'll do your nails."

Savannah has about a million jars of nail polish on her dresser, with ridiculous names. She knows I couldn't care less about that stuff, but she was trying. My cloud of anger lifted.

"Fine. But not what you have on. It looks like you just clawed someone to death."

"Ha." Savannah hopped up to read the titles of her little treasures. *"Plum Passion, Desiree, Sultry Smoke, Whisper Kiss, Seduction, Hot Lava…"*

"Jeez, Savannah, it sounds like those little bottles're all having sex up there on your dresser."

"Oh, shut up. What about *Bodacious*? That'd look good on you. Or *Flygirl*. Or *Dazzling Des*—"

"That last one."

"Dazzling Desire?" Savannah looked doubtful.

"Flygirl."

Turns out my own, personalized nail polish was a sort of red-dish-pink that made my fingertips look like little lipsticks. But Savannah worked carefully, and didn't ask how I'd hurt my hand. Somehow, her hovering over me like there was no more important job in the universe—well, it was comforting. Even with that awful smell. *If I fly tonight, maybe I'll tell her tomorrow…*

Then, just as she was finishing up my left pinkie, she had to go and ruin it.

"So, Nate told me he likes you," she said, and then immediately squawked "Joss!" as I jerked away.

"What're you talking about?" The room seemed to heat up suddenly.

"Don't clench 'em, you idiot, you'll mess 'em all up! Jeez! Now I have to do that hand again."

"Never mind," I said grimly. "When did you talk to those guys? I thought you said you were never going to speak to them again." *But what did Nate say?* floated up from somewhere in my brain.

"Oh, so you *were* listening to me last night," Savannah said, arching her brows. "Well, for your information Nate called me this morning. To apologize."

"To you? What for?"

"No, not to me, dummy, that's what I'm saying. He wanted me to tell you he's sorry. See what I mean? He obviously likes you. Why else would he call *me*?"

Huh. "So…" *So he didn't actually say he liked me?* No way was I going to ask. *Like it matters! Nathan Cowper's a jerk.*

"So I told him you were cool with it," Savannah went on. "I mean, I told you they were just being guys, right? Oh, and I said you'd call him later so he could tell you himself."

You know those sped-up films of flowers opening? I felt like someone was messing with the rewind and fast-forward buttons, opening and closing me at crazy speed. Suddenly I wanted to cry. *What's the matter with everybody?* All I wanted to do was get through the day, wait for a little darkness, and see if I was still magic, was that too much to ask? And all these stupid people-issues kept swarming over me like vines, trying to tie me down.

Mrs. Mac would tell me I'm mixing my metaphors. But I'll bet Mrs. Mac never had to deal with jerks who may or may not like you but are too jerky to let you know.

"Hell no, I'm not calling him," I snapped. "You call him if you want to."

Savannah looked taken aback. "No, no, I don't need to talk to him. He was just being nice, Joss, 'cause he knew you were upset last night."

I examined my ruined nails, feeling the flower go open-shut, open-shut.

"I keep telling you I'm *sorry,*" she added, and even though this wasn't quite true, well, it also was, so I let it go.

I waved my left hand. "Hey, why'n't you get this stuff off me."

She sighed, but didn't argue. Out came the polish remover. But when Savannah reached for my right hand with her little cotton puffs, I pulled it away.

"No, that's okay, I'll keep this one," I told her. "I'm still at least half Flygirl."

Mrs. Mac always made us keep Journals, the dorky kind that teachers read, where we have to Reflect on our Reaction to the end of *Hatchet,* or Freewrite on the High Points of our Winter Break. Now and then she'd read from some famous journal like Anne Frank's, and then she'd sigh and say that Journaling is a Lost Art. "It's also cheap therapy," she would add. I was beginning to understand that.

Should I call Nate? What would I say? How the hell am I going to live alone with Dad and Lorraine? Why doesn't Mom want me in McClenton too? And most of all, *why, why, when the biggest miracle of my life—of anyone's life!—just opened up, is everything so clogged with complications?*

70

I needed Mrs. Mac to assign me a Reflection to sort it all out on paper. But there was nothing to do but get through the day as fast as possible, so I biked home and spent the rest of the afternoon finishing the shed. My "therapist" was going to be the sky. *But what if I can't get back up there?*

"I just want you to know, Joss," Dad said, hours later, "Michael's not going on vacation. He's going to work all summer in McClenton."

I had just walked into the pizza-smelling kitchen for dinner. *Hah, so Lorraine talked to him and he's feeling guilty for not telling me himself. Good.* But I was so distracted by the clock, I had almost forgotten about Michael. My stomach tightened.

Eight-thirty was when I had to leave the house for Big Leap Number Two: late enough for a darkening sky, but still enough time for me to get out, get up—*oh, it has to work!*—and get back in time for the movie. Two and a half HOURS to wait.

Lorraine drifted in, speaking softly, like she expected everyone to hush up just to hear her. "I made a plain cheese one, in case you don't like feta and olives."

"I like 'em fine," I told her automatically. *Shoot. Now I have to eat that stinky, salty crap just to prove it.*

Michael clumped in as we were sitting down, looking tired and grumpy.

"So you're going to Mom's?"

"Yeah."

"Aren't you upset you're gonna miss Battle of the Bands?"

"Pfff."

It sucked that he wasn't upset about his banishment. It sucked even worse that I was. And it sucked worst of all that I had to get through two more HOURS before I could try my magic again. If I hung around after dinner, Dad would suggest starting earlier, and then where would I be?

Michael helped a little: when Dad asked him about job appli-
cations, he grunted. That started another argument, the slo-mo
kind where both sides clench their anger behind their teeth. But
eventually Michael muttered, "I *said* Mom's apartment super's
gonna give me a job, okay?" And everyone left the table before
they unclenched.

After washing up, I tried hiding out in my room with a book,
but that didn't work; I was way too nervous to concentrate on
reading, and if Dad called to start the movie I wouldn't be able
to pretend I wasn't there. Outside, then: *I can always say I didn't
hear him, right?* I tried lying on the grass behind the picnic table,
invisible from the house, staring up at the sky I might soon be
whooshing through. A pale, skinny moon already lounged above
the woods, but the sun looked in no mood to set. Seven-fifteen,
my watch said. *ARGHH.* What if the magic is gone already? *But
oh, my flying dreams…*

A bat dipped wildly past. The moon grew a shade brighter, but
the sky remained as stubbornly light as a piece of paper. 7:22. An
ant crawled on my wrist and I let it skitter all the way up to my
elbow before it tickled so much I had to brush it off. Probably
looking for some more fried chicken scraps. Boy, could Louis eat
chicken. *Is he mad at me now?* He should be. *Maybe I should go
over*—Louis doesn't have a phone—but Louis knew about Movie
Night, so how could I keep from inviting him? *Yeah, come on over,
buddy. Or, wait, on second thought—gimme about fifteen minutes to
turn into Batgirl, then come over.* Oh wow, though, his face sure had
looked sad last night when he left with that carrot cake.

7:28.

I rolled over on my stomach, pillowed my head on my arms
and closed my eyes, willing the time to pass. I would not look at
my watch. Not for at least another fifteen minutes. Should *I call
Nate?* What would I say? *Hey, if you promise not to be a jerk I'll tell
you the biggest secret in the world…whoops, too late, you're already a*

jerk! No, don't look at your watch. Seven-thirty. Damn.

At one point I tried to visualize my takeoff—*step step BOOM*—but then stopped hastily. What if thinking about it too much messed you up? I felt another ant crawling, this time over my bare ankle, and I gritted my teeth and let it crawl.

And a new idea skittered into my brain. *If it works...when it works...I can show Michael! No way he'd want to leave then!*

I rolled back over, staring at a knothole in the picnic table bench. *Maybe I can take him flying, like Superman and Lois. Maybe I can fly the truck home for him! Then he won't even owe Dad...*My brain began to hum with plans. Jobs for both of us, right here on Dalby. Flying in the evenings. A whole new secret bond. I closed my eyes, picturing my rescued summer.

The moon was huge, a giant pearl. I flew across it, seeing my own silhouette crossing the dimples and crags of its glowing surface, and Louis was right alongside, and he was smiling at me through eyelashes as long as a girl's. "It's all right," he said in someone else's voice, "she's right here."

"You called it, Lorraine—she's right here. Hey, sleepyhead—still want to stay up till midnight?"

Dad's voice above me. His hand on my shoulder. *What in the world?*

"What time is it?" I gasped, rolling over and clonking my shoulder on the picnic table. The sky was no sheet of paper now; it had turned the color of gravel.

"No idea," Dad said, sounding amused, "except time to talk to your mother. She's on the phone for you."

Still shaking the dream-flight out of my head, I tottered into the kitchen. As I reached for the phone I saw the stove clock: 8:55.

I'd been asleep in the yard for an hour and a half.

"H'lo?" I mumbled.

"Hey, babe. Hippo birdie, finally." My mom's crackly voice always reminded me of the sound a bean-bag chair makes when you sit in it. Kind of comforting usually, but all I could think was, *If I don't get off the phone in about three minutes, there'll be no time to fly.*

"Thanks…"

"So, whaddja get? Anything good?" She sounded sober, just a regular telephone-mom settling in for a good, girl-to-girl chat.

"Um…yeah. I got a book from Dad."

"Well, sorry I didn't get your present yet. I need your help to pick out something out of all the crap they sell here. It's like they think all girls want to dress like whores. You haven't caved into the fashion gods yet, have you, Joss? Tell me you don't want to dress like a whore."

"No, I don't." 8:57.

"Did you have a good party? Must've been good, they couldn't even get you to the phone."

Ouch. In spite of myself, she started to pull me in. "Mom, I didn't not call you on purpose, okay? There was a lot of stuff going on and nobody told me—"

"Hey, don't worry about it. We're talking now, aren't we? So tell me, babe, you okay with the idea of Michael coming over here? That crazy kid. No wonder they want to ship him off to me. Don't you want to come too?"

"Mom…" 8:59. I looked desperately around the kitchen, but there was no helpful family emergency to call me away. "I don't know. I mean, it's fine, I guess."

"You don't know if it's okay, or you don't know if you want to come?" The scratches in her voice got deeper, but I was past caring.

"I don't know! Mom, look, I have to go, okay? There's something I gotta do—look, I'll call you tomorrow, all right? Okay?"

She was silent. The clock showed nine.

"Okay, Mom?" I pressed.

She sighed. "Whatever, babe. Let me know when you've got an opening in your schedule." Then a click, and silence.

Any normal girl would've felt horrible, any normal girl would've called right back and talked until everything was fixed.

But I was no longer a normal girl. And I was almost out of time to fly. I burst out the door and raced across the lawn toward the woods, past Dad and Lorraine at the picnic table.

"Hey, Turbo, where ya going?" he called after me and I yelled, "Be right back!" But even as I tore onto the Toad shortcut, I knew I wouldn't make it there in time. Ten minutes to get to the Toad at a dead run, ten minutes back, that only left ten minutes in the air, and what if it didn't work? What if the landing was just as rough as last night? I couldn't run back into my living room all bruised and gasping...

I screeched to a halt on the scratchy path. *Stupid, stupid, stupid!* Now I was going to have to wait another twenty-four hours to fly again, and maybe whatever Solstice Magic had been at work would have worn out! What would I have to show Michael then? Out of time, out of sorts, out of my mind with frustration, I made a startling discovery.

Sorry, old Toad. You're a friend in need, a refuge, and the world's best spot to eat a sandwich, but you are not the only magic launch pad on Dalby Island. I closed my eyes and clenched my fists, ready to scream with outrage at the way the world was conspiring against me, and shot straight up through the trees.

CHAPTER EIGHT

FLYING
BURGOWSKI

*C*runch.

That was the sound my head made when it zoomed straight into a fir branch. The pain wrung me like a rag. As I fought not to spray the remains of my pizza over the underbrush, my arms took over and flailed like crazy. I must've looked like some sort of drunken helicopter, hovering in a face-down, moaning spin.

Big, open-topped rocks aren't required for takeoff, turns out. They're just way safer.

I have no idea how long it took me, in slow-mo rotation, to breathe away the nausea and the throbbing pain. But finally I opened my eyes to realize that my head, though wearing a lump like the Toad, was still attached...and I was flying!

The last of the pain disappeared into a whoop of joy. Like an idiot I nearly knocked myself out again, but at the last second I flailed just right and went shooting along, safely horizontal, about ten feet above the path where there was a little room to maneuver below the lowest branches of the firs. In a flash I was through the woods and angling up to soar above the arching of the Toad and out—*at last!*—into the freedom of the sky.

My heart was shrieking with delight. *Itworked! Itworked! Itworked! Oh, thankyouthankyouthankyou!* I flew a while without thought, without a plan, without awareness of anything but this giant swirl of triumph, glowing like a firefly.

Around me the air grew cooler and I suddenly realized I was very high; from up here I could see the just-past-Solstice sun lowering itself into the ocean. I angled down to settle myself at what felt like a safer altitude, although that seemed silly. *How'm I supposed to know what's safe?* I seemed to have skipped the whole pilot training thing, and no one had exactly given me a manual to thumb through. *But who cares?* For the second time my body had taken over, and that was enough for me.

"Ladies and gentlemen, I give you...the Flying Jocelyn!" I said to the night. Sounded lame. "The Amazing Flying...Burgowski." That fit.

You know how it feels in a swimming pool, pushing through the water but it's still holding you up, like it wants you to succeed? When you fly, the air doesn't need pushing. It's all the love and none of the resistance of water. I'd been so busy that first flight trying not to panic, learning how to turn and rise and swoop, that I hadn't bothered to notice this fact: flying felt like no work at all.

This is bogus, of course. I've already mentioned how hungry I get when I fly. Burns a ton of calories. But, oh, wow, what a feeling to flail and kick, to veer and roll and flap my arms, the soft air giving way to my skin, limitless as possibility. I flew toward the center of the island, where sleeping sheep and cows dotted their pastures like lumpy little mushrooms. And as I flew, I tried some tricks.

Running in place with big, silly strides: fun! Pointless, but fun. Using my feet like flippers and waving my body like a seal: a little insecure. I felt better in Superman position. I was on the verge of trying out an aerial cartwheel, over a dwarf apple orchard, when I heard someone chuckle below me. Right below. I was about to whoosh directly over the heads of two people who were walking through the shoulder-high trees, and there were no woods in sight for me to hide in while they passed.

And no brakes! I flailed, hoping like crazy I wasn't creating a whirlwind that would cause them to look up. It took a second, but sure enough, just as I was right on top of them, I started flying backward. Like an idiot, I closed my eyes so they wouldn't see me.

Then one of the people laughed, up and down like a musical scale.

My eyes flew open. Even in the growing dusk it was easy to tell Savannah, her white shorts practically glowing, the miniature pony tail sprouting from the top of her head like a handle. But I couldn't tell who she was walking with—someone taller and quieter. *What in the world is she doing here?* Then a face turned toward the moonlight.

"What the hell is that?" a male voice said distinctly.

I cartwheeled. Not on purpose, I just flung my body sideways, out of the line of that pale face's sight and kept going, tumbling through the air toward the nearest barn, which was still nowhere close enough. My heart was pounding so loudly I didn't hear Savannah's response, but the boy with her was plenty loud now.

"Look!" he shouted. "It's a frickin' condor or something!"

It was Nate. And he'd seen me. Savannah's face lifted skyward too, luckily the wrong direction from me. "Where? Where?"

I flailed some more, then made an intelligent choice and turned tail. You can fly a lot faster forward than backward. With Nate's voice in my ears, I flew.

The barn was huge. I flew right through the open hayloft doors and landed on a hay bale as delicately as a kingfisher on a branch, then I turned around, gasping, and hid myself in the moonshadow of the doorway to peep out. Nate and Savannah were running through the little orchard like hounds on a scent, still a hundred yards away but headed right toward me, their voices carrying clearly in the stillness.

"It flew right in there! I swear!"

"You're crazy," my friend said, but she kept with him.

Forget flying; I climbed up those bales like they were some kind of scratchy pyramid and I was a human sacrifice escaping the priests. It was pitch black in there, and I only discovered the top of the pile by bumping my head on one of the rafters, but I was so grateful to be hidden, I didn't mind the throbbing of my original head-lump that leapt back to life. The hay smelled fresh and sweet, but I stifled my breathing as best I could, straining to hear what was going on below me.

Don't let them find me. I had no idea why this was so important.

"Well, that is weird and a half," Nate's voice said from below. "It couldn't've flown indoors, right? I mean don't those things, like, roost on crags and stuff?"

"Don't be an idiot," Savannah told him. "They don't have condors here. You just saw an owl or something. A barn owl!" For once I was grateful for Savannah's know-it-allness.

But what's she doing walking through an orchard with Nate? my mind wanted to know.

"No way, owls don't get that big," Nate insisted. "Wonder if we could climb up there?"

Of its own accord, my body stuffed itself higher up into the crevice beneath the rafters. Something rustled behind me. *Do snakes live in haylofts?* I don't mind snakes when I can see them, but I wasn't wild about cuddling up with one in the dark.

Savannah said, "Well, you go right ahead. Just don't come crying to me when you get owl-pecked," and then I couldn't hear the rest, but it involved laughter.

Savannah and Nate. *What-ever.* No wonder she kept making like she didn't like him. Good thing I hadn't called him! Normally I would've seen this a mile off, but I'd been so distracted all week. *Still, what's so bad about them seeing me?*

Well, I don't want anyone to see me. Duh.

Them especially, though. How come?

They wouldn't get it. The whole flying thing. They'd want to make a dumb video and put it on the internet.

Well, who wouldn't? That's not the point and you know it.

Fine. Whatever. But the voices were gone. Cautiously I clambered back down my hay-pyramid and peeked out the hayloft door.

The moonlight, brighter than ever, showed an empty barnyard. So far, so good, and—*hey!* It suddenly occurred to me: I had landed on a dime! Well, on a hay bale. But no crash, no thud, no feeling the need to puke. *I'm getting good at this.*

The smug feeling didn't last long. That moonlight was telling me something. *Oh jeez, it's getting late.* This was supposed to be a short flight, only a test, to see if my new talent was real and not just Solstice magic.

Well, mission accomplished, but now I was totally late for Movie Night.

Without a second thought, I flung myself out of the hayloft.

Takeoff Number Three was the best of all. For a moment I forgot everything—the panic at being nearly seen, the confusing glop of feelings about who had nearly seen me, the frantic need to get back home—and lost myself in the glory of that leap, when my body simply joined the air, and nothing bad happened. No fright, no pain, no need to flail. I cartwheeled, just for the heck of it, right there over the barnyard. And then I sped for home.

I checked my watch: 9:38. Oh, Dad was going to be pissed. My stress distracted me so much that I didn't even notice the *Whssshh* turning into a *WHSSSHH!!*

Then it hit me: I'm *fast!*

I had no idea how fast; I mean, it's not like I had a speedometer. But then I spotted a car coming along Bay Road and I couldn't resist a little test. Veering to the left, I positioned myself above the car and flew along about fifty feet above it.

The speed limit there is twenty-five, which of course no one does. That car might have been going thirty, more likely thirty-five. I left it in my dust, the air just flowing around me, welcoming me through.

Oh, Michael's gonna love this! I mean, this wasn't just Peter Pan anymore. I could rocket.

"I'm a superhero," I said aloud, but that sounded ridiculous. *No... The Flying Burgowski. That's me.*

But The Flying Burgowski needed to pay attention—she nearly flew straight over the center of the village. We don't have much night life on Dalby, but on a nice June night there were several people walking around down there, in couples and clumps. Even though it was pretty dark now, I'd be plenty visible to anyone smart enough to look up. Luckily, people hardly ever do; it's something I've noticed since I became a Flyer. That's how come I know Michael's video was a fake; if someone saw something like that, they wouldn't whisper about it, they'd yell, right? But I veered again, taking the less direct route to my house. Straight over Louis's.

His house is tiny. I think it actually used to be a storage shed attached to the food co-op, but Shasta, his mom, lives there as caretaker. Dad helped Shasta build a tiny addition next to the goat-pen so Louis didn't have to share a bedroom with her. And a light was on in Louis's room.

I couldn't help myself. Late as I was, I slowed in midair and swooped down to window level. The tangy smell of goat filled the air, and one of them said, "Meh-eh-eh," probably Goat for, "What the—?"

Thinking back, I probably was going to do something dumb like whisper, "Hey, Louis! I can fly! I can even hover!" just for the sheer need of bragging on myself, then zoom away. But one peek into the little room killed that idea.

Louis was crying. I couldn't see his face, but when someone's curled up on the bed like a puppy, you can kind of guess the reason: either they have a terrible stomachache, or they're hugging their misery close because they don't have anything else to hug.

I didn't think Louis had a stomachache.

Half of me wanted to fly right down, walk through their front door and yell, "Hey, Louis! Let's go clamming!" Anything to un-curl him, let him know I was still his friend even if I was such a crappy one.

The other half said, "You're late. You'll never be able to explain that to Dad. You can talk to him tomorrow."

I listened to the second half—not the better. And it got me home in time, but a little piece of Louis's hurt stuck in my stom-ach. I no longer felt like eating popcorn. The stove clock said 9:43 as I breezed in from the dark yard. The living room flickered in TV-light, showing Dad and Lorraine on the couch, Michael in the armchair on the other side of the room. They had started without me.

"'Bout time," Michael said, but he sounded slightly admiring.

"Young lady, where've you—" Dad hissed, but Lorraine shushed him.

"Watch the movie, Ron. This is the good part."

Whoa, Lorraine to the rescue! I could live with that. "What're you guys watching?" I whispered.

Turns out it was this really ancient movie from the 1980s, *Ed-ward Scissorhands*, about a guy who is seriously different. He finds cool and useful things to do with his freakish hands, which are not just scissors but all kinds of blades like a really disorganized Swiss Army knife. For a while everything's great and he thinks he's fitting in, but in the end he's just too different and he can't help hurting somebody even though he doesn't want to. I was kind of surprised Michael watched the whole thing. At first I thought he was trying to be a good boy for once, but when I glanced over at him, his hair was pushed all the way back and his face told me he was really into poor old Edward.

When it was over we all sat there in the darkness, listening to the twinkly credits music. My heart sped up: now I just needed to get Michael alone! But first we'd have to sit through Lorraine asking, "So? What did you guys think?" It was her movie choice, after all, and she's the librarian—they're practically teachers, right? But she didn't.

Finally Michael said, "See, that's what you get for trying to do what everyone else wants you to do."

Dad looked up quickly, and I realized he had been resting his head on Lorraine's shoulder. "That's what the movie says to you, huh?" he asked, but he sounded more sympathetic than challenging.

Michael shrugged, which for him was like being on his best behavior. Lorraine said, "I love this movie. I just think it's a shame all the stories of freakish people trying to fit into the normal world are about boys." For some reason she was looking at me when she said it. *Freakish people, huh? You have no idea, lady.*

The image of Louis stabbed back into me then. I might be the Flygirl, but he was the freak who didn't fit in. And I knew it, and I wasn't doing anything about it.

"Well, all I know is, I'm choosing *Spider-Man* next time," my brother said. "When I get back, anyway. That dude had it figured out. Secret identity, yeah—but none of that bat-cave or Kryptonite crap. Just keep the ol' mask and tights handy and you're outta there whenever things get hairy."

"'With great power comes great responsibility,'" Lorraine said softly, and we all stared at her. "What? I used to read Spidey comics when I was a kid," she added, and actually giggled.

I could see Dad's grin clear across the room in the darkness. The air around my tense little "family" relaxed a teensy bit.

"Well, good night, all," Dad said. "Jocelyn, if us old people are useless tomorrow, it's your fault." But he came over and gave me a hug. "Mm, don't you smell nice," he said into my hair.

"Doesn't she, Ron?" Lorraine sounded like she was smiling. "It's almost like…" But she didn't say what my smell was like or why she was so weirdly into it. Then Dad kissed the top of my head.

Right on my lump—*oww. Damn.* He never noticed my wince, though, 'cause he was taking Lorraine's hand and they were definitely heading toward his bedroom together—no more pretending.

Michael disappeared into his room. *Now's my chance. With great power comes great responsibility.* Right, Spidey: first my brother— then I could take care of Louis.

I tapped on his door. "Hey. Want to know a secret?" Like I was five years old.

"What," he said. I entered the Michael-cave, heart racing. He'd turned on his lava lamp; orange blobs lit the black netting on the ceiling in a shifting glow.

I took a deep breath. "I can fly."

Michael looked at me through his hair.

"Really! I've done it three times now. First on my birthday, and I thought it was like a kind of special Solstice magic or something, but I just did it again. Tonight. Twice, and it's not just the Toad either, I flew right off the path, and off a hay bale, and some people almost saw me…"

Michael kept looking at me. In my opinion when someone doesn't reply, what they're really doing is sucking up the conversation-air, so pretty soon there's not enough left for the person talking.

"I'm serious!" I managed before I had to stop for breath.

"Wow," my brother said. "And they think I'm the pothead."

"I am NOT—"

"Oh, keep your pants on," Michael sneered. "Too many books, overexcited imagination, not enough attention. Call it whatever you want. I'm sure *they* will. You gonna share this little secret with *them?*"

"Are you crazy? You think they'd believe me?"

"You think I do?" Michael asked. "You've been looking at that video I showed you, is that it? Shee-it, Joss, you know that thing's a fake."

I wanted to cry with frustration. "I'll show you!" I said fiercely. "C'mon outside, now, out to the woods, I'll show you! But you have to promise not to tell."

"Okay, Joss, cut it out." Now he sounded like Dad. "It never was particularly funny, now it's just getting old. You like to play flying. Whoopee for you. It'll give you something to do while I'm in McClenton."

"Please, Michael, just come outside," I begged.

"F--- that. Fly right here if you're so...gifted. Go ahead, I'm watching. Fly."

"It doesn't work inside," I mumbled. Of course it does—if only I'd known that then! I could have hovered right over my bed. But the last thing I wanted was to mess up in front of Michael.

"Yeah. Right. Nice talking to ya, Sis," Michael snorted. "Shee-it, I can't wait to leave this place. Now get your ass out of my room."

So I had no choice. I had to go get that truck by myself.

I know—I'm an idiot. Why not go outside and fly to Michael's window like I did with Louis? Seeing is believing, right? But a single thought rescued me from the paralyzing fury of Michael's rejection: *I'll show him.* I'm Superwoman, right? If I can fly me, why not the truck? Just pick it up and fly that puppy home. Michael will see it in the driveway, without a single tire track. Plus— he knows I can't drive! He'll have to believe me then. And if the truck's back, he won't have to pay for the tow, and he won't have to go to McClenton.

SO many things wrong with that plan. Forget the fact that Dad would have wondered just as much about the missing tire tracks, so I'd have had to tell him too. Forget the fact that Michael didn't want to be saved from exile. What got me in the end was my stupid bedroom door. In my rush to save the day, I left it open.

Dad wouldn't have noticed his missing daughter otherwise, when he got up to pee around one in the morning. Wouldn't have known a thing about my plan. My failure.

'Cause it's not like I could fly a truck. Not like I could have washed off all the greasy, muddy evidence of all my attempts to lift it from that ditch, hovering in the dark like a stupid dragonfly over a rock. A rock that wasn't going anywhere.

But Dad saw my open door, my empty bed. And when I stumbled back in, close to two, filthy and glum, he was sitting in the kitchen, gathering his anger.

"What the hell do you think you're up to?"

I had just been wondering the same thing.

CHAPTER NINE

MY BROTHER'S KEEPER

"Who were you out with? Do you have any idea what time it is? Did your brother put you up to this? What the hell's the matter with my kids?"

Turns out leaving my door open was only Mistake Number One. Number Two was not preparing a cover story. That happens when you're too busy being rolled by wave after wave of emotion. My rage at Michael had given way to the exhilaration of midnight flight, only to get slammed by the humiliation of discovering, in the muddy truck-darkness, that I am not Superman. Or Spider-Man. I am, in fact, a teenage idiot whose family thinks she's a stupid little girl.

"Sorry," muttered the stupid little girl.

"'Sorry?' That's it?" my father roared. "Out in the middle of the night, not a word to anyone? Wearing perfume? And—is that mud on your jeans?" His face darkened and his eyes narrowed. "Jocelyn, I swear. Whoever he is, if this is his idea of dating, you can forget him right now."

"What? No, Dad! It's not like that." *Whoa.* Maybe little girl was better than slut. "I'm...I'm not seeing anybody." *But he thinks I could be? Whoa.*

Dad stared a hole in me, his face returning to normal. "What am I supposed to think, then, huh? That's twice tonight you've jetted out of here. You've always been truthful with me before, Jocelyn. So if you say it's not a boy, okay. I'm ready to believe you. Just tell me what the hell is going on."

I opened my mouth, but nothing came out.

"What's up?" Michael stuck his bed head into the kitchen.

"None of your business," I snapped. Still, no answer for Dad. *Went for a walk? Star-gazing?* How could I have not seen this coming? "I…just felt like being alone."

Dad threw up his hands. "Great. Wonderful. And I thought I only had one kid to worry about." He stood up. "I can't deal with this right now. I have half a mind to send you both to Mc-Clenton."

"Wait—what?" Michael and I said together.

"Go to bed," Dad ordered.

"She can't come with—"

"I can't go to—"

"Go. To. Bed." Dad repeated. "NOW."

The moment I woke up Sunday morning, my stomach knew something was wrong. Took my brain a moment to catch up. But then…

Oh yeah… Dad's pissed. I may be banished with Michael.

Mom's pissed too. She hung up on me and she wasn't even drunk.

And I saw Louis crying.

So I tried staying in bed to see if anything got better.

If I went to McClenton, at least I'd be with Michael. *But he doesn't want you. He'd be worse than ever.*

I could make it up with Mom face to face. *Yeah, when she knows it wasn't your idea to come? Right.*

I could get a job there too. Dad would see he could trust me after all. *Ouch. Yeah.*

Louis would understand I'm not ditching him 'cause I want to.

That last one got me out of bed. *Can't ditch Louis.* I could give

Dad some time to think it over, I could talk to him, apologize my head off—he'd back down. He didn't really want to send me away.

And I couldn't possibly go. Mom would hate me.

I promised myself I'd call her first thing later on (which Mrs. Mac would call an Oxymoron, and then give us about twenty more, like "Twelve-Ounce Pound Cake"). No Dad around—*phew*—so I grabbed a piece of leftover pizza for breakfast and headed out for my bike.

Dad had pumped my tires to life without even telling me. I swallowed my pizza, and a large chunk of guilt, with difficulty.

I could still tell him about my magic. But how? Michael only sneered at me. Dad would send me to a shrink. So I rode away.

At Louis's, I did what I've always done since we were little: walked in the front door saying, "Hey."

"Hey, sweetie." Shasta was having breakfast in the miniature kitchen with some new shaggy guy. He looked startled to see this strange chick breezing into his girlfriend's house, but nodded and went back to his breakfast—probably thirty-seven-grain cereal. "He's in his room," Shasta added, same as always. She grinned like her son, lighting up the kitchen as I passed through.

Louis, sitting on his bed, was not grinning. His face wasn't doing much of anything, and I'm not even sure he was reading the big astronomy book propped on his lap. I didn't give myself time to feel guilty.

"Hey," I said. "Seal Rocks?" For some reason the Toad seemed the wrong place to go...or *do I want to keep it to myself now?* I didn't give myself time to think about that either. "It's a negative two point something tide pretty soon," I added. Negative tides mean lots of tide pool critters to examine.

"Okay," Louis said gravely. He put on one sandal and started hunting for the other. Same grimy T-shirt as last night, but that's normal for Louis. "Hey, your birthday cake was good. Want a piece?"

Ah, Louis and food. Nice and normal. "Yeah, let's take some with us," I said, and we did.

The sun was hot by the time we got to Seal Rocks, and I was glad for the water we brought to wash down the cake. It wasn't bad, for carrot, but in my opinion vegetables really ought to stick with being vegetables.

Tide-pooling is all about finding stuff: the weirder, the better, like the chunk of dead orca we found years ago. Here's what we scored that morning: two eating-sized kelp crabs; one skinny, bloodred starfish; and about a gazillion mini-hermit crabs. We also counted thirty-eight seals lounging like big, blotchy kidney beans on the rock-island beyond the fast-rushing narrows, plus a whole bunch swimming. One of 'em started slapping his tail on the water, which they do sometimes when they're feeling frisky. The morning got sunnier, and we lay on our stomachs moving hermit crabs around the tide pool like we were gods of a tiny ocean.

Louis told me his mom's new boyfriend's name was Al.

"Really? Al? I thought he'd be called something like Star Child," I said. Louis giggled. "Or, I don't know, Cedar Wind. Is he from here?"

"He just moved here," said Louis. "He lives in a tent. And," he giggled again, "Al believes in angels."

Now this was different. Al looked like he might believe in animal spirits, but angels? "How do you know?"

"When he came over last night he was all excited. Said he'd been meditating out by his tent and something whooshed over him. It wasn't a bird, he said, but big, huge, and it whooshed."

I knelt suddenly on my sore knee and nearly toppled into the tide pool. "Last night?"

"Yeah, just after dusk, he said. Hey, that's a cool word: 'dusk.'"

"Uh-huh," I murmured. "So…what'd he say the angel looked

like?" And then to cover for my unnatural interest I added, "Probably playing a golden harp, huh."

"Aw, I asked him, he didn't know," Louis replied, and a little bitterness crept into his voice. "He kept saying the Experience was what mattered. I think he was trying to impress my mom."

Looks like it worked, I thought, and felt a throb of guilty pity for Louis's crazy home life. *All my dad did was marry a perfectly normal lady, and I spent a whole week feeling sorry for myself.* But the Flying Burgowski was going to have to watch it. Angels! Condors! And I'd only flown twice.

Condors. Between Edward Scissorhands and Louis last night, I'd forgotten all about Savannah and Nate in the orchard. *Were they on some kind of date? And how'd it end?* I wasn't sure I wanted to know.

"What?" Louis asked, staring at me.

I quickly rearranged my face. "Nothing," I lied. "Just trying to imagine what an angel *would* look like."

"My mom says we're our own angels." Louis stared at the ocean. *Now would be a good time to tell him. Why not?* "But I don't believe her," he added, and I answered myself with the old favorite: *Because.*

But I owed him something. "So Michael's going to stay with my mom for the summer," I told Louis. He glanced over, like, *So?*

"And...my dad's kinda thinking of sending me too."

His face turned—what's that word? Stricken. "Why?"

"He's kinda mad at me. 'Cause, um..." *Go ahead, Flying Burgowski. Tell Louis about trying to rescue the truck.* That'd be harder to believe than angels.

"Found anything good?" a voice above us called.

This time Louis and I both nearly went into the pool, grabbing each other to keep our balance.

"Oh, whoops, looks like I'm interrupting something." The sun was right in our eyes when we turned around to see our visitor, but there was no mistaking that lazy, smiling voice. For a moment I was confused. *Did I somehow conjure up Nate by thinking about him?*

"What're you doing here?" I demanded. *And where's your girlfriend?* I wanted and didn't want to add.

Nate shrugged and moved slightly so his head blocked the sun, giving him a brilliant halo. "I was going to my aunt's. Saw your bike. Thought I'd see what's up."

You know what my bike looks like? "Nothing," I said defensively. Too many thoughts were competing for space. Nate and Tyler messing up my party. "*Nate said he likes you.*" Nate and Savannah strolling in the dusky orchard.

"Oh, cool—is that an abalone?" Nate hopped down onto our rock. His big toe stuck through a hole in his Adidas.

"No, it's just baloney," I heard myself sass. Nate chuckled, and next to me I felt Louis stiffen.

"Hah, good one," said Nate, and his grin seemed to invite me. "How 'bout: are those anemones?"

"Nope, enemas," I answered, falling effortlessly into the game. "You go," I added. "Is that a starfish?"

Nate thought hard. "No, it's a…fart dish! Hah! Top that, Hamburger!" But it sounded kind of cute the way he said it. I found I was giggling. "Okay, this'll get you," he said: "Hey, is that a Moray eel?"

"No, it's a limpet," Louis answered. I turned to see him frowning into the tide pool. *C'mon, Louis, don't be such a dud. Can't you just play along for once?*

"Hah!" Nate repeated, and slapped his knee. "Awesome, dude. I never realized limpet rhymes with Moray eel. You should definitely write poetry." The funny thing is, his face looked just as smooth and happy as if he were giving Louis a compliment.

Louis frowned harder, and this is where I was supposed to tell Nate not to be a jerk. Instead I said, "No, it's a Hooray Squeal," and even though that was incredibly lame I got rewarded by another Nate Cowper chuckle, as warm as the sun on my back.

"Hey, Joss, wanna go home?" Louis asked me.

Nate said, "Aw, don't leave, we're just getting warmed up. Hey, try this: Octopus!"

"Joss?"

"Block of pus," I said, ignoring Louis. It was his own fault; if he wasn't such a dweeb, maybe he could have some fun once in a while.

"Eww," Nate said appreciatively. "The Burger gets down and dir-tay."

Louis stood up. I stared hard into the tide pool. There was a limpet in there, a big one. A hermit crab was trying to nibble its way under the protective shell.

"Hey," Nate said. "If something's full of pus, is it pus-y? Or pussy?" He pronounced it both ways.

I couldn't help it. A honk of laughter jolted out my nose, pushed by a train of giggles. And when Louis hopped off our rock and started climbing the bank toward the woods all I could do was choke, "I'm sorry! It's not funny at all!" through laughter that said what a liar I was.

"I'm taking the rest of the cake," was all Louis said, and he disappeared in the direction of our bikes.

My laughter disappeared with him. *Oh, great—what's the matter with me?*

"Jeez, what a 'tard," Nate said, shaking his head. "No offense, Joss, but seriously, that kid is…"

I didn't wait to find out what Louis seriously was. "Don't be such a jerk," I snapped, standing up, but I was talking more to myself. Or I should have been—because, even then, in the middle of feeling properly ashamed for being such a rotten friend, a little part of my brain was saying, *Did he just call me Joss?*

Nate smiled at me. "Ohh-kay. Sorry. Hey, is that a squid?"

"I'm not playing anymore," I informed him. But I looked back into the tide pool.

"Get anything cool for your birthday?"

"Tons of stuff." But I knelt back down on my sore knees.

"Oh, good," Nate said, kneeling down next to me to pick up a hermit crab, "'Cause I just hate it when I only get a couple pounds of stuff. I mean, what are birthdays for, unless you get a couple of truckloads, right?"

Oh, I could've used Mrs. Mac to assign me a Reflection right then: *"Explain how it is possible to like and dislike something at the same time."* I would've been all over that. Except it would have taken me about five pages. And I didn't have any paper. All I had was the infuriating feeling that I was more like Savannah than I'd ever realized. Louis now felt worse than before, thanks to me. And here I was, tide-pooling with the enemy.

"Why are you always such an idiot?"

"What can I say?" Nate spread his arms; they were way browner than mine. "I'm like that T-shirt my dad wears, y'know? 'Fish Fear Me, Women Want Me'—"

"Oh, please." But still I had to bite the inside of my cheek to keep from smiling back at him.

Hard. A real chomp. Maybe that's what did it, the taste of my own blood. Suddenly I felt swamped, like a limpet pried from its rock. *I need to re-anchor.* But not here. Not in the glow of Nate's jokes, where I might start laughing like a music scale. *I gotta find Louis. Call Mom. Start over.*

I bolted out of there. Nate might have said something to my retreating back, but I can't be sure. He might have just knelt there and smiled.

Me—I flew. Oh, not in front of Nate, but yeah, as soon as I reached the woods, I took off like an idiot, right there in broad daylight. Only I'd learned enough from last time to leap at more of an angle and avoid another lump on my head. Still, winding

my way a few feet above the woodsy path to the Seal Rocks
parking lot, I knew it would take a miracle not to run slap into
some family with a picnic basket. It was the middle of a beautiful
summer day.

Didn't deserve it, but I got my miracle: the parking lot was
empty. Just two bikes, mine and Nate's.

I swept right past and over the treetops. My mind was churning like a broken wave, full of fragments, nothing smooth and
logical like, *How are you going to explain how you got home without
your bike?* Up high the sun felt hotter than ever on my skin,
and an illustration flashed through my mind from Mrs. Mac's
Greek Mythology Unit, of Icarus's death-fall when the wax of
his homemade wings began to melt. The look on his face was
one serious *Uh-oh.* Immediately my wingless body lowered itself
to skim the treetops instead of flying high and free, and I headed
for the village.

But where was Louis? He didn't have that much of a head
start, and he's not that fast a biker. Had he dragged his bike behind some trees to cry in private? "I'm sorry, I'm sorry," I murmured as I flew. It made me feel better. *Is this what Savannah does?
No wonder she can hurt my feelings so often.* What about Nate? Was
he feeling bad right now too? *Do guys like Nate ever feel bad?*

I'm a moron. All those people whirling around my head had
choked out the biggest thought of all, but it suddenly surged
through: *I'm flying! In the daytime! The magic doesn't need darkness
after all, I can just—*

Someone squawked. *Ohjeezohjeezohjeez*—daylight! I had forgotten about cover and was flying straight over the harbor, which
on a beautiful Sunday morning was filled with tourists messing
with their sailboats. Luckily all those people spend their time
on the water looking everywhere *but* up—and the cry had been
nothing but a grumpy old heron, now flapping his dignified way
to another part of the beach. I showed a lot less dignity; I pedaled

my feet in the air like those old *Flintstones* cartoons Dad loves. But I managed to change direction in about two seconds, and hid myself in the treetops over the Spit.

Great. Now how'm I going to get across the channel?

The obvious solution was to land on the Spit and walk around the harbor on the road. It would only take twenty minutes. Maybe I could even get a ride with someone.

Or I could fly across.

Don't be an idiot. How could they not see you?

Yeah, well, if they do they'll make up some kind of explanation, right? Maybe this time I'll be a UFO!

Yeah, an Unbelievably Foolish…ummm…

Hah, can't even think of an "O."

And what if someone has a camera? Or points their cell phone and takes a video of you flying? Is that what happened to the Dalby Island Ghost? But no, that's stupid. I would know by now if there was another flying person on the island.

That's when I saw my brother.

See, Dalby Channel is teeny. Sailboats barely squeeze through. On the other side of that opening perches a handful of buildings: the Village. The main building is everybody's favorite, because that's where you find the bakery. That was also, at the moment, where you found Michael. But since he was crouched behind the building, visible to no one but flying people, I didn't think my brother was there for a caramel brownie.

And someone else was crouching with him.

In my opinion, people crouch for only two reasons: they're about to start sprinting, or they're in the middle of something so absorbing they don't think how weird they look crouching.

Michael's no sprinter. You can't blame me for being curious.

Okay, flying across the channel was pretty stupid. But nobody saw me, I'm totally positive. And for sure nobody got me on video. How do I know? Because nobody squawked, not even a blue heron. I flew fast and straight to the bakery, hovered by the back corner, and looked down at the crouchers in the shade.

They were giggling. I couldn't remember the last time I heard Michael giggle. But the other one—oh yeah. Just two days ago, laughing over Nate's joke about chicken meat: Tyler. Only where Nate's laugh makes you feel warm, Tyler's makes you feel dirty.

Then I smelled it.

I know the smell of pot, okay—sweet and rough. I even know what it tastes like, thanks to Savannah last fall, who agreed afterward that the smoke felt like a nasty person groping around inside your lungs.

But my brother smoking weed with Tyler the Jerk?

I landed. Not like Icarus, I just…came down. Luckily around the other back corner of the building, hidden both from Michael and the happy croissant-eaters in front.

Well, no huge surprise. Michael's been acting like a stoner since he turned sixteen. The hair, the heavy metal, the potty-mouth, shutting himself up in his room. But with *Tyler?* That ogre? I'd never even seen Michael talk to Tyler!

But that wasn't the point. I didn't plan to snitch, but if Michael got caught he'd be grounded right here on Dalby. *Isn't that what you want?* But then he'd be more caged-up and pissed off than ever…and taking it out on me.

"Well, hello there." I whirled to find my new stepmother behind me, holding two long baguettes in a paper bag. Her hair was down, and with the sun directly overhead she looked, well, radiant.

"Hi," I managed. *Okay, nice cheerful Lorraine—she obviously hasn't seen either Flying Stepdaughter or Smoking Stepson.* "Um, are those the plain ones or the sun-dried tomato?" I asked, nodding at the baguettes.

"One of each," Lorraine beamed. "Oh, I have you guys figured out, don't worry. Know what I got for Michael's going-away tea? Chocolate-covered macaroons."

Going-away tea? Are you for real? But macaroons *are* his favorite. Which he was going to be plenty hungry for, if it's true what everybody says about pot and the munchies. And here's Lorraine, all happy 'cause she's got just the right treat for him, and cool old Michael's gonna sneer about her all the way to McClenton. I had half a mind to snitch after all.

But she saved me from having to decide. "Do you smell what I smell?" she asked me. *Kinda cool she assumes I know the smell of weed.* I nodded.

Any normal person would shrug, like, "Oh well, that's just Dalby." Not Lorraine. That might be somebody's kid behind that pot smoke, and she was going to find out who and then call his mom.

So she did. At least with Michael, she saved herself a phone call.

I should've gotten the hell away from there. But I couldn't help it: I had to hear the first Burgowski scene starring Lorraine in a real stepmothering role. Too bad Michael turned his head as Lorraine finished her whispery confrontation and left. He caught me hunkered there by corner of the building.

"You bitch," he hissed, and Tyler flipped me off as they shouldered past me.

I knelt in the dirt, feeling punched. My brother's called me a ton of names in my life, but never that one. When my breath came back, it kept punching. My brother hates me. Louis hates me. Savannah…I cringed inside, remembering how I had turned into her on the tide-pool rocks.

*Gotta get my stupid bike…*but I couldn't move. The shade felt good. A tourist family came by with the world's fuzziest puppy, and we hung out a while. But eventually they moved on and I had no excuse not to go home.

Dad's truck had been returned to the driveway. *Oh jeez…*from thirty feet away I could see my handprints all over the rim of the bed where I'd tried to lift it last night from the air. What a moron! No point rubbing them off now. At least Dad's focus was back on Michael. *How much does a tow on Dalby cost, anyway?*

Slipping into the kitchen, I could see that Michael's tea clearly wasn't happening. Well, he wouldn't be going away now, would he? Probably grounded to his room for the rest of the summer. *He can't stay mad at me that long, right?* Dad was on the phone; Lorraine must have taken over the store. I headed for the fridge for some lunch when Dad caught my arm.

"Hold up, Bethany, she just walked in," he said, and thrust the phone at me. "Your mom wants to talk to you." He picked up a scrubby and started working on the stove burners, frowning.

I found myself trying Savannah's trick without even planning to. "Hey-mom-sorry-I-didn't-call-sooner-I've-been-trying-to-deal-with-my-friend-Louis-he's-kind-of-depressed-right-now-you-know?" all came out on the same breath. *Wow, what a little jerk I'm turning into.* But Mom was ready for me.

"Don't worry about it, babe." I could almost see her waving the thought lazily away. "So, hey, sounds like your brother's gone and got himself into even more of a mess, huh? You wearing the family halo again now, even after sneaking out?"

"'Course not," I said. "Wait, you know about—"

"Well, keep that halo on," Mom continued as though I hadn't said anything. "We're both gonna need it, sounds like. Gonna need all the divine intervention we can get, holding ourselves together this summer."

Ourselves? Scrub-scrub-scrub went Dad. "Mom, what are you—"

"Don't worry, you don't have to babysit him. I think that was Lorraine's idea, or maybe your dad's. But they're right—" she paused and I heard ice cubes clinking—"having his little sister to take care of in dangerous old McClenton will make that kid grow up some."

"What are you talking about?" I burst out. "I'm not coming to McClenton!"

The phone was silent. So was the kitchen. Dad had stopped scrubbing and was nodding at me gravely.

"Why am I going to McClenton?" I demanded of the kitchen in general.

Mom's voice came from near my hip, where I must have lowered the phone: "Hm, sounds like someone needs to discuss something with her dad. Thought you'd already talked to her, Ron!" She raised her voice on that last part, but Dad didn't react. He was still nodding.

"Mom," I said, then remembered to bring the phone back up, "Mom, no one talked to me about this! I don't..."

What? Want to come live with you? Yeah, I'm gonna tell her that?

"Hey, whatever you want, babe," Mom's voice said, sounding like she was making an effort to mean it. "One kid for the summer, two kids, it's all the same to me, okay? So you talk it over with your dad and get back to me. See ya—maybe."

"See ya," I mouthed automatically, then stood there.

"She's right, I should have told you first," Dad said firmly, going back to his scrubbing. "But I did warn you I was thinking about it, Jocelyn. Things are...worse than we thought with Michael. He has to get out of here. But we can't just pack him off to McClenton to be on his own all day. Beth has to work. Your brother needs a job, but he also needs someone to look after, to touch base with. That's you."

I hung up the phone.

"And you need it too," Dad continued. "More responsibility than you have here. Last night was a wake-up call for us, Jocelyn. We're concerned about you."

"We?" I demanded. "You and Mom decided this?"

"Ah, no," Dad replied, turning back to the sink. "You heard your mom, she's okay with anything. No, it was Lorraine's idea... and mine, of course."

Something moved at the edge of my vision. Lorraine stood at the curtain, her face flushed. "That's not quite what I said, Ron. It was for Beth."

Dad made a polite little bow, like, *Whatever you say, honey.*

"For Beth, not Michael," Lorraine insisted. "Joss, I said I thought you and your mom would be good for each other now."

I stared back at her. *All that buddy-buddy stuff about baguettes, and now she's telling Dad to pack me away?* "What would you know about that?"

She looked down. "You're right. I just thought…I'm sorry."

I kept staring until she stepped back and the curtain closed behind her.

CHAPTER TEN

SEE YA, WOULDN'T WANNA BE YA

Of course I didn't have to go.

I was fourteen! I could have wielded arguments like Mrs. Mac's high-noon cowboy. I could have pitched a fit and pouted till I got my way.

But if I stayed on Dalby, they'd be watching me like hawks. Plus Mom would feel rejected. Again.

They told me it was up to me. Parents are great at that: they push you off a cliff, then say, "It's up to you if you want to climb up from that ledge you landed on." Oh, Dad did most of the talking, but I knew who was behind the plan all right. Lorraine kept taking all my arguments and tossing them back and forth with Dad like a kid playing catch.

Lorraine: "So you're sure Beth's up for this?"

Dad: "Oh, absolutely, Bethany's a whole new woman these days. I'd trust her with my own kids!" *Ha ha.*

Lorraine: "Don't you think Michael will need more supervision? I mean, Beth will be at work…"

Dad: "You kidding? No one makes a better parole officer than a former offender. Beth'll have Michael under her thumb before he steps off the ferry, and he won't even know it."

Lorraine: "If Michael's working for the apartment super—Arnie? — what's Joss going to do all day?"

Dad: "Well, maybe Arnie can use her too. She's fourteen, she can work— painting, maybe, or pool maintenance. And she can keep her earnings, no tow truck to pay for."

Lorraine: "But won't it be kind of lonely for Joss, without her buddies?"

Dad: "Joss can call 'em every day if she wants; I'll pay the phone bill."

Joss: "Louis doesn't have a phone."

Dad: "Well, we can have him over here to use ours. Anyway, it's only a month. Your girlfriends will all be jealous, Joss, all those malls out there to shop in."

Joss: "I hate shopping."

Lorraine: "That's true, Ron—maybe we could get her a one-month pass to the Seattle Science Center."

That sort of thing.

So why didn't I bring up Mom's drunken phone call last week? One word from me about Mom backsliding into old habits, and Dad would keep both me and Michael safely on Dalby. But then he'd go off: "Why didn't you speak up sooner? What else about Beth have you been keeping from me? You think I'm ever letting you stay with her till she's completely clean?"

Mom drives me crazy, okay? Sometimes she hurts my heart. But I can't stand to hear Dad talk about her that way.

In the end, I didn't even say the words, "Okay, I'll go to McClenton." I just yelled "Fine!" and marched off to my room to pack, leaving Dad and Lorraine to toss their happy little ideas back and forth without me.

Michael must have been waiting for the sound of my door. No sooner had I closed it than he pushed it open again, super-quietly so the Parents wouldn't hear.

"Feelin' pretty good, snitch?"

I backed up to my bed. "I didn't tell 'em, Michael! They didn't hear about it from me."

"Hear about what?" he demanded. "How'd you know what happened if you didn't see? And how'd *they* know if you didn't tell?"

"I…I did see, okay? But so did Lorraine. Just on her own, I never said—"

"HOW?" Michael snarled in a stage-whisper, leaning over me. His arms quivered; I couldn't look at his face. "Ty and I've hung out there for a month, no one ever sees. Then suddenly you're spying on me and I'm in deeper s--- than ever."

"I told you!" I whispered back. "I can fly." The words gave me courage: I put my hands on my hips. "I saw you from the air, and I landed. Right there. And that's when Lorraine came by, and she smelled you guys."

"Oh right, she must've been flying too. What a crazy f---ing liar you're turning into."

"I'm not a—"

"Shut up. Just shut up. I don't care what you are, all right? I don't care what lies you tell. I don't even care if you're coming to McClenton. Just stay the f--- away from me."

Fury is a great distraction; it leaves no brain space for anything else. But eventually it leaks away and you have to think real thoughts again. That happened to me halfway through the evening, packing books. I looked up from *Eragon* and thought, *Damn. How am I supposed to fly in McClenton?*

I know, I'm an idiot. But that wave of rage had washed my new power right out of my brain.

McClenton's a city. Sure, it's not Seattle, no skyscrapers, but still: houses and stores everywhere, and stupid identical apartments like Mom's. And a big old freeway running through everything. The one park there is teeny. What was I supposed to do, fly along the interstate?

Like Michael was gonna "touch base" with me. Like I was

gonna make any difference at all to him, halfway up his own cliff. I could see it now: the three of us, sitting around and snapping at each other on Mom's little balcony that looked over stupid, concrete McClenton.

I stopped packing and stared at the cover of *Eragon*, counting the colors in the dragon's eye.

Another knock, soft. I didn't answer. But Dad was now taking my cooperation for granted; he stuck his head in anyway. "Jocelyn? You want to bring your bike, honey?"

My bike.

"I dunno." *Seal Rocks. Right where I'd left it.*

"Well, think about it, okay? Just give me enough time to load it up tomorrow. We're taking the nine-thirty boat." There was a pause; Dad was probably deciding whether he should attempt a good-night hug. "Set your alarm, okay?"

"'Kay," I said, too distracted even to snark about him saying "we" were taking the ferry.

"G'night, honey." His head withdrew.

The paralysis was gone, replaced by a stab of adrenaline. If I'd been a cartoon, my thought balloon would've said, "Oh, shoot. Now what?"

I didn't see a lot of options. Except to do a better job than I had with the truck. Pillows and rolled-up towels in the bed if somebody peeked in. Wait until late. And this time, close the damn door.

Surveying my Joss-bed, I realized that a flying mission was a pretty decent cure for the rotten powerlessness of the afternoon. I checked my watch: nine. Great for flying time, but biking home in the dark? Okay. Bike light, then. Yellow windbreaker. Don't want to get hit by a...

Wait. Bicycles. Flying. Bicycles and flying.

What movie scene does that sound like? *E.T.* is one of the few DVDs my family actually owns. I always crack up when the little girl looks at the alien and says, "I don't like his fee-eet." And I always get a throat-lump at the end when the boys go soaring across the full moon on their flying bikes.

Oh, come on. It didn't work with the truck. Why should it work with a bike?

Bikes are so much lighter...

Sneaking out was a cinch. I waited a half-hour, till Dad and Lorraine were laughing loudly at something on TV—well, Dad was; Lorraine never does anything loudly. I took off right from the yard and spent the flight to Seal Rocks trying to visualize my return trip. *Make a little ramp for a riding takeoff, or just grab a handlebar and leap, then mount the seat in the air?*

It was another beautiful night, although the moon was only a glow behind clouds. If I had let myself pay attention, I probably would've cried to think what I was leaving behind for smelly old McClenton: the tree frogs in the marsh, the chatter of starlings, the gleam of a far-off ferry gliding between islands. The lily smell of the sky. But that night I was focused on my mission, the image of E.T.'s ride burning in my brain.

Turns out I should've let myself soak up the Sensory Details. I'm no E.T. any more than I am Superman, okay? Trying to leap into the air while holding my bike ended up being just as ridiculous as it sounds, and I don't even want to talk about the ramp idea. At least I didn't get all muddy this time.

Swearing in the Seal Rocks parking lot, I finally realized that a), I was going to have to ride home in the dark after all, and b), in the excitement of planning to bike-fly, I had forgotten my light and my yellow windbreaker. And by now thickening clouds covered the moon's glow. It was just me and my bike, and seven miles of DARK.

I started riding. What else was I going to do?

Luckily there's not a lot of traffic on Dalby, especially on that end of the island. I kept my senses sharp, ready to pull over if a car came up behind me. Two cars did, and I began to settle into the weird rhythm of biking by feel, noticing all the little bumps in the pavement.

The third car stopped.

On Dalby, you never think about being attacked or kidnapped or anything—that's mainland stuff. I braked.

"Jocelyn?" called a woman's voice. "Is that you, sweetie? Want a ride?"

Only Louis's mom wouldn't bother to ask what I was doing out here.

Turns out I sure did want a ride in her old VW. As Shasta chattered to me—she'd been dropping off Al at his new campsite, the positive energy was so much stronger on the west side of the island—I realized this was exactly what needed to happen before my month of exile.

"Can I come over for a minute?" I asked Shasta.

"Sure, sweetie! Louis will be thrilled to see you. You guys can make oatmeal cookies if you want." Only Shasta would suggest cookies at nine forty-five p.m.

Poor old Louis may not have been thrilled, but he was nice about it. That's the thing: Louis is always nice.

"I have something to tell you," I whispered as soon as Shasta had bustled away. We were sitting at the kitchen table surrounded by the cookie ingredients she had taken out for us—honey, of course, no sugar. "I can fly. I just found out two days ago. Michael doesn't believe me, but I knew you would."

Louis looked at me. "Does Savannah believe you?"

"I haven't told Savannah. Don't think I'm going to."

And that was all it took. "Okay," said Louis. "Wow. That's really cool."

Now *that's* a friend.

"Don't you want to see me do it?" I asked.

"Yeah!!! Here?"

"We have to go outside. I don't need a runway or anything, all I do is...hey!"

"What?" Louis said. His eyes were shining more than usual.

"I wonder if I could...if we held hands...you're lighter than a truck—but no, it didn't work with the bike..."

"What're you talking about, Joss?" But he must have known; his eyes were practically popping.

"C'mon, I'll show you!" There was no need to sneak at Shasta's house; we banged outside, past the smell of the goat pen, into the field behind the Co-op.

And this is how much I'd gotten used to my new Flying Burgowski self, after only three days: when I looked down at him from twenty feet up, I was surprised to see Louis sitting in a heap on the ground.

Once he got over his shock, Louis was thrilled. By the time I'd shown him how I could do somersaults in the air and hover like a giant hummingbird, he'd said "Cool!!!" about a thousand times. But I should never have gotten his hopes up that he could fly alongside me, like Lois and Superman. I guess I just wanted so badly for it to work. Louis is kind of used to swallowing disappointment, and I hate adding to it. So I made him a promise.

"When I'm in McClenton, I'll practice every day, and try to carry heavy stuff around with me when I fly. Then maybe I can take you up with me when I get back."

I'm such an idiot. I'd forgotten I hadn't told him that I really was going to McClenton. So that took a while. And by the time I was done, his face was split about half-and-half, misery at being left alone for a whole month of summer, and crazy hope that he'd go flying with me at the end of that month.

I really, really wanted to see his whole face happy before I left. So I kept talking, imagining out loud all the trouble we could get into if we could fly places together. When I got to the part about dropping rotten eggs down Tyler's chimney, Louis's eyes squinched up and he finally laughed out loud.

So I decided to stay and make cookies with him. It was after eleven, but so what? Dad and Lorraine were for sure asleep by then, and what was I going to need my beauty rest for—Mc-Clenton?

"Looks like somebody slept through her alarm," Dad said next morning, smiling.

"Oops," I said. No point in telling him I'd forgotten to set it.

"Let's go, sleepyhead. Pancakes are ready." Pancakes on a Monday? *So he's feeling guilty about sending me away. Good.*

We were walking onto the ferry, not driving, so there was no need to get in line early. Breakfast was quiet, the pancakes jumpy in the pit of my stomach. Michael and I had been to Mom's together tons of times since my parents split, but we'd never been bundled off like this. Not speaking to each other. *So much for keeping my family together.* The anger from the night before puffed in my chest, and I resolved to make sure Dad knew exactly what he was doing to me.

I didn't have much chance, though. He loaded our bags into the pickup without the usual parent chatter about, "Do you have this-or-that?" I noticed my bike in there next to Michael's. *Hooray for my Bike Rescue Mission last night...* which made me remember my promise to Louis. "I'll practice in McClenton," I'd told him. Stupid. Probably the flying power wouldn't work at all. Probably it was a Dalby thing. But with any luck, Louis would forget all about my promise in a month, he'd be so glad to see me back...

Yeah, right.

In the blur of these thoughts I found myself in the cab of the pickup between Dad and Michael with the motor starting. Lorraine was waving, and I dimly registered that she'd been there the whole time, watching as we packed up. *Like this whole exile thing wasn't her idea! Raising all my arguments with Dad, pretending to be on my side!* I refused to look at her as we pulled away.

Dad pulled up to the passenger area and dropped us off with our bikes, Michael's guitar and duffle and my old rolly-suitcase. "I've already called your mom to remind her which boat you're on," he told us. "She'll be there to meet you."

"That would be a shock," muttered Michael.

"Hey," said Dad, "you be nice." But he looked sympathetic. And firm. And guilty. All at once. *Good.*

Michael and I did the hug-Dad-good-bye thing pretty quick; leaving without hugs would have created more drama than it was worth.

"See you in a month!" Dad called behind us, but we didn't turn. It's pretty hard walking a bike while dragging a suitcase. Besides, you don't wave on your way into exile.

Not until I was safely on the boat, watching the bright-barked, twisty madrona trees of my island fade into a blur of green, did it occur to me: I had never called Savannah. But hey—she'd never called me either.

Now she could spend a whole month walking around with Nate. *Fine with me.* Why hang around with people who made me feel bad, or made me make other people feel bad? Savannah and Nate could explore every orchard on the island while I was gone. *They can join Tyler now he's lost his smoking-buddy, all three of 'em getting high up there on the Toad.*

I sat and brooded for the whole forty-five-minute trip, my book unread on my lap. Across from me, Michael stared at the ocean, lost in his MP3. By the time the boat rumbled its way into the mainland dock, it would have been tough to tell who was in a fouler mood.

And when Mom failed to meet us, it felt so rottenly perfect, I was secretly pleased.

CHAPTER ELEVEN

WHY WE BRUSH OUR TEETH

But Mom brought doughnuts. That's why she was late to the ferry. And on the drive back to McClenton she stopped again at a Starbucks and let us choose any drink we wanted. And she drives way faster than Dad.

So even though we started out mega-crabby, we were all in great moods by the time we got to her apartment.

Mom talked Harry Potter with me and music with Michael. She's the only grown-up he doesn't roll his eyes at when she asks who he likes these days, because she actually listens to the same stuff. Kinda immature, in my opinion, but she got all excited talking about drum solos, and I decided anything that made her look so young and happy must be okay.

For dinner she took us out to McDonald's.

"Now don't get used to this," she told us around a mouthful of fries. "I know how starved you guys are for this kind of thing, so, yeah, I'm spoiling you a little tonight. But tomorrow it's back to the real world."

The thing is, Mom's real world included things like canned ravioli, which Michael and I would kill for. It's not like Dad's a health-food freak; it's more like he's worked so hard to prove he's the World's Best Single Dad, canned ravioli would be a sign of defeat. Mom just bought stuff.

And Michael's real world included marijuana—until Mom discovered his little baggie cleverly hidden in his guitar case.

"Honestly, Michael, you are such a cliché," she snapped, and then jerked her head at him like a movie bad guy signaling "Let's go," and my brother followed her meekly out to the little balcony. Mom shut the door so I couldn't hear their conversation, but from Michael's expression it was nothing like he'd ever had with Dad. I swear his face turned white, and when he came back in he wouldn't look at me.

"What did she *say*?" I hissed later as we were brushing our teeth, but all I got was a grunt, leaving me to imagine their conversation:

Mom: "Do you want to end up like me? Look at what I've done with my life!"

Michael: (whining) "It's only pot…I bet you've done it yourself…"

Mom: "Yes, and look where it's taken me. I. Clean. TOILETS. For a living. Is that what you want?"

Michael: (whimpering) "I'm sorry, Mom…"

He never did tell me what they talked about. But Dad was right. After that first night, Michael was under Mom's thumb, and strangely enough, he seemed to enjoy it there, at least enough to start speaking to me again. And me? I was suddenly psyched. Mom even tucked me in that first night—or her version of it: a pat on the head and "'Night, babe." This terrible McClenton exile was starting to *rock*.

Only then did I realize, lying on my sofa-bed in the not-very-dark living room, that I hadn't even thought about a plan for flying. Where in the world was I going to…? And when, and how…? *Oh jeez,* my tired brain said, *I'll think about that tomorrow.*

But tomorrow came and went. Mom had managed to get a half-day off work, so she made a picnic lunch and took us to the McClenton pool, which is way bigger than the dinky one by her apartment, with a waterslide! And after that we went to see *Pirates of the Caribbean II* and she bought us drinks and popcorn. So by the time we were having take 'n' bake pizza on the balcony it was ten o'clock and I nearly fell asleep at the table.

Phone call from Dad:
Him: "So how's your mom doing?"
Me: "Good, I guess. She hasn't had a single beer."
Him: "Of course not! I told you, Joss—your mom's a whole different person these days. Think I'd let you stay there if she weren't?"
Me: "Yeah...I mean no."
Him: "How 'bout your brother?"
Me: "He's starting his job with Arnie tomorrow when Mom goes back to work. Weeding or something. I'm gonna ask him if I can do it too. Arnie, I mean."
Him: "Hey, great initiative, hon. Michael will appreciate the company. Is he there? Let me talk to him."
Me: "Um, I think he's in the bathroom ..."
Him: "Oh. Okay. Well, tell him hey for me, good luck with the weeding..."
Me: "Tell Louis to call me tomorrow, okay? We had McDonald's last night, he'd love that."

Top Ten List of Cool Things in McClenton:
1. Cereal. Mom buys whatever we want, and I try all sorts of combinations, like Cap'n Crunch with Froot Loops sprinkled on top.
2. Mom's notes. She's gone to work by the time Michael and I get up, but she leaves us little smiley-face messages just like a real mom.
3. Weeding. Arnie hired me too! And he doesn't believe in wasting energy, so all we do is squirt poison on the weeds and then

pick them up later with gloves on. I know it's horrible for the environment, but apartments don't really count as environment, do they? It's fun. And he pays us minimum wage.

4. PlayStation. Yeah, Mom got one! Well, it's not exactly new, but it works fine. We're getting addicted to *Spider-Man*.

5. Dinners. In the late afternoon Mom shows up, complaining that her knees hurt but smiling kinda shy, then plops some cool thing on the counter. Turkey hot dogs. Frozen enchiladas. Fried chicken! Since she remembered how much I love fried chicken, we started having it every Friday to celebrate the weekend.

6. Strawberry milkshakes at Dairy Queen. Michael and I ride our bikes over, and I'm getting totally addicted.

7. Ummm... Painting. Well, priming, actually, but close enough. Arnie promoted us to re-doing his utility house. At least with priming you don't have to worry about brush-strokes. It's fun.

Okay, I can only think of seven things. But life's good.

I did get homesick, once, on the Fourth of July. That morning it suddenly hit me that I was going to miss the Dalby fireworks show for the first time in my life. For a little island, we have a pretty crazy-big bunch of fireworks; we raise money for it all year. I remembered how Savannah and I zipped our sleeping bags together last year and piled up pillows, then lay in luxury to watch the show. So I called her, but she was grumpy that I hadn't called earlier, and spent the whole time bragging that Tyler had invited her to a "real party." I ended up wishing I hadn't bothered.

But Mom took us to Dairy Queen *and* Starbucks, and then to Seattle for their giant show by the lake, and they had fiery hearts *and* planets *and* that golden rain-shower thing that sprouts purple at the end, and I forgot all about Savannah. Dalby fireworks were probably way lamer.

So I guess Seattle fireworks is Number Eight on the list.

Phone call from Dad:

Michael: "Yeah, Arnie says he'll hire me again next year if I want to come back for the whole summer…Yeah, that'd be cool. Mom got me a Drivers Ed book so I can…yeah. Did Ed play with the band on the Fourth? Oh well. He pretty much sucks anyway. I'm gettin' so much practice here, I'll be way better than him by the time I get back. Yeah, okay, here she is…"

Me: "Hi, Dad."

Him: "Hi, sweetie. Sounds like your brother's a man on fire! What's Beth been feeding him?"

Me: "Well, we had pizza again last night, the kind that puffs up when you bake it…"

Him: "Oh, I didn't mean literally—but thanks for the menu update. You havin' fun out there?"

Me: "Yeah! Did you know Mom has cable now? We've been watching all these *South Park* reruns."

Him: "*South Park*, huh? I've heard of it…Well, long as you're happy, kiddo. You getting outside any, or do you guys just sit around and watch TV all day?…I mean, when you're not working for that slave-driver, Arnie."

Me: "Oh, no, Arnie's hella nice. He can sing 'The Star Spangled Banner' backward. And we go biking. There's a river here, sort of. You can bike along it on this path, and we saw a heron yesterday…"

Him: "Well, great. I tell ya, I wasn't so sure about this idea, but…"

What Joss did NOT say: "Yeah, right."

What I did say: "Yeah. Hey, guess what, Michael said Mom could cut his hair tomorrow."

Him: "No kidding! Breakthrough. Wow, can't wait to see that boy's face again. Hey, speaking of boys, I saw Louis this morning, asked him if he wanted to use our phone to call you. But I guess he's too shy to come over when you're not here. So he just said hi."

And this is how sucked in to my new life I was, after nearly three weeks: even the mention of Louis failed to make me fly.

I know that sounds idiotic, but I was distracted, okay? Just a little distracted by this really cool mom who said things like, "Yeah, I loved *The Horse Whisperer*, but don't you think the ending *sucked*?" and taught Michael how to play a real F-sharp minor chord so he could quit faking it. And then there was Arnie, and the milkshakes, and *Spider-Man*. Who needs flying when you can swing between skyscrapers? I guess I thought about it off and on for the first few days, and then I just…put it off. The skies of McClenton weren't exactly calling to me.

"We don't have glaciers on Dalby," I said. It was the third Friday since we'd arrived, and we were having our fried chicken out on the balcony. You could feel the heat rising up from the parking lot below, but there was a nice breeze blowing through the apartment, and so what if it smelled like asphalt? Balconies are cool. But even the balcony didn't remind me about flying; it took my brother to do that.

"We don't have water parks on Dalby either," Michael shot back. We were arguing—nicely, so far—about what to do with our weekend. Michael was for going to Wild Waves; I wanted Mount Rainier. You can see the mountain from the south end of Dalby on a really clear day, but it's tiny—just this pale little cone on the horizon. It doesn't look real. From Mom's apartment—okay, you have to kind of lean off the balcony to see it—it looks real, all right, and huge. Ginormous. More like a monster than a mountain, with big grey bones and white fur. It had never occurred to me that you could just go up and walk around on it, until Mom said, "Well, what about a hike? You guys don't have anything like The Mountain on Dalby, right?"

Now we were a little stuck, and coming closer to a real fight than we'd been in three weeks.

"Giant water slides!" Michael argued, and I countered with, "Real snow that you can throw at each other!"

"They have a wave machine!"

"They have marmots! Mom said so."

"You didn't even know what a marmot was," Michael accused.

He was right, I'd had to ask—turns out they're kind of like groundhogs, and they whistle ...I just *had* to see one. But I told Michael, "So what, I do now."

"You know, you guys—" Mom began in her scratchy old voice. She was probably going to say something reasonable like, "We have one more weekend before you go back, so why don't we do both?" but then again, it might have been something totally random like, "Mangoes are the world's most popular fruit, so why don't we get one?" She has a tendency to change the subject when people start getting mad. But I'll never find out, because this is where Michael decided to get personal.

"What's so special about being on a mountain? You can see it from here!"

"Yeah, but I want to get way up high and see what everything looks like from up there! Look how tall it is! Water parks are just...there."

"Oh, well, if you want to get way up high, why don't you just fly up there, Joss?" Michael turned to Mom, smirking. "Joss can fly, did she tell you?"

It was the weirdest feeling, like my body had been divided up and painted in all these different colors and shapes, like those Picasso paintings Mrs. Mac showed us. My face would have been a big, red balloon: *He told! He doesn't even believe me and he told!* but my stomach shrunk down into a kind of pale rectangle of shock: *Flying? Flying! Joss can fly...How had I managed to ground myself?* And my arms and legs felt all grey and droopy.

Then I looked at Mom. She held a drumstick in midair and stared at me as though Michael had just told her I'd been hit by a train.

"You can *what?*" It came out almost as a whisper.

Michael seemed delighted with the reaction he'd caused. "Oh, wow, Joss, I can't believe you didn't tell her first thing. What's the matter, was I sworn to secrecy? Funny, I don't remember that part."

That woke me up; I became all one piece, bright red and furious. "You're such an *a--hole,*" I told him. "He is, Mom! I was joking with him about stuff, and he—"

"Wait, wait," she interrupted . "I just want to make sure I heard you right. Michael said you can *fly,* is that what he said?"

My face was boiling. "Yeah, but he's just being stupid and he knows it. It's just this stupid joke of mine, okay, and I told stupid Michael about it and now he's trying to make me feel stupid—"

"Yeah, like that's hard! I'm not the one who said I could—"

"I wasn't for real, you creep! What do you think, I'm like six years old or something?"

"I don't know," Michael shrugged, "you sounded pretty convincing to me."

"All right, that's enough." Through the haze of my humiliation I could see Mom sitting up, as stiff as her voice. "Michael, she's right: you are being a creep. Knock it off. We're going to Mount Rainier tomorrow, and if you don't want to come, fine. Now eat your chicken." But she put her own drumstick down and looked at it.

"Naw, I'll come," mumbled my brother.

Me, I fled into the living room, slamming the balcony door behind me. I had lost my appetite, even for chicken. And for the first time since we'd come to Mom's that summer, I needed to cry. Even though I knew they would talk about me behind my back, even though Mom would probably start asking Michael all kinds of embarrassing questions like, "Has she started getting her period?" or "Has she been telling other lies like that lately?", I had to get out of there, had to throw myself on the sofa and cry quietly into the cushion. I cried because things had been going so well and I suddenly remembered that my family was still a mess. And I cried because I had put aside my magic, and now it must be gone for sure.

After a while I heard my "family" come in as they cleared the table, but I kept my head buried under the cushion and no one tried to talk to me. I heard the dishwasher being loaded, and Mom saying something to Michael in a low voice, and a few minutes later the front door opened and closed.

"Okay, babe, he's gone, you can come out now," Mom's voice said above me. "Shove over." She sat down by my feet.

I didn't have much choice, and besides, it wasn't her I was mad at. Unfortunately I was also in that shivery, snotty phase of crying, where you've stopped but not completely. Not a time when you want to look at anybody, even a mom who's being strangely nice to you. I got up and went into the kitchen to splash my face.

Mom seemed to understand. She sat there and waited for me like she knew I'd come back and sit down beside her, so I did. She was having a beer.

"Want a sip?" She offered me the bottle.

I shook my head.

"Oh, Joss, don't look like that. I'm just kidding. I know what you guys think, I'm the Wild Mom, right? Just trying to stay in character."

"We don't think that," I lied. "At least, not lately," I added, more honestly. It felt weird to be sitting there, just the two of us.

"Hm, nice of you," she said, but she didn't sound sarcastic. She drank her beer. I looked at the painting on the opposite wall, a cheery farmhouse. It must have come with the apartment; it didn't look like something Mom would own.

"Where'd Michael go?" I asked.

"He went for a walk."

"Michael doesn't go for walks."

"He does when I tell him to," Mom said firmly. She hesitated then and began, "So..."

She wasn't just here to comfort me, I could tell; she wanted to say something. It's freaky when a grown-up acts shy. That's supposed to be our job.

"So are you and Michael getting in lots of fights back on Dalby?"

That one was easy. "Yeah," I said. "Lots more than here."

"Why is that, do you think?" She sounded cheerful, like, *hey, guess I'm a pretty good parent after all, huh?*

I said, "I dunno. I guess maybe Dad pushes us more. There's all these chores and stuff."

"Oh," Mom said. I wondered if I'd hurt her feelings.

"Well, and there's the Lorraine thing," I added. "I mean, that was kind of a shock, I think it stressed everybody out. And now she's there all the time..." I figured Mom might like the idea of trashing the new wife. But she didn't.

"I always liked her," she murmured. "Do you remember when we used to go over to the library for Storytime? She read that book about the little mouse and the bear and the red, ripe strawberry, and after that you used to ask for that same story every week...Funny how she could make that little voice of hers all deep and gruff."

I looked at my mom in surprise. This was the most she had talked about my childhood that I could remember. It was not a topic she was comfy with, and I had long ago given up asking those questions all kids like to ask, "Did I do such-and-such when I was little?" It's not fun to hear your mother snap, "I don't remember" about your golden years of youth.

"One thing you can say for Ron," Mom added with a sad smile, "he has great taste in women."

"Yeah," I said. My sniffles had finally disappeared. "You look good, Mom."

Her eyes widened, and I hoped I hadn't hurt her feelings again by suggesting that she used to look not-good. But then she smiled for real.

"Why thank you, dahling," she said, and stretched out her leg, pointy-toed like a dancer. She had changed into shorts after work, so we both admired her smooth, muscley leg. I guess you stay in pretty good shape cleaning big buildings all day, because I never saw Mom exercise.

I laughed, and a little left-over crying-shiver caught up with me, and that made Mom laugh, so I laughed some more. It was starting to feel downright cozy.

"So," she said, "what was all that about you flying? Why's Michael giving you a hard time about that? Was there something...?"

My expression must have stopped her; I could feel my jaw hardening. "I told you, it was just a stupid joke I made."

"Really? It just seemed like...Okay, never mind," Mom said. But her face went back to normal: pale and pointy like a white mouse, big dark eyes looking down, and the cozy feeling evaporated. "So...wanna rent a movie tonight?"

Michael came back in then, and we fell back into our pattern of suggesting activities and things to eat, where everyone knew what to say and the hardest choice in life was *Pirates of the Caribbean I* or *Ocean's Eleven*. But my insides felt roughed up, and I knew why: I had my own choice to make, one that I had conveniently forgotten for two and a half weeks: To fly or not to fly.

Don't you mean, To try or not to try? my brain asked. I didn't like the way it sounded, but I had to admit that was probably more accurate.

Michael and Mom were gazing at me like they had asked me a question. "Whichever you want," I mumbled, and Mom looked at me hard, but didn't say anything. *Tomorrow night,* I told myself. *I'll fly—I'll try, tomorrow night.*

The three of us walked around the block to the video store,

then stopped at the 7-Eleven for Slurpees, plus some candy bars for our hike on Mt. Rainier. I found myself inspecting the corner of every building we passed, wondering, *Could this give me enough cover to take off without being seen? Maybe I should go a ways down that bike path on the river...but how would I get there by myself?* That's like the only thing Mom's strict about, us going around alone in McClenton. *What if I try going off the balcony? The fourth floor isn't that much higher than Greta's uncle's hayloft...*

Honestly, it's just as well I didn't get the chance. I wouldn't have bet on the results.

We made microwave popcorn and unfolded my sofa-bed and everybody crowded on. I decided to eat my Milky Way for second dessert, and Mom laughed at me but didn't say no. Captain Jack Sparrow gets funnier when you've seen the movie like ten times, and there was nothing in it about flying, so I forgot about fretting and just watched, giggling into sleepiness. At one point I heard Mom saying, "'Night, babe,'" and smelled her shampoo or something, right up close for a minute—not the smell of apples, not lilies, but something darker and a little sour...

I woke up briefly some time later. My teeth felt disgusting; no one had insisted on brushing before bed. For the first time I understood, sleepily, that annoying grown-up idea about too much of a good thing.

Too bad I wasn't paying more attention. But Mom and Michael and me, we were having so much fun. Mom was acting healthy and happy, and all these treats we were getting, like Milky Ways and Mt. Rainier, those were just the icing on the cake.

But in my opinion, that expression has another meaning. Cake is perfectly good by itself. When you cover it all over with gooey sweet icing, it's only a matter of time before you realize you need to stop and brush your teeth. Either that, or keep on eating frosted cake until you puke.

MY NATURAL HABITAT

Well, the marmots were cool, anyway.

And the wildflowers. They were *insane*. In the middle of the hike, we dropped down into this bright green valley crammed with bluebells—that was the one flower-name I remembered—and some yellow and pink things. It looked like one of those famous garden paintings and smelled like springtime. We saw two marmots fighting up on their hind legs like short, fat kangaroos, and some baby marmots scurried right over to us when we stopped for sandwiches. Mom said they were begging, but she wouldn't let us feed them. "Animals don't understand what's not good for them," she said.

Oh, and the Mountain? I take it back, it wasn't a monster after all. It was... overwhelming.

I couldn't take my eyes off it—just kept staring at the shining white dome hulking over this ancient-looking wall of reddish gray, and thinking, *That's* snow. *That's* rock. *It's* real. *It's just a big old Toad with snow on it...* Then my eyes would light on the icy-blue edge of a glacier, which Mom said is made up of accumulated snow that probably fell two hundred years ago, and my brain would go, *No way. That can't be real. An hour and a half from McClenton? No way.*

We didn't actually get to throw snowballs at each other; turns out in July there's only a teensy bit of snow where we were, and you're not allowed to walk off the trail. But the hiking wasn't hard at all. We stopped to look at everything, flowers, marmotholes, funny lightweight pieces of rock which Mom said was pumice and a reminder that this mountain was really a volcano, which freaked me out all over again. The scenery made the sandwiches taste amazing, and Mom shared her Milky Way with me since I'd already eaten mine. The sun made you feel like stretching out on a rock like a marmot. So we did that for a while, but finally Mom said we should head back or we'd have trouble with the traffic on the way home.

But traffic was not the problem.

On the way back to the car I asked for the water bottle, and that's when we realized there was only one sip left, and the extra bottle Mom had meant to pack was still sitting on her kitchen counter. Instantly, of course, we all became as dry as Saltines. Michael and I fell over ourselves insisting we were fine, but every time one of us cleared our throats I saw Mom wince a little, like it was her fault we were dying of thirst.

Maybe that's what made Mom's mood cloud over. Or maybe, after almost a month, she had run out of easygoingness. It's not like water; you can't pack something you don't have.

"So, Wild Waves tomorrow?" Mom said in a mega-cheery voice. "Or maybe we should wait till next week? It's supposed to be colder tomorrow."

"That would be good," I said, huffing a little up a steep bend in the trail. "It's our last weekend, so that would be kind of a fun whaddya-call-it...finale."

Mom didn't stop hiking, but her back straightened up underneath the little pack she was carrying. "Really? Next week? I didn't realize you guys were going back to Dalby so soon."

Behind me Michael's voice said, "It's been a month, Mom."

"More than that," I piped up helpfully. "By next weekend it'll be closer to five weeks."

"I didn't realize you were counting the days," Mom said. I felt like a jerk; Michael didn't even need to shove me.

"It's been amazing, Mom," I said quickly, and Michael added, "Yeah, really," but she just said "Uh-huh."

The hike seemed to get a little faster after that. As we crested the rim of the valley I wanted to stop and say good-bye to all that flowery greenness, but Mom kept going, so Michael shoved me again.

"Cut it out," I muttered.

"Well, walk faster," he snarled, and suddenly we were marching along, heads down, as if someone had waved a wand and magicked the beauty of The Mountain away. The tons of people coming toward us along the trail kept us from falling into an all-out argument, but we sniped at each other in low voices all the way back. It was like someone had left our little bottle of family-goodwill juice sitting on the counter with the water.

Finally, finally, we reached the parking lot. The clouds had moved in over the Mountain, but it was still plenty hot, and my feet hurt. "*Damn*, I'm thirsty," Michael blurted, and then shot a guilty look at Mom. "But awesome hike. Thanks for taking us."

"Sure thing," Mom said, smiling tightly. "Tell you what, let's hit the snack bar before we hit the road. I'm thirsty too. Let me just…"

She was checking her purse. Michael and I looked at each other, feeling guiltier than ever.

"We got money," Michael said, after I shoved him for a change. "Arnie's been giving us—"

"It's fine," Mom snapped. "I'm loaded. C'mon, before we all die of dehydration."

I'm pretty sure the next thing that happened was my fault. I'm pretty sure we all would have had different kinds of soda, trading sips of the different flavors, if I hadn't done what I did. But I was feeling bad. Mom hadn't packed enough water and now she was feeling like a rotten provider, and she was probably down to her last dollar after spoiling us for a month. I didn't want her to feel like that.

So I ordered a glass of water.

Michael, who probably had his eye on a large root beer, quickly took my cue and ordered the same thing. *See what a good mother you are? We're hardly thirsty at all, and we don't even cost you anything.*

"Oh, for Chrissake," Mom rasped, her voice dryer than ever. She stepped up to the counter like she was seizing the reins of a stagecoach or something. "Forget that, give 'em two large Mountain Dews. And I'll have a Bud."

"Thanks, Mom," we chorused, looking at our feet. Mountain Dew did sound wonderful.

"How 'bout some ice cream?" Mom pursued relentlessly. "Or a milkshake? That way you for sure won't get thirsty on the way home."

"No, we're fine," we protested, "we're perfect, thank you," and Michael and I stared avidly out the window at the half-clouded Mountain so Mom wouldn't think we were watching her drink. But we didn't have to fake it too long, since she finished her beer in about two seconds. And decided to order another.

That one I think was Michael's fault, but I helped.

"I'm still thirsty," she sighed as the Bud disappeared, and Michael said hastily, "Want some of my drink?"

Mom shot him a look. "No, thank you," she said. "I think I'll have one of my own. Unless you're in a real hurry to get home?"

Michael and I wrestled in whispered combat like marmots as soon as she left to order.

"What'll we do?" I hissed. "She's gotta drive us down the mountain, did you see how twisty that road was?"

"Don't have a cow, it's just beer," Michael hissed back, but he looked worried. "Maybe if I offer to drive…"

"That's stupid, you don't have your license, plus she'll just bite your head off if you make it seem like you don't trust her..."

"Well, I do, it's just that..."

I kicked him under the table; Mom was heading back our way. We sipped our sodas innocently, trying to make them last through Mom's second beer, trying to make it okay. Michael didn't need to finish his sentence, I knew what he meant: It's just that two-beer Mom is a whole different person, it's just that two-beer Mom is already in a foul mood which is probably why she needed that second beer; it's just that there's a really good chance now that everything's going to go downhill, not just us in Mom's little car.

The drive home wasn't all that bad, if "bad" means going straight through a hairpin turn and crashing down the mountainside. We didn't do that.

On the other hand, if "bad" means driving an hour and a half in silence as glaring and cold as those Mt. Rainier glaciers, cracked only by the occasional whispered insult between Michael and me—well, yeah...we did that.

When we got back to the apartment Mom didn't even bother with the sarcastic politeness. She went straight to her version of Louis curled up on his bed, which for her is the fridge for another beer which she drank right there, standing up, then the TV and the sofa (my sofa!), with the volume turned up loud enough to drown out us kids, and the rest of the six-pack to drown out the TV.

And my brother and I? We huddled in his little bedroom with the door closed as though she'd locked us in there, and we both did what we do in times of stress.

After reading page 309 of Harry Potter Five about six times, I grumbled, "Quit swearing so loud. I can't read."

"Well, read louder." But that made me giggle, and finally we could talk again, me sprawled on Michael's bed, he pacing around the tiny space by the window.

"What are we gonna do?" I must've sounded about seven years old, but honestly, that's how I felt. "This is just like that time at Easter..."

"I know," Michael said grimly. Neither of us had to paint each other a memory-picture; Mom's binges and breakdowns were burned into our brains. Last year at my birthday. Easter the year before. That time when she first moved to McClenton and Dad wouldn't let us visit, and she called every half hour till we unplugged our phone...

"'Least she doesn't have to work tomorrow," he added.

"But what if she doesn't stop?"

"It's just beer," Michael said. I hate when older, stronger people sound as helpless as I do. "She's gotta go to sleep pretty soon, and then..."

"What if she doesn't? What if she keeps taking those pills?"

"What pills?" Michael whirled on me. "You saw her taking pills? When? What color were they? Why didn't you say something?"

"I don't know," I wailed. "You were in the bathroom, and she went into her room and said something about staying awake, and when she came out I saw her swallowing them. I'm sorry, I'm sorry...I couldn't, like, knock 'em out of her hand or anything, could I?"

Of all the responses he could have made, my brother chose the one that surprised me most. "No, no, it's okay, Joss. It's okay," and he patted my foot. It made me want to cry, but I kept it in. "Speed," he added, more to himself. "Or some kind of uppers." My drug knowledge was only enough to make me think, *Uh-oh*.

We were quiet for a while, listening to the blare of an old black-and-white movie from the next room, men talking fast and clipped. Mom was apparently a Turner Classics drunk these days.

Finally, Michael said, "Okay. Here's the plan. You go in there and talk to Mom. Cheer her up a little, make her some coffee— but decaf, so she'll go to sleep. Then when she does, I'll sneak into her room and grab all the pills, and then we can flush 'em down the toilet."

"That'll never work," I protested, a million arguments fighting to get out first. "Talk about what? And I don't know how to make coffee. And she'll see you. And—"

"Read the directions on the jar," Michael said firmly, choosing to address the easiest problem.

Turns out I can make coffee. But who knows what it tasted like, since Mom never tried it. Not even close. Here's what our conversation sounded like:

"Hey, Mom…can I watch with you?"

Shrug.

"I like these kinds of shows. What's this one called?"

Head turn. Stare. Slow blink.

"Ummm…you want a cup of coffee? I think I'd like a cup of coffee. Shall I make one for you too?"

"Coffee?" A faint murmur.

"Yeah, a nice cup of coffee. And I think maybe I'll make some macaroni and cheese, is that okay? You might want some when you…you might want some later on."

Blink. Whisper: "Gotta stay 'wake."

"Right, Mom, the coffee will help. You like lots of sugar, right?"

Endless nodding. "Yup. Gotta stay 'wake. Watch m'kids. Kid's're staying over, gotta keepaneyeonem."

"It's okay, Mom, we're fine."

Nodding continues. (Michael emerges from his room, sees Mom's wide eyes, and retreats.)

"So, a cup of coffee, then?"

"Coffee?"

You get the idea. I followed the directions for the coffee and brought Mom a cup, half-full of milk so she wouldn't burn herself, and it sat there on the coffee table and turned cold while she continued to stare at the black-and-white actors. Michael stuck his head out a couple more times, but he never did work up his nerve to enter Mom's bedroom while she was awake. Me, I sat there, glancing over at Mom every now and then to see how her eyes were doing. The one movie ended in a blare of trumpets and a close-up of a smoking gun, and another movie started, full of fur coats and satin dressing gowns. Mom's eyes stayed wide. Every now and then she shook back the hair that was hanging out of her ponytail, then let it fall across her face again. I felt trapped.

She did eventually go to sleep around eleven. I guess the eight beers in her system finally beat out whatever sneaky little chemicals those pills had set racing around. We turned off the TV, put a pillow behind her head and covered her up with a blanket. And then, with my heart beating like a criminal's, I helped Michael on his search-and-destroy mission.

Mom keeps her bedroom weirdly bare, like she just moved in. Not even a calendar on the walls, no little doodads on the dresser. Even Dad has stupid stuff, like the pumpkin-shaped clay bowl I made in third grade. The only hints of life in Mom's room were two little photos in a hinged frame: me and Michael. Not recent ones; in mine, I was showing off my new ninth-birthday bike.

Her night table drawer was sure lively, though: a whole drugstore full of those little brown plastic bottles, with typed labels that sounded like the names of aliens.

Michael and I looked at each other. What's sad is, he didn't look shocked, so I guess I didn't either.

We only got in one short argument over how many pills we should try to whoosh away at a time.

"I bet her downstairs neighbors think she's got terrible diarrhea," I said on the seventh or eighth flush.

Michael looked at me. "What, you think they haven't heard this before?" he said, and I got a sudden, vivid picture of my mother, all alone in her tiny blue bathroom, hugging her toilet like I'd seen her do at our house that time at Easter.

"We have to tell Dad," I said. It just popped out, but as soon as I said it I felt like I was wielding a Harry-Potter Shield Charm. Dad! The one who fixed my flat tires without asking. Dad would know what to do.

Or not. "No, no, Joss, are you crazy?" Michael was emphatic. "He'll bring us right home, he won't let us come out here anymore..."

"So?" I said brutally. "Don't you want to go home? Why would you want to come on back here again?"

Michael frowned. The meanness of my words echoed around the little bathroom.

"I meant," I amended, "we can't do anything, right? I couldn't even get her to drink a cup of coffee! And when she wakes up, she's gonna...oh, jeez."

"When she wakes up," Michael said, "she's gonna need us more than ever. D'you really think that would be a good time for us to disappear? Back to Dalby? Rescued by Dad on his white horse? 'Sorry, Mom, you blew it, we're outta here—'"

"Okay, okay, okay." I knew he was right, it was just weird hearing Michael be the responsible one. "So we won't tell Dad. What's gonna stop her from doing this all over again next week when we have to leave anyway?" *Other than the fact that she's out of pills*, but I didn't say that. We both knew she had other ways to knock herself out.

"Joss, you just don't get it," Michael said. His dark eyes bored into me, same shape and color as Mom's but with an urgency hers never showed. "We have to stay with her. This week, and the week after. The rest of the summer. The minute we pull out, she is going to fall apart again, and you know it."

"But—but—" My thoughts were as breathless as I was. *The rest of the sum—? It's not even Aug—! Are you nuts?*

Michael plowed on, "Joss, look at her. Look what happened. She's been doing great all month, then the minute we start talking about leaving—boom. Right back where she started."

"Yeah, but—!!!" *Where to start?* "If that's true, then we have to stay here forever, we can't ever leave! That's just crazy, Michael. I want to help Mom too, but I…" *I want to go home.*

"There's no point in getting hysterical," Michael said maddeningly. "I didn't say forever, I said all summer."

"What happens at the end of the summer?"

"By then she'll have gone back into therapy. Maybe AA. She'll have coping skills."

"Hah!" Not much of an argument, but I was feeling more trapped than ever. Michael seemed so sure of himself. *What if he's right? What if we leave and Mom does something crazy?* That would be our fault.

"Just think," Michael continued, "if we convince her that we'd rather stay with her, how much better that'll make her feel. I mean, this visit was Dad's idea and we just went along with it, but what if the next one's our idea? That'll be like therapy in itself."

But what about how we feel? I wanted to yell. But Michael was being so grown-up and generous, I couldn't face opening my mouth and showing him what a baby I was.

Luckily he gave me a moment to pull myself together. "Okay," I said finally, "let's say we stay another month. Or even another six weeks, till school starts. What if she's not 'coping' by then?"

I give my brother credit for this next part. He had obviously thought it through, probably all the way home from Mount Rainier, and he knew what my reaction would be. So he actually leaned down and put his hand on my shoulder, like Dad. His face was grave.

"Well, if she's not ready for us to leave then, Joss," he said, "there's nothing else we can do. We'll have to go to school in McClenton for a while."

In the end, it was the macaroni and cheese that did it. Exhausted from battling Michael's insistence that Mom's life depended on us "being there" for her, I forgot about normal things like time and food, until Michael saw the clock and asked if I was hungry. It was midnight, and I was starving. Nobody had eaten anything since our hiking sandwiches—unless you count pills.

"C'mon, I'll make us some mac and cheese," Michael said, and it was the way he said it, all caring and protective, that won me over. You can't fight very long against someone who's more mature and nicer than you are, and I had to admit, even in my defeated, empty-bellied lightheadedness, that I liked this new brother a lot. And when the mac and cheese hit my tongue, I started to see his point about making Mom's life better. It's hard not to be optimistic when your mouth is full of bright-orange, saucy noodles.

We ate that box, then fixed another and ate it too. We drank milk, careful to leave enough for Mom's morning coffee, which she would definitely want. We even decided to set the alarm to make sure we were awake first, and settled on pancakes as the best first step in wooing our mother back.

The food fueled Michael's optimism too. Already it seemed things were better because we had decided they would be. We would call Dad first thing tomorrow; he'd need some convincing, but Michael was sure he'd go for it: "Hey, what guy doesn't want to spend more time alone with his new bride?" It sounded reasonable, but then I was totally tired.

So why couldn't I fall asleep? Maybe because Mom was passed out on my sofa, leaving me her hard bed in that strangely bare room. Maybe my body knew, better than my mac-and-cheese-addled brain, that Michael's idea was horrible. Maybe it was just the stress; I've learned a little something about my reaction to that. I shut down, yeah—but then the flying urge takes over.

Because that's what happened: in the dark of Mom's room, I suddenly remembered I'd promised myself to fly today. "Today" was passed; it was tomorrow already, almost one a.m., and I knew it was time. No stroke of midnight, no Solstice, no Toad, no Dalby anywhere in sight—but I had to go.

Silently I got up and pulled my shorts back on; I had lain down in T-shirt and undies. Mom was breathing quietly in the living room. The city light through the balcony window made her face look pretty.

The balcony? Tempting, but no—I was being drawn to the door, to the stairs. I even remembered my key. At the front door downstairs I briefly wondered if I was about to set off some kind of alarm system, but then I was out in the cool McClenton night—or morning—and all I heard was the river of car-sound flowing from the interstate.

If I'm making it sound a little like I was in a trance, then fine. It did feel pretty dreamy, at least until I took a few fast pavement steps and found myself back in the air.

Then everything got normal really fast. Flying just felt, at that moment, like the most appropriate thing I could possibly be doing. Like I was an animal in the zoo and the sky was my natural habitat. But what's really weird is this: along with exhaust fumes and that nasty gas-station smell, the McClenton sky still smelled a bit like lilies.

Must've been the smell that peeled my heart open like an orange. Where had I been for the past three weeks? Tangled up, face down, in a net of TV and fast food and desperate cheerfulness about Mom, that's where. *But I'm free again. I'm back. I am the Flying Burgowski.* The magic was mine, or it was with me, or inside me—who cared which? *I can fly in McClenton!*

And if I could fly here, I could live here, at least for the next six weeks. As long as I could sneak out at night I'd be fine, since I could sleep as late as I wanted next morning. And, oh wow, flying was even freer than on Dalby, no one to look up at me, no one to care. *I can start exploring!* Who knew what there was to see, so close to so many thousands of people and yet invisible above the streetlights. And the darkness would only fall earlier and earlier the longer we stayed... *This'll be downright cool.*

A pink glow lit up my outstretched arms and I looked down. Without realizing it I had begun a slow circle of the humongous Furniture Warehouse Savings Mart just down the highway from Mom's. From up close the big neon sofa on their sign looked creepy, like giant lips. The store was obviously closed, but a few cars still dotted the edges of the parking lot. Had people just left them there and walked away? Were they resting up for a long drive home? Or maybe each car was full of six-packs and empty pill bottles, and a smelly, drooling driver sleeping them off in the back seat. For the first time since I had become a Flyer, my heart gained weight in my chest and I tilted myself upward to compensate for the heaviness. *Six more weeks. Maybe a little longer.* That was Michael's plan. *Then Mom'll be better and we can go home...* leaving her stranded in big, concrete McClenton, like one of those pathetic cars.

"Damnit," I said out loud. Didn't help. I veered left and headed for the twisting patch of darkness that was the river. I followed it, the freeway noise constant as a headache.

Skimming the tops of those scruffy, city trees, I felt zero urge to plunge into the darkness of the bike path that should have called me to adventure. "I can fly, I can fly," I murmured to myself, but after a while I realized I was repeating those words not in celebration, but as a kind of engine to keep myself aloft.

Time to turn around. Suddenly I felt exhausted. My arms sagged; keeping them outstretched felt like punishment. I tried kicking like a swimmer. Didn't help. Whatever my flight-fuel was, the tank was empty.

Here came the sofa-lips, pink and horrible, level with my shoulders. *Almost there.* Aching weights pulled on every limb. "I can fly," I grunted hopelessly. *I have to! I can't walk home! It's a scary, dark parking lot. And I'm only fourteen.*

Landing felt like being dumped out of a laundry basket: I sort of tumbled, then lay there for a second catching my breath. Then the fear kicked back in and I sat up. I was in the corner of the parking lot, right next to one of those abandoned cars. My skeleton felt hollow.

I'll never know if anyone was sleeping in those cars; I sure didn't check. I did what any self-respecting, terrified girl out alone after midnight in a strange city would do: I picked myself up off the pavement and ran.

All my muscles whimpered. But I struggled on, powered by fear. Around the corner of the closed 7-Eleven I almost stepped on a guy lying curled up on the sidewalk. I was so scared I nearly threw up, but he never stirred.

And neither did Mom when I slipped back inside. My legs still felt trembly, and I wished I could slide into the sofa bed with her and cuddle like a little kid. *Oh jeez, when she wakes up and finds me sleeping in her bed…* The shakiness turned back into something more familiar: good old dread. But dread would have to wait. I was wiped.

The clock by Mom's bed said one forty-five. Such a short interval, to rediscover my sky-world, revel in my powers, then fade out of my very own habitat. *It can't just be Dalby,* my brain mumbled as it hit Mom's pillow. *The magic's in me, right?* I lay in the dark, smelling the sour spice of my mother. I had answered one question: I could fly in McClenton. Barely. The only question now was, did I want to?

CHAPTER THIRTEEN

MEAN MUSTANGS

N ext morning the weather turned back into February. So did Mom. Grey and grim.

She woke up, found herself in the living room—Michael and I peeking anxiously from the kitchen—and went straight to her bedside table with its now-empty drawer.

Her door slammed. We heard her punching something soft. Guess Mom's pillows were taking the beating she wanted to give us.

For the next twenty minutes, Michael and I made pancakes, arguing about whether or not to cook her some. We were still at it when she reappeared. Her eyes were red. She looked...well... like our mom.

"Okay, you two—I get it. I'm done, all right?" she rasped. "I'm good. Gimme a pancake."

We served her and she ate with a reassuring appetite. February thawed into March.

Of course it wasn't that easy. I'm skipping a lot of Blah blah blah, like that evening when Mom wandered back into her bedroom, swore like Michael, then stormed out of the apartment and disappeared for two hours. But she came back with fried chicken, and no alcohol breath, and she let me teach her how to play *Spider-Man*. Then the next day after work, Mom told us she'd made herself another appointment with her therapist. Michael looked at me pointedly.

My brother's little Burgowski-kids-to-the-rescue scheme worked even better than he'd hoped. Over the phone, Dad totally bought our cheesy plan to stay the rest of the summer with Mom. "Jeez, I'll have to skip the Fair, it just won't seem right without you two bugging me for money," he said, but he sounded enthusiastic about the idea of us feeling at home in McClenton after all these years.

So there we stayed, enjoying our cool routine with a little more caution, like people on a tightrope. I added the apartment pool to my McClenton Top Ten list—okay, nine—and Michael and I made tons of money from Arnie's multiplying jobs. I guess Mom made the same as always, and obviously she couldn't keep feeding two teenagers with KFC and Subway and still make the rent. But Dad started sending checks once a week. I missed him horribly, especially Saturday mornings, since Mom never got into the fancy breakfast thing.

Some nights when I flew, it was all I could do to force myself to turn around and head back to the apartment.

Oh yeah. I got back into the sky, but I had to fight my way up there just like that August sun, pushing through clouds of fear and self-doubt. After that first disaster of a landing in the parking lot, it took me over a week to try again. But I did, and here's how: I promised myself I would only fly once around the apartment building, and I made myself take a nap first, like a boring grown-up, so I could stay up past midnight and still have enough energy to fly without that horrible weighty feeling.

It worked! I flew around twice to celebrate. Next night—after another nap, ignoring Michael's sarcasm— I flew just to the river and back, flexing my arms and legs to make sure they still felt lively, and that triumphant sky-habitat feeling came trickling back.

By the third night that feeling was a flood. I steered clear of the industrial areas and insanely big parking lots with their stink of diesel and garbage, and headed for the neighborhoods where the sky-lily scent mingled with cut grass and the fumes of grilled hot dogs. Once or twice I even flew across part of Lake Washington to cruise the really ritzy houses—damn, they have some huge ones! But the memory of my first exhausted flight kept me from getting too far from Mom's, just like it kept me from trying something as stupid as flying home to Dalby. Don't think that idea didn't cross my mind every single flight. But I'm not a total idiot.

"Four more weeks till school," I told Michael. "Dude, Savannah's gonna be SO jealous about our mall trip." We only bought me a bathing suit, but we tried on a whole bunch of ridiculous stuff, like matching mother–daughter camo miniskirts, just for fun. And it was.

"Three more weeks," I told myself. Was Louis going out of his mind with boredom? Maybe Shasta's shaggy boyfriend was taking him fishing or something. Had he forgotten all about me? But then I forgot about Louis for days at a time.

"Two more weeks." What in the world was I going to write about when Mr. Evans, who I'd have for ninth grade, assigned the traditional Summer Vacation essay? Rentin' in McClenton?

One night *Edward Scissorhands* came on Mom's TV, and I got a sudden flash of Dad, sitting on the living room couch in the T-glow, with his head on Lorraine's shoulder. I missed him so much my stomach hurt, and I didn't even mind that Lorraine had barged into my memories too.

August zoomed along. A week to go. Then, on a perfect Saturday afternoon, lounging by the apartment pool, Mom said, "You know, I guess I better get you guys enrolled, huh."

My whole body froze, feet in the water. I became a poolside statue in a new purple bathing suit.

"Oh, ummm," said Michael. He was deep into his eighth Stephen King book, but Mom's comment seemed to have jolted him right out of there.

"I mean, you can't just show up on the first day of school," Mom continued. "Well, you can, but it'd be a big pain in the—it'd be a bad idea." She slowly pulled herself up from her beached-whale position and examined the towel imprints on her thighs.

Joss-the-statue sat there and stared at Michael. *Do something! This whole stay-all-summer thing was your brilliant idea!*

"Mom, do you," he started, then he actually had to clear his throat. "Do you really, um…don't you think we should, like…"

Mom seemed to be turning into cement too. She stared heavily at Michael. "Think you should what?"

"You know, go on…back…" Michael struggled. I knew he had just stopped himself in time from saying "home."

Suddenly I was furious, and the anger breathed my muscles back into life. I yanked my feet out of the pool and turned to face my mom. How could she pretend she didn't know how homesick we were?

"Back to Dalby, Mom—duh!"

She turned to me. The towel-mark on her cheek made her look all young and innocent, which added to my fury. *Who does she think she's fooling?*

"We want to go to our school, not some lame McClenton school! We want to see our friends! We want to see D—"

"It's been great here," Michael interrupted loudly. He looked scared. "It's been a cool summer, Mom. But Joss is kinda right. We really should be—I mean, everyone's expecting us to come back, you know…"

"And we want to!" I burst out. Somehow I had to drive that into my mom's little-cement-girl expression: she had to face the facts. "We want to go home, Mom."

"Our other home, Mom—" Michael gasped. But the damage was done. The statue shattered itself and stood up. I felt viciously pleased.

"Of course!" she said. She gave us a large smile. "Of course, of course you do. I'm so sorry, guys. I'm so sorry I didn't notice." And she picked up her towel and walked back into the building.

"Oh s--t," said Michael's voice, muffled into his towel, and then he said a whole bunch of other things I don't want to write here. Finally he raised his head and said clearly, "We are in deep doo-doo now."

"Why?" I demanded. My whole body felt energized. "About time someone stood up around here! You saw that, she took it great! Now we can go home and quit worrying about hurting someone's feelings every time we open our mouth."

"Oh, come on, Joss, don't be as moronic as you look," my brother said. "Do you really think everything's fine and dandy now?"

Of course I do. Well, of course I don't. But my big brother just called me moronic. First things first.

Jocelyn said blah blah blah. Michael said blah blah blah. They both knew their mom would blah blah blah if they didn't blah blah blah. It went on FOREVER.

We forgot to eat lunch, we were so busy arguing, and by the time we noticed and went upstairs for a sandwich, Mom had locked herself in her room. We were pretty sure there weren't any more pills in there, but that didn't seem to matter. Her voice through the door was so high-pitched and cheerful it scared the pants off both of us, even though I refused to admit this. We kept on fighting.

Blah blah blah.

This time Dad wasn't buying.

"Put Beth on the phone," he demanded. "I want to hear this from her."

"She's taking a nap," I told him as convincingly as I could. She might have been; our last timid knock on her door had been greeted with silence.

"It's dinnertime! Who's making dinner for you guys?" My

heart clenched; it was just like Dad to worry about food, just like Mom to ignore it.

"Oh, we are. We always do Saturday nights," I said, which was true enough.

"You guys wanted to stay the summer, fine. It really sounds like it's been a good situation," Dad said. "But it's time to come home. You're starting high school, Jocelyn! I just can't fathom... school in McClenton? That makes no sense to me."

Me neither! I wanted to scream. "We just...Michael and I really just want to see what it's like. To get out of our comfort zone." Michael had coached me into this supposedly grown-up phrase. I was already out of mine; I hadn't felt comfortable for hours. "They have a rock band at McClenton High, Dad. Michael's totally psyched. And there's, like, poetry classes and this stained-glass program..."

"You can make stained glass right here on Dalby," Dad sighed, not bothering to point out that our nearest neighbor was a stained-glass artist. "You're not being straight with me, Joss. What's really going on over there?"

I had to cover up the phone for a second so he wouldn't hear me sniffle. What was really going on? Reality, in my brother's voice, had worn me down over the past few hours. *We go, and Mom falls apart. What choice do we have?* My brain had accepted this, but my heart was still kicking its feet and pounding the floor.

Now was the moment to tell Dad. He'd understand. He'd come get us in a flash—well, more like midnight, after the ferry ride and the drive. And he wouldn't blame us, he'd blame Mom for putting us in this situation, and he'd be right.

And she'd be on her own again.

At that moment, I felt the push-off power rising in my left foot, like someone started an engine in there. I took a step across the living room floor, still holding the phone. "Joss?" I heard

Dad's voice, sounding far away. My fingers quivered, feeling for the open air.

"Gimme that," Michael snapped, grabbing the phone. "Dad? Hey, it's me...look, it's no big deal, okay?"

I sat myself, hard, on a kitchen chair. The take-off feeling drained away. Just as well—I would have killed myself smashing into the ceiling. But I had never, ever come so close to flying not-on-purpose before. Indoors? In front of Michael? My body still hummed, and my knees felt shaky.

"...might even go out for cross-country," Michael was saying. "And they have all these high-tech classes, you know, like broadcasting and stuff, and they have Chinese, how cool is that..."

He's good, my brain said. *Mrs. Mac would call that world-champion persuasion.* I put my hands on my knees to still them.

That's when Mom joined us. Pale, but her eyes were focused and normal-looking. "Is that Ron?" she asked, as if she hadn't just made herself invisible for the past six hours. Michael handed over the phone. "Hi. No, I haven't brainwashed them." The scratches in her voice were deeper than ever, but she sounded calm. "I think it's a lousy idea too. Why in the world would they want to go to school in McClenton?"

Nope—Michael's not the world champion. In three minutes of agreement, Mom turned Dad's mind around. Hey, anyone that self-sacrificing must be one heck of a parent. She actually convinced *me*.

"If you're sure that's what you want," was the last thing Dad said to me when the phone made the rounds again. "But if you change your mind, Joss, I'll come get you. Just say the word."

"Thanks," was the word I chose to say.

The rest of the evening was taken up with school-supply shopping plans. Blah blah blah.

Too bad no one warned me and Michael about Dress Code.

At Dalby School, everyone wears what they want. Even the teachers wear shorts and flip-flops when it's warm. No one cares. At McClenton, they cared. Apparently there'd been a problem with gangsta wannabes, or bullying, or slutty girls, or who knows what, so: no headgear or bandannas. No tank tops or visible bra straps or skirts shorter than an inch above the knee. And the rule that sent Michael on the world's grumpiest shopping trip: no shirts with writing. Oh, and those shirts had to be tucked in.

I remembered Mrs. Mac teaching us, "If you don't stand for something, you'll fall for anything," when we had to write our Character Essay last year. At McClenton High School, home of the Mustangs, I decided to stand for Being Different.

Like that was hard.

These Mustangs made sure I knew I wasn't part of the herd. When they spoke to me it was usually something like, "Seriously, you don't have a phone?" or "Are those your brother's shoes?" Mostly they spoke past me, to each other. "Guess someone thinks she's all that, right?" this one girl, Crystal, whispered loudly to her friend Kaylee on our third day in History when I was the only one who knew that Asia wasn't a country, and Kaylee, who I had thought might be my friend, laughed and wouldn't look at me.

That was the girls. Crystal and Kristen and Kaylee ran the biggest clique, but it had little offshoot-cliques in every one of my classes, with little Crystal wannabes just dying to prove how popular they were by putting down the smart new girl. One of 'em, Mariah, started calling me "Bossy-lyn" after I tried to organize our relay-race group better in P.E., and the name stuck. So after the first week, Bossy-lyn kept her mouth shut.

"Don't let those little bitches get you down," Mom urged me when I told her Kristen accused me of making Dalby Island up. I couldn't help smiling at the thought of Mom in a cat-fight with Kristen and Crystal. She'd kick their little Mustang asses. But I wasn't about to get in a fight, and arguing back just made them taunt me more. Being ignored was easier.

The boys in my classes decided I wasn't worth it, and after a couple of times when I wouldn't let Dwayne and Erik, the hottest ones, copy my math homework, they all decided to ignore me. I could've started flying right there in class, and they'd have gone on whispering about playing *Halo*.

Ignoring was something Michael was getting pretty good at, too; he practiced on me every afternoon. Our walk home from the bus stop sounded like this:

Joss: "This is so screwed up! I can't believe you made us stay here. Mrs. LaFrance actually told us today we *have* to write 'In my opinion' in our essays. She's such an idiot!"

Michael:

Joss: "And in P.E., Crystal kept whispering stuff to Kaylee when we were lined up for roll, and they both kept laughing and looking at me."

Michael: (fiddles with his earbuds)

Joss: "I want to go home! This was all your lame idea! This place SUCKS!"

Michael: (Whiny guitar chords start leaking out of his ears.)

I didn't yank his earbuds out, I didn't throw a screaming fit there in the apartment parking lot, I didn't leap up and fly away home. I didn't do a lot of things. Including asking Michael how he was liking eleventh grade. Including my homework, which reminded me every night of the horrible teacher who'd assigned it or the horrible girls whispering or the horrible boys ignoring me in that class. Much easier to stop thinking about it at all.

And Michael must've been thinking the same way all along. He never did any homework either. We just turned on the TV and lost ourselves in *Simpsons* re-runs. And when Mom came home with the pizza or whatever she'd picked up for dinner and asked the homework question all good parents have to ask, all we had to say was, "Yup, we did it already."

For the first couple of weeks she asked about school, but "Fine," isn't much of a discussion topic. In my opinion, that was fine with her. We talked about the pizza, or the *Simpsons*, or the way people at Boeing acted like the custodians were invisible. As invisible as I felt at McClenton High.

Being invisible is pretty tiring, turns out.

I don't ever remember feeling so exhausted. Ninth grade was killing me. I flew three times in the first two weeks, fueled mostly by frustration at the trap Michael had caught us in. Flew again in the third week, when I found out that a humiliating memory can drag a Flyer down like an anchor. Every time I tried to gain altitude, I remembered Dwayne, the one who looks like Harry Potter, waving at me across the room in math, and thrilled old Joss waving back…not realizing Dwayne was waving to Kaylee behind me. After five minutes of trying to shed that memory, I landed and walked back to the apartment.

Week number four, I decided to take a little nap before flying, maybe give myself enough energy to fly above the rotten, heavy school-thoughts. Lying down on the couch after dinner felt like a joke. Who takes evening naps? But pretty soon my eyes were stuck shut and the buzz of the TV had faded into a weird dream about flying with a swarm of giant, friendly bees. Mom covered me with a blanket and woke me up the next morning for school. Next night, same thing. Sleeping left no time for flying.

After that, I quit pretending I didn't know what was going to happen when my eyelids started sagging at seven-thirty. I unfolded my couch-bed right in the middle of Mom and Michael and *Law and Order*, brushed my teeth like a good little girl, and went to sleep. After the third night, Mom asked me if I was maybe coming down with something, but I pretended I was already asleep. So she patted my head and left me alone.

Next day, I skipped English. It was easy. I just hid in the bathroom and re-read Harry Potter Five. Invisible, remember? And I didn't even need a magic cloak.

Mom's answering machine was blinking when we got home. I'm not stupid, I knew what the message was going to say even before I heard the recording of our Attendance Secretary announcing the absence of Jocelyn Burgowski from Fourth Period on Tuesday, October Third. What surprised me was Michael; he was the one who played the message because he beat me to the machine. But I understood a minute later when he smirked at me. "Great minds think alike," he said, and pressed the button again.

"This is Mrs. Burton, Attendance Secretary from McClenton High School—again," the machine chirped. Different kid, same message, except Michael had apparently skipped two classes, not just one. We looked at each other.

Michael shrugged. "Like it matters."

What's sad is, I agreed with him.

I started skipping every couple of days, mixing it up between English, P.E., and history—which just happened to be the classes containing the three meanest girls. I knocked myself out on the excuse notes I forged; my best one said that My Daughter Jocelyn's presence had been required at the bedside of her cousin who was giving birth to triplets, signed, Bethany Burgowski. Mrs. Mac would've been proud of my creativity.

When mid-quarter progress reports came in the mail, it was a cinch to snag them and forge Mom's signature. As far as McClenton High was concerned, Mrs. Burgowski was fully aware that both her kids were failing half their classes (which just shows how ridiculously easy school is; we should've been failing all of them). Their job was done; I'm sure they thought we were now grounded for our terrible grades, no TV or internet privilege. Neither of us had ever failed a class in our lives, so it was kind of fun being bad together for a change.

"Shouldn't you guys be getting, like, grades or something?" Mom asked in the middle of October. Michael and I were ready for her.

"No, Mom, remember? It's not about grades anymore, it's about your Performance Portfolio," I said like we'd had the conversation a million times. "At the end of the semester we'll have our conferences and you get to see what-all we've been doing in our classes." By which time, Michael and I decided, we could sadly admit that *McClenton High was just too much for us, Mom, we're really sorry, but it looks like we'd better go on back to Dalby for our own good.* That way it wouldn't be our choice, and she couldn't blame herself for being a bad parent if her kids were just plain stupid, could she?

Mom was too smart to buy this right away, but Michael and I pulled out some old work—with the dates carefully rewritten—to show her the amazing stuff we were working on, like a Literary Essay on *The Scarlet Letter* (Michael) and an Annotated Timeline of Washington Territory (me).

She studied my timeline thoughtfully. "Your handwriting's better than mine," she finally said.

"Thanks," I said, getting up from the table. My stomach was not happy with the compliment.

But Mom wasn't done. "Do you mean this, Joss? This part in the summary where you say life must have been better back before there was electricity?"

Of course not; what idiot thinks that? Life without refrigerators and TV? I had just been trying to provoke Mr. Horchak, who's not only my fattest teacher but also one who thinks Crystal is smart because she agrees with him in class debates. "Nn—yeah," I muttered. "Sort of."

"Well, you make a pretty good point here." Mom put her finger along my lame-o timeline. "'Before the discovery of electricity, people did fun things that needed darkness, like sitting around campfires.' That's true, right? I used to think that way myself, how it was such a shame that we had to, I don't know, lose touch with our wilder, outdoorsy selves, and move inside and turn on the lights all the time."

I stood behind my chair feeling like a complete phony. Here was Mom trying to have this deep conversation with me about something I had only written to bug Mr. Horchak, back when I cared enough even to turn anything in. "Well, yeah," I said again. Michael rolled his eyes at me and carried his plate into the kitchen. I started to follow.

"Is that it?" Mom asked, and her voice sounded funny. Not mad or sarcastic or wild-girl-funny or any of the other versions I'd become familiar with in the past few weeks. It didn't sound scratchy at all. "I'm just wondering, Joss. What's the matter, you don't believe that part about electricity anymore?"

"No, no, I do," I lied. Or maybe I wasn't lying. All I knew was, talking about school with my mom was the last thing I felt like doing, or second-to-last. Talking about magic, now *that* was right down at the bottom of my list. The last time I'd been in touch with my "wild, outdoorsy self" was over three weeks ago, up in the sky...or was it four? "It's just, I've gotta go do my reading now," I added vaguely, and wandered away, but not before I caught her expression. She looked like she'd rung a doorbell and had the door slammed in her face.

That was the last we heard from Mom about school for a while. The following week, for the first time since we'd come to stay, she stopped by Ricky's Tavern for Happy Hour. "Hey, it's no big deal," she grinned that evening, when Michael and I greeted her beer-breathed late arrival with accusing stares, even as we helped ourselves to the deli packages she'd tossed on the counter. She giggled. "Sometimes people need to let off a little steam, y'know?"

Oh, I knew all right—or I did the next day. That was the day I decided never, ever to go back to McClenton High. The day I found out I couldn't fly anymore.

CHAPTER FOURTEEN

FLIGHT

The whole thing started with English. I skipped every other day, so Mrs. LaFrance wouldn't get too suspicious, right? Turns out she was a little smarter than she looked.

We were fixing Run-on Sentences, totally boring because Mrs. Mac had already taught me. So I was zoning out in the back of the room where Mrs. LaFrance put me to break up the cluster of cool kids who whisper and pass notes. It didn't work; they just used me as their personal mailman, and Crystal would kick my desk if I didn't play along. But that day Crystal was busily writing, Mrs. LaFrance was droning on, and I was free to wonder what Mom was bringing home for dinner that night. I'd been starving all morning. Then it hit me: that's not hunger I'm feeling, below my stomach, like machinery grinding to life. My period had barged in early. And I had just barely noticed in time.

Must have been the stress; my body'd been whacko ever since I came to McClenton. *Do I even have any tampons in my purse?* I raised my hand.

Mrs. LaFrance ignored me.

I waggled my fingers. Usually teachers will just wave you along to get rid of you.

But instead of nodding me toward the bathroom pass, Mrs. LaFrance looked right at me, hard. "Go ahead, Jocelyn. We're looking for the difference between a period and a semi-colon. Help us out."

"Oh, I know that," I blurted, "but I just wanted to ask, Can I use the bathroom?"

"I don't know, can you?" Mrs. LaFrance responded. *Wow, didn't know teachers still did that after kindergarten.* Mariah giggled. "Don't you mean—"

"*May* I," I amended quickly. "Please?"

"Didn't I ask you a question first?" Mrs. LaFrance replied, all fake-polite, and even though technically she hadn't *asked* me about the frickin' difference between a frickin' period and a frickin' semi-colon, I played along for the sake of that bathroom pass.

"A-semi-colon-is-like-a-junior-varsity-period-it-does-the-same-thing-as-a-period-just-not-as-strong!" Mrs. Mac's old lesson poured out of my mouth. Mrs. LaFrance looked taken aback.

"Interesting notion, but essentially correct," she nodded, eyebrows arched, already turning away from me. "Now, what happens if we—"

"So can I—may I go now?" My machinery was grinding into high gear down there.

She smiled sweetly. "Leave my class? Oh, my, I hardly think so. You're in here so rarely these days, do you really think I'm going to let go of you when I do finally have you in my clutches?"

My face caught on fire. I dropped my head to let my hair fall like a curtain, like Michael does, but it's not as thick and dark as his. I couldn't shut out the giggles swirling around me. *Trapped!* I crossed my legs.

Someone kicked my chair. I looked around through my hair to see Crystal holding out a note in her demanding way. *No way, I'm not playing.* She kicked my chair again, hitting my foot.

There was nothing I could do. Mrs. LaFrance was over by her desk, and she wouldn't come to my rescue anyway. I snatched Crystal's stupid note and looked to see which stupid cool kid I was supposed to pass it to.

"Yo Dwayne: Bossy-lyn got SERVED!!!! LMAO!!!" is what it said, in pink pen. She hadn't bothered to fold it over.

I don't know how I got over to the window. I don't even remember heaving it open. All I remember is my hands on the window sill, gripping so hard they looked like somebody else's, and my body scooched sideways so the class couldn't see the huge stain I could feel announcing itself. And the fleeting thought, *So this is how Louis feels.* And Mrs. LaFrance's voice at my back, "Jocelyn, what are you DOING?"

Flying the hell away from here, I thought, and lifted my right foot, my takeoff foot, to the sill. And with one push I soared away from those losers, up and up, away from all the cute smirks and the tucked-in shirts and the sarcastic, arched eyebrows. Higher and higher I flew, leaving those mean Mustangs gasping in amazement at my powers…

At least that's what should have happened.

Here's what did: I pushed off, and fell out the window.

Good thing Mrs. LaFrance's classroom is on the first floor. I guess.

My wrist started bleeding from the scratchy landscaping, but inside I felt… nothing. My flight-engines stayed silent.

Where'd the power go? I thought wildly. *I almost flew by accident yesterday… Did my power get mad at me and leave?*

"Hey, nice one, Bossy," said a voice above me. I looked up to see my entire Ninth Grade English class crowded to the window to catch the action. Dwayne's smile looked appreciative.

"Look out, here comes the teacher," someone called. I scrambled to my feet and took off around the side of the building, toward the playing fields. Running, I mean. The only kind of taking off I could do.

Turns out there aren't a lot of hiding places around a high school. I couldn't sneak back into the bathrooms—that barky-voiced security guard, Mr. Wright, would be looking for me. I was in trouble. Skipping was one thing. So was failing. But I'd never heard of anyone jumping out of a classroom and running away before. I should have been all panicked, wondering *what to do, what to do?*

But I felt numb.

Oh, and my machinery? It stopped grinding. The joke was on me. When I finally found a good hiding place underneath the football bleachers, and, you know, *checked*—there was no huge embarrassing stain. Oh, I got my period all right. It was just taking its time, and *by the way humiliating me in front of half the school by sending me out to fly when my power's probably been gone for weeks and weeks.* I was a normal girl now, all right. I fit right in. Ha ha. Ouch.

I could've made the long walk home, but I didn't want a policeman to stop me. And I had no other plans, down there in the sour-smelling dirt with the old soda cups, lines of sun falling through the bleachers above me. I was out of magic and out of ideas. So I curled up in the sticky dirt and went to sleep.

Barking voices woke me. I swam up from a confused dream— a pack of bloodhounds? No, not a dream. Someone really was calling my name.

The stripes of sunlight had shifted, but it wasn't any darker than before. I shook my head hard, then moved my watch into one of the light-stripes: eleven-thirty. A long, bleeding scratch had scabbed its way down to my watchband. I was freezing, and filthy from lying in about twenty years' worth of spilled soda and bits of popcorn. I'd been asleep under the bleachers for a good couple of hours. And someone had finally figured out I hadn't gone home.

A bunch of someones, sounded like. I recognized Mr. Wright's voice, even though the only thing I'd ever heard him say was, "Hey! Tuck that shirt in!" Now he was repeating my name, "Jocelyn Olivia Burgowski," like someone making an important announcement. *JOB, my old signature. Before I turned into The Flying Burgowski.*

"Jocelyn?" called another voice, scratchy with emotion. I had never heard such a hopeless sound.

Wait—Mom's here. In the middle of the day. That meant that someone had reached her at work. Now she'd be in major trouble for leaving without notice.

"Jocelyn Olivia Burgowski." Mr. Wright was coming closer, and he knew enough about kids to check under the bleachers. He'd shine his stupid flashlight. *Not you. Mom can find me. Not you.*

But Mom's pathetic calls were drifting in the other direction.

"Jocelyn Olivia Burgowski." I heard a click, then a pale beam competed briefly with the light-stripes.

I bolted. Third time that day. Only what's sad is, I didn't even think of flying. I had learned my lesson and I used my feet like a normal girl.

But no one shouted "There she goes!" They kept calling my name like the boring chorus of a boring song.

I got a little lost in those confusing streets, but I felt too dazed to be scared. When I finally made it back to Mom's, up those four flights of stairs, I collapsed, all sweaty, on the couch.

And cried, okay? A whole lot.

I stopped eventually. Duh.

Then I took a shower and put on clean clothes and checked my Feminine Products collection: one solitary tampon. Mom might have some, but I really, really did not want to go through Mom's drawers again. Who knew what-all I'd find? I could go down to the 7-Eleven, but, not working for Arnie anymore, I only had a dollar-fifty. *Gotta wait for Michael. Has he heard about his crazy escaping sister yet?*

Then I realized I was starving. It was lunchtime back in Mustang-land. So I snarfed some peanut butter-and-Saltine sandwiches. And for a long stretch, I forgot to wonder where my mom could be.

Guess I just didn't want to think about it. Because when I started to, I suddenly got real sleepy again.

Next thing I knew the apartment door was slamming, my watch said 3:35, and my brother was in my face.

"What the hell, Joss?"

"Oh," I said, and yawned. "Hey. Got any money?"

"I missed the frickin' bus waiting for you! Why didn't you *tell* me you were skipping? And where'd you get that scratch?"

I had NOT planned to tell Michael. Anything. Number One, it wasn't any of his business if I skipped. Number Two, who tells their brother about their period? Number Three...one look at that scratch and I was back in the bush below my classroom window, breathless...that line of faces above me... *"Nice one, Bossy..."*

"Nowhere."

"You get in a fight?"

"'Course not." I should've just said Yes. But all of a sudden I felt so sorry for myself, I couldn't think at all.

"Joss..." He used the Dad-voice.

So much for plans. First I lost it again. Then I told him everything.

Well, not *every*thing. I just said Mrs. LaFrance wouldn't let me go to the bathroom. And, duh, I left out the flying part. Like there was a point in trying to convince my brother of my magic now.

Michael was impressed. "Right out the window?" he kept repeating. "Damn! Wish I'd seen that." He shook his head, and I felt a teensy bit better. Until Michael added, "So what're you gonna do tomorrow?"

We agreed that simply erasing the school's messages wasn't going to do it this time; Mom already knew I was in trouble. And that's when Michael figured out what my brain had been refusing to deal with all afternoon: "Hey, if Mom knows—how come she's not here?"

We stared at each other. Michael swore.

By dinnertime, neither of us felt like eating. Not because our choices were Shrimp Ramen or more peanut butter crackers, but because we were slowly going nuts trying to figure out what to do. Go look for Mom? Where to start? Call Dad? And tell him what? Every now and then we'd take a break from fretting and try to watch TV, but we couldn't concentrate.

"Maybe we should call the police," I suggested at eight-thirty.

"That's a lame-ass idea," Michael snorted. But he didn't have any better ones.

"I'm going out to look for her," my brother announced an hour later.

"That's ridiculous, it's totally dark, how would you know where to look, where would you go?"

"Fine, then."

It scared me how fast I deflated him. "I'm hungry," I heard myself whine.

"I'm starved," Michael admitted. "Look, let's make some noodles, okay?"

When the water boiled, Michael added the little packet of shrimp-flavor and the steam turned fishy. "Remember when Dad dumped the leftover tuna casserole in the Ramen that time?" I said. Michael and I looked at each other over the steam.

"After this we'll go home," he said quietly.

I nodded, afraid of crying again. Neither of us said what "after this" might mean. We slurped our noodles, ate crackers for dessert, then a bowl of dry cereal. It got later.

In all our worry about Mom, I actually forgot about my Feminine Products Problem. My body reminded me.

"Hey Michael, remember when I asked you if you had any money?"

"Huh," he grunted. We were watching *Men in Black*, one of our Saturday Night movies back home.

"Well, do you? I need to go to the 7-Eleven."

That got his attention. "Are you insane? It's like, eleven o'clock."

"It's quarter of. So it's still open, right? But I need, like, five dollars."

"You can't go by yourself. And I can't go with you. What if Mom calls? And anyway…" Michael shook his hair out of the way to glare at me, "what the hell's so important you can't get it tomorrow?"

"None of your business," muttered brilliant Joss, blushing her head off.

Michael's pretty smart, for a guy. "Oh," he said.

We watched as Will Smith punched out a monster with tentacles.

"You could've told me," Michael sounded more embarrassed than annoyed. "Here."

I looked up to see him holding out a bill, his eyes still on the TV. I took it and unfolded it: a ten. "Hey, thanks. I'll pay you back."

"Just go fast, okay? Run, so no one messes with you. And I'll watch out from the balcony."

The creepy fat guy behind the 7-Eleven counter showed no sign of locking up when I arrived at 10:59. He was watching Will Smith too, and his eyes never left the tiny screen as he took my money. I got Michael a pack of peanut M&M's with some of the change.

Big-city Joss, out on her own at practically midnight, buying treats for her brother. For a moment I forgot about Mom and my horrible day, forgot that Michael was waiting out on the balcony for me. I came around the side of the 7-Eleven and there it was, my old take-off spot, hidden from the street by those lame, pointy evergreens in giant pots. I felt suddenly at home, there on the oily pavement. It wasn't the Toad, but it was my first McClenton launching pad, the place that had convinced me that my magic wasn't stuck back on Dalby Island.

I should give it another try, I thought. *This is my spot. What's there to lose?*

That thought sent my mind soaring. *Oh, yesss! The Flying Burgowski lives in the sky, wind in her face, lily-smell in her nose, to infinity and beyond!*

I took two fast strides and pushed off.

And smashed right into one of those concrete planters. My knee hit the edge and I went down, hugging the scrawny tree.

It's a good thing Michael couldn't see me from the balcony. So he wouldn't wonder why his little sister just threw herself onto a potted tree. Or why she was now lying crumpled next to an oily puddle.

The pain hit like a tidal wave, swamping me in nausea. But when that wave sucked back, it whispered a message worse than pain: *The magic's done. You let it go. Your fault. Your fault.*

I'm not sure how long I lay there, groaning like a wounded animal. It was my limping Michael noticed when I finally made it back to the apartment.

"What the *hell*?" Then he said a bunch of other things. Some of them were questions.

I chose the easiest one. "I tripped."

More questions, more swearing. What was I thinking, did I know how long he'd been waiting, did I think he was ever, ever letting me pull something like that again, and by the way had I noticed Mom hadn't come home yet?

I nodded a lot. I felt so, so sleepy. Then somewhere in there, I heard Michael say, "Are you *okay*, or what?"

The tears rushed up again from my stomach. But for the first time in my life, I shut the floodgates. *No. Damnit. No. Can't fly, won't cry.*

It felt like a burial. Like…it's official now. Show's over.

"Got you some M&M's," I muttered, and slid them out of the bag. "'M going to bed now, 'kay?"

And this is how bad I must have looked: my brother didn't even try to argue with me. "Okay. I'll just…I'll wait up for Mom."

I sleepwalked through my bathroom business. Then, still in my clothes, I went to bed.

Invisible ropes crisscrossed my shoulders. I rubbed at them, trying to loosen their grip, but there was nothing there but bone and muscles, my own body keeping me from the air, my natural habitat… "'Me go," I mumbled, and woke up to my brother's face a few inches from mine in the dark living room.

"Joss-stay-here-'m-gonna-get-Mom," Michael jabbered. By the time I sat up he was at the door.

"Huh? What time is it?"

"Stay *here*," he repeated fiercely, and slammed out the door.

I turned my wrist toward the dim light from the parking lot. 2:20. The room was freezing. Michael had left the balcony door open, watching out for Mom. Like he said he would. While I slept like a little kid. I felt so ashamed, I was glad Michael wasn't there to see me.

Then my brain woke up. Did he say he was going to get Mom? Where?

Like an answer, I heard her voice, down in the parking lot.

"Getcherf---in handsoffme," my mother said.

I scrambled to the balcony. Four floors down, there she was, leaning on a car, her streetlight shadow looking stronger and straighter than she did. Even with her chin tilted up and her hands on her hips, my mom looked tiny and vulnerable.

And drunk. From my perch I could see she was barely staying upright; her hands dug into her waist like useless clamps. She was in trouble, anyone could see that.

Anyone obviously had.

There were two of them, identical dark bundles from my view, until one stepped forward and the streetlight shone off his giant bald spot. He spoke to my mother, something too low for me to hear, but it made his buddy laugh from the darkness. If they were seeing a lady home, they were doing a pretty crappy job of it. I started to shiver in the clammy air.

"I f---in' told you, Jim or Todd or wha'ever the f--- your name is, I'm fine, so leave me th' hell alone, I gotta go take care of m'kids." *Way to go, Mom,* I thought, but then she added, "Okay? I'm fine," in a little-girl voice and I knew she wasn't, and I knew Jim and Todd knew, and when bald Jim-or-Todd said clearly, "Hey, sorry, baby, but you're the one who invited us, 'member?" I knew they weren't sorry about this at all.

And then Michael was there, racing into the lamplight and screeching to a halt like a cartoon character. "Hey, Mom," he said in a very cheery, un-Michael voice, "What's up? Let's go home now, huh?"

Oh, Dad would've been so proud. So straight he stood there, his hair pushed back and his face shining pale in the light, while Mom crumpled on his shoulder like a slung backpack. Michael put his arm around her, saying something encouraging, and they took a couple of shaky steps toward our building. *You da man, Michael,* I thought.

"Hey, you da *man,* bro!" someone said smirkily, and for a second I was freaked out—was that my voice? But no, it was Todd-or-Jim, the other one, stepping out of the shadows, and he turned out to be a lot bigger than Baldy. "Way to go, Sir Knight, way to ride in on your white horse. Thing is, your mama ain't quite ready for rescue. How 'bout you come back in a couple hours." He didn't make it a question. He was really big.

"Yeah," Baldy added, "don't call us, we'll call you!"

"We're fine," Michael said, but it came out quavery. *He's having trouble holding Mom up, that's all. Of course he's fine.* Jim-and-Todd cracked up. The big dude had to bend down and grab his knees to recover.

"Oh, yes *sir*, you are fine, young sir, and your mama's even finer," he gasped, and I swear I could smell his fumes from four floors up. "Thing is, she kinda promised us, y'know? Like a business proposition? Cost us—what, Jim?"

"Forty bucks," said Baldy Jim.

"Forty," repeated Todd. "Bucks." He laid a massive hand on Michael's other shoulder, and I saw my brother sway. "Your mama c'n sure put 'em away, kid. But me 'n' Jim don't buy like that outta the goodness of our hearts, a'right?"

"Business proposition," Jim nodded. He moved in closer, like a lion on one of those nature programs. A stupid, drunk, dangerous lion. And Michael was the mama wildebeest, protecting her young.

"Go f--- yourself," the wildebeest said. But this time Todd and Jim did not crack up. They snarled like the animals they were.

"I don't think so, a--hole," Todd said, and with one little shove sent Michael and Mom into a heap on the pavement.

Call 9-1-1. Call Arnie. Scream. Do something.

I stood frozen on the balcony.

Four floors below me, Todd was trying to haul Michael off our mother. Michael was fighting like a cat now, all claws and teeth. I think he was growling. Todd kept swearing in a low, disgusting stream.

Call 9-1-1!

They'd never get there in time.

Jim got hold of Mom, dragging her by the armpits to the edge of the parking lot. Her face in the light looked like my old baby-doll, eyes closed, serene as death. Then she faded out of view.

A giant shudder shot through me. My whole body buzzed. I gripped the railing.

From the darkness, Jim laughed a panting laugh.

A heave. Bare feet on the freezing rail. Four floors up.

You'll kill yourself.

Can't fly, won't cry.

Michael whimpered, a ragged, animal sound.

"I'm coming!" I bellowed. "Mom, I'm coming!" and pushed off.

In the sky, in the sky, in the sky! One second—two—of rocketing exultation. And then I took my triumph and I shaped it like a pointy missile and I aimed it straight down, at the back of Todd's nasty, fat head.

Feet first. At the last second I locked my knees and a good thing, too; I probably would've broken my ankle, but instead Todd got the full force of Joss-the-missile through bare feet as hard as concrete.

Todd made a sound like a baby goat and fell sideways, over Michael's legs. My brother's eyes looked up, enormous over a bleeding nose. He said something that I didn't hear. What do missiles need with hearing? Already I was lighting the fuse, leaping high, aiming myself and *boom!* There went Jim. I honestly don't remember if I flew at him or just plain old punched him out. My hands hurt later, but that could've been the other thing. Once I'd pushed Jim off my mother, I mean. And seen his unzipped pants.

Michael must have stopped me. One minute I was flailing in a red storm of grief and fury so wild my arms and legs whirled like Arnie's weed-cutter. The next, I was a girl again, a skinny, sobbing one with stinging hands, being yanked out of the red world by her bleeding brother, being cradled on the damp grass, his arms around my shoulders, his breath whooshing "Sshhh," in my ear, the two of us rocking from some inner motion that might have come from either of us, or from both.

My brother let me cry. Probably we should have rushed right over to check on Mom. Woken up Arnie. Called the cops. Oh, we did all that. Dad told us how good and responsible we were, later on. But in those moments as the storm passed and the bad guys lay around us limp as seaweed, Michael sheltered me until my sobs turned into shivers, and the blood from his nose started sticking to my hair.

"We gotta get out of here," he finally said. "Let's get her inside, okay? Do you think you can help me carry her?"

I nodded, sniffed a huge sniff, wiped my nose on my T-shirt.

My hair pulled as he heaved to his feet, then he reached to help me up. "You okay?"

I snorted. "You look way worse than me!" The nose-blood was everywhere by now, but Michael shrugged, turning to where Mom lay sleeping peacefully on Arnie's carefully trimmed grass. She looked so perfect I wanted to cry again.

"C'mon," Michael said softly. He knelt to slide one arm beneath her shoulder. "I think I can maybe lift her if you, like, grab her legs or something."

"Okay."

"On three, okay? One…"

"Michael?"

"What."

I couldn't help it. "I told you, huh," I said. "I told you I could fly."

CHAPTER FIFTEEN

RECOVERY AND REVENGE

Here's what I remember from the rest of that night:

1. Michael saying he was sorry for not believing me before.
2. The Doritos-and-diesel smell of Arnie's truck when he drove us all to the emergency room at three-something in the morning.
3. My mom's smile when she woke up in a vinyl chair with her head on my lap.
4. The lady cop who winked at me behind the back of the man cop who was lecturing me and Michael for putting ourselves in such a dangerous situation.
5. My brother whispering, "Can you show me how you do it?"
6. This thought, which has not gone away: maybe I should be a cop.
7. Dad's voice on the phone, after his first shocked syllables warmed into sentences: "Okay, you guys. I'm on my way."

That's pretty much it.

At some point, Arnie must have driven us back to the apartment, 'cause that's where we were when Dad woke us up next morning by hammering on the door. I made it there first, groggy with dreams, still dressed in my bloody T-shirt.

"Oh, Jocelyn," Dad sighed into my hair after we'd been hugging for like twenty minutes. "You are such an island girl. Have you been opening the door all this time to anyone who knocks?"

"It's okay," I heard Michael's voice behind us. "No one ever comes here. It's just been us, the whole time."

Then something amazing happened. The tight loop of Dad's hug loosened and then pulled close again, and this time Michael was inside it too. I couldn't see anything, mashed against Dad's engine-oil-smelling jacket, but I could feel Michael in there with me, and I swear he was hugging Dad back.

"So," Dad said, on the elevator ride up to Mom's hospital room, after we'd been over all the facts a few hundred times. Arnie hadn't called the cops till after he got Mom to the hospital, so Jim and Todd must have managed to crawl away. And since Mom refused to talk about it, there was no "crime" to investigate. After badgering her for a while the cops gave up, like, *Yup, you probably deserved it, lady.*

All Dad's questions started with "So," as if that could get a harness on his confusion. He was having a tough time accepting that his kids had somehow beaten up a guy attacking his ex-wife. We made it one guy instead of two so he and Arnie would believe us, but still.

"So can you promise me you won't pull any of this skipping-class stuff when you get back to your real school?"

"Hah! Like you can get away with that on Dalby," Michael said, but smiling.

"Right. Back to Dalby rules. Act like everyone knows you, 'cause they do. I'll feed you healthy food again, or Lorraine will…"

Oh yeah. Her. Believe it or not, I'd forgotten all about my new step-mom since McClenton had taken me over.

Now we were going back home to live with Lorraine.

"Okay," I said. *Guess there's always gonna be something.*

But I can fly again, my brain reminded me, and I walked into Mom's room on that little pulse of happiness.

She was sitting on the edge of her bed in one of those stupid hospital gowns. My happy feeling fluttered and I noticed Michael looking down, so I guess I wasn't really looking at Mom either. But then there she was, hopping off the bed and hugging us hard—my tough little Mom who hadn't given me more than a head-pat in about three years. So I did look at her, right up close.

She looked like crap, to be honest, her face puffy, a bruise on her chin I hadn't noticed before. And she still smelled like—well, garbage. But she was smiling, and when I decided to hug her again, just to make up for all the missed ones, she squeezed me so tight I couldn't breathe.

"I'm sorry, kiddo," she whispered into my hair. "I'm sorry you had to see all that. I'm sorry I've been such a crappy mom. I'm sorry you had to take care of me. It's supposed to be the other way around, huh."

"It's okay, Mom," I said, or maybe just thought—she was squeezing me awfully hard.

"So," Dad said, when we'd finally separated and everyone was pretending they weren't crying.

That's when a social worker with amazing jeweled fingernails came in and talked about Inpatient Recovery and Personnel Plans and Sick Leave Benefits.

"Bottom line?" Mom finally asked, her voice tired, and the social worker smiled and patted her hand, jewels flashing.

"Bottom line, your insurance will cover all this. Six weeks of recovery. You picked a good company to work for, Mrs. Burgowski. Make it work for you, okay?" and Mom closed her eyes.

"I will. Oh, believe me. I will," she said, like she was talking more to herself.

Funny thing is, I believed her.

Saying good-bye to Mom was easier than I had thought. After all those months when Michael and I had convinced ourselves we'd be killing our mother if we left her behind, she ended up shooing us back to our Dalby lives. Everything was taken care of: yes, six weeks of rest and addiction therapy, paid for by her company. Yes, she was going to be okay by herself. Yes, it had been a fun experiment and we were sweet to want to stay with her, but Dalby was our home. Yes, we were going to work really hard now and make our parents proud of us.

"Even the ones who've got no business asking that of you," Mom added in a trace of her old sarcasm. "Now off you go. Things'll get better."

It was that simple.

Walking back to the elevators, Michael and I looked at each other, like, *Why didn't we just leave back in August when we wanted to?* But he gave me a tiny headshake, and I understood. Sometimes stuff just has to happen.

"So," Dad repeated, back at the apartment, "we need to get you guys checked out of school, huh?"

"Why?" Michael shrugged over a spoonful of dry cereal which he was eating very carefully. His nose wasn't broken, but the bruised swelling made it look like a boulder on his face. "Like they'll even notice we're gone."

"My backpack's still there," I suddenly remembered. Wow, it felt like a million years ago, but it had only been yesterday when everything came unraveled. *But! I'm a superhero now, and Michael knows it.*

"Okay, here's the plan," Dad said. "You guys pack up all your stuff, and I'll pack a suitcase for your mom. We'll stop by the school and fill out all the paperwork so they don't think you just flew away." Michael and I stifled grins at the same time, which felt cool. "Then we can drop off Beth's suitcase, beat rush hour and make the six-thirty ferry. Sound good?"

I could tell he liked feeling back in charge. But...I shook my head vigorously. "No way am I going back to that school, Dad."

All those grinning faces, looking down at me from the window. Dwayne. Crystal. *"Bossy-lyn got served."* "Can't you just pick up my stuff for me?"

"Well," Dad hesitated. "Don't you want to say good-bye to your friends?"

I snorted.

"I'll go," Michael said. His expression was sending me some kind of message, but I couldn't read it. "LaFrance's room, right? I'll get your stuff while Dad signs things. Want me to pick up your project too?"

"What project?"

"You know," Michael nodded significantly, "the ones on display over by the *window*."

"Oh," I said like I understood. "Sure. That'd be great." At least I wasn't dumb enough to ask Michael to explain himself in front of Dad. Michael hatching a plan involving me—that was plenty.

So after our whirlwind of packing and leaving, I stayed in the parking lot, scrunched down in the truck where no one could see, while my father and brother made one final visit inside Mc-Clenton High School. Or what I thought was final.

They came back out fifteen minutes later, Michael with my backpack and a smug look on his face. "Couldn't find your project," he announced, "but there were a bunch of cool ones, all lined up on the *windowsill*." Then he gave me a thumbs-up behind Dad's back. I was beginning to get annoyed with his mystery.

But heading back to the hospital, Dad stopped for gas. That gave me my chance.

"What was all that about the window?" I demanded as soon as Dad was out of the truck.

"I unlocked it. Behind somebody's big ol' A-plus project where no one will check."

"So what?"

He raised one eyebrow at me. "So didn't you tell me you tried to fly out that window? C'mon, Joss, use your imagination. If I could fly, and if my school had been total jerks to me, and if they had windows that opened that much, hey, I'd be planning my revenge. But maybe that's just me."

Revenge? The thought brought a whiff of something exciting and spicy. "But what should I—"

"Never mind that now. Tell me more about the flying."

So I did. Mrs. Mac would've subtracted a bunch of points for Organization, 'cause I started with the middle and told the story in all directions at once, but Michael got the idea. The take-offs from anywhere. The lily smell. The way the power just came, the way it left me after I neglected it, the way I got it back last night when I could have killed myself leaping from the balcony.

"Hey," Michael interrupted. "Maybe that's why you got it back! D'you think maybe risking your life, you know, kind of showed the…the flying-power or whatever…that you were, like, worthy or something?"

I'd had the same thought, but it was weird to hear it from my brother. I nodded.

"Maybe. 'Cause it felt different that time. I remember how—" I stopped.

"What?"

"Feet first," I breathed as the scene came back to me. "I leaped off, but then I put my feet together and went down that way…" Connecting with Todd's head. So that's why my knees hurt so much.

"Yeah, I know, I saw you. It was amazing," Michael said. "My own f—, my own frickin' sister, flying like Superman!"

"No, not like Superman! That's what I mean!" Dad was replacing the nozzle. "I always thought I had to fly that way, arms ahead. I've been doing it ever since June. And now it turns out I can go feet first!"

"What's so important about that?"

"Well…it means…what else is there about my flying that I don't even know about yet?" And then Dad was opening the door and we couldn't talk about it anymore.

Instead we talked about our grades. Or Dad did. It was kind of a one-way conversation.

Good thing he was feeling guilty for leaving us in McClenton so long. Michael and I let him talk for a while about Choices and Personal Responsibility, and by the time we got back to the hospital he was pretty much done.

"So," he said, sitting there for a moment after turning off the truck, "I guess you guys are sending me a message here, huh."

"What message, Dad?" I asked helpfully, since he seemed more solemn than angry.

"You can take the kid off the island," he replied, and smiled for the first time since he'd arrived in McClenton, "but you sure can't take the island out of the kid. You guys don't belong here, that's pretty obvious. So why…?"

We waited.

"Never mind, stupid question," Dad said. "You did tell me. I just wasn't listening."

It was a very adult moment.

"So," Dad said for the millionth time, after dropping off Mom's suitcase, "let's go catch a ferry, shall we?"

"But I'm starving," Michael moaned. His whiny tone caught me by surprise; he sounded…well…like me. "Can't we get a real meal before we split? At a restaurant or something?"

"But the traffic," Dad began. "If we wait too long…"

My brother gave him his best puppy-dog look, and I joined in. Come to think of it, I was starving too. And we were about to leave the land of fast-food forever.

"All right," Dad sighed. "I guess we can wait it out and aim for the eight o'clock. We'll never make the six-thirty."

"And," Michael put in, "we can use the extra time to fix up Mom's apartment real nice, you know, so she has something cool to come home to." His voice was so enthusiastic I looked at him suspiciously, but his face was all innocence.

Dad bought it, though. He took his poor, starving children out to Denny's, where they proceeded to stuff themselves on fried chicken, mashed potatoes and cheesecake.

"'M gonna mish dish plashe," I managed, around a mouthful.

"What, Denny's? They have 'em everywhere," Dad said, but I could tell Michael knew what I meant. There's something about being normal that's so comforting; something about blending in and wearing and eating what everyone else wears and eats. Like Crystal and Dwayne and all the others. It wasn't a life I wanted, exactly—but I didn't want it to reject me either.

Turns out Michael was thinking the same way. And he wanted to make sure McClenton knew *it* was the one being rejected.

Back at the apartment, he busied himself making to-do lists for me and Dad. Yes, I know, this is Michael we're talking about. Dad had to go to the 7-Eleven for cleaning supplies so Mom could come home to a scrubbed kitchen and bathroom. Joss had to make a string of Welcome Back cards to hang in Mom's bedroom. Michael actually started dusting, even though I pointed out that all that dust would be back before Mom would. He just snorted and looked at his watch.

"It's quarter to five," he said significantly.

"So?"

"Dark soon." Dad was in the kitchen, but Michael lowered his voice anyway. "How dark does it need to be for you to… you know."

"Fly?" He nodded, and I glanced out the window. "Darker than this."

"Well, we don't have a ton of options here. I've stalled as long as I can, Dad's gonna want to leave pretty soon. You're gonna have to head on out there and take your chances on being seen."

"Head on out where?" I was so confused.

"Shee-it, Joss! Do I have to spell it out for you? School. Fly. Open window. Take care of business. Fly on back." He glared at me. "I'd do it myself if I could. But since you're the only Superman in the family, how's about taking advantage for both of us?"

"Ohhh."

So we pretended that Arnie owed us some money and clattered downstairs before Dad could protest. Michael ran with me to my favorite take-off spot by the 7-Eleven, "to give you some cover," he said, but really I think he just wanted to watch me take off. It was pretty cool to hear my own brother say, "Whoa..." as I leapt off the pavement.

But not as cool as flying. *Nothing is—nothing, nothing, nothing!*

It was super tricky getting to my school in the not-quite-dark, and I had to force myself not to hide behind billboards, 'cause people look at billboards. Where they don't look is straight up, so that's where I went—higher than I'd ever been, wondering how low the TV helicopters flew, 'cause I could hear one somewhere. But then, there it was, McClenton High, like the world's ugliest Lego construction, and I dropped straight down. Feet first I went, because I could, and I even tried a little barrel roll on the way down just to see what it felt like. Answer: like a dizzy dolphin.

Lights were on for the custodians to clean up the candy wrappers of my darling classmates. But Mrs. LaFrance's room was empty, and, sure enough, the first window I tried was unlocked—the same one I'd fallen out of the day before. I scrambled through.

Oh, there were so many tricks I could have played. Michael had suggested a ton: Empty out the teacher's desk. Write weird messages on the whiteboard. Turn the computer upside down.

"Halloween's next week," he urged, "they'll just think someone's getting a head start on the pranking."

But I didn't want to be just another stupid vandal, and I sure didn't want my prank mistaken for anything but Jocelyn's Revenge. The message I wanted to send was very, very specific.

So in the end, I went with the simple touch. Michael was disgusted; he called my idea lame. But it only took a second, and when I flew back out of there, showing that classroom and that whole school who was boss, I pictured Crystal's face tomorrow, when she reached in her desk and found the card I'd made out of the same blue construction paper as Mom's welcome-home ones.

"NOW WHO'S BEEN SERVED???" she'd read, and when she turned the message over, looking for clues, she'd find my signature, black and swoopy and dripping with the power she and all the rest of McClenton could never hope to have: "THE FLYING BURGOWSKI."

CHAPTER SIXTEEN

SAME OLD, SAME OLD–NOT!

I think I deserve a little break. I mean, I've been writing every spare moment for, like, days, and my hand is seriously tired. Plus now that I'm home I'm dying to get back to my routine of hanging out with my friends. And trying to find time to fly. And avoiding the stepmother.

Okay, scratch the routine idea. Gonna need a new routine now.

But I had to write it down, right? Without putting it on paper, I don't even want to think about how crazy I'd be feeling, after all the flying, and the not-flying, and the flying again. And Mom. Harry Potter? I totally know how he feels—not the magic part. I mean all the scraggled-up emotions, what Mrs. Mac calls Internal Conflict.

I did warn you it was that kind of story.

Plus, I have homework to do—tons of it. You'd think my new English teacher, Mr. Evans, would go easy on the new kid, but instead he says I need to read *The Secret Life of Bees* double-fast because the rest of the class started it two weeks ago. I tried complaining about him to Mrs. Mac, but it's hard to get sympathy from people when you can't look them in the eye.

I can't look Mrs. Mac in the eye just yet. Mrs. Mac has lost all her hair.

"Oh yeah," Louis says with big eyes the first morning I'm back. "There's this thing about Mrs. Mac."

Turns out she has breast cancer. Turns out everyone's known about it since the start of school, and I would have too if I'd stayed in touch with Louis. I know the phone thing didn't really work out, but I could've sent a letter, a real one on paper. Some people still do that. Or I could've called Savannah.

Anyway, point is—my favorite teacher in the whole world, and I didn't even know. So every time I look at her it reminds me of how rotten I can be, or not rotten so much as blah, weak, blurry. McClentonish.

I sure am glad I'm home.

"You've said that, like, three times already," Savannah says. We're back in her room, in a sea of stuffed animals, supposedly doing our math homework. I'm a little behind on some geometry concepts that probably got taught during my skipping days, and Savannah's great at math. On some other things, though, I'm starting to have my doubts. Like loyalty. She didn't even call me, my first day back, I had to call her, and then she got all mad because I hung out with Louis before I hung out with her! I know, I said I was the rotten friend…but after McClenton High, I don't have much patience for drama.

"Yeah, well, three times the charm," I say. Mrs. Mac says that sometimes. "I still can't believe it," I add, even though I've probably said that way more than three times.

"What?" Savannah says. "No, look, on number seven you forgot to multiply times *r*."

"About Mrs. Mac," I say, kind of shocked that she can't figure that out. I guess she's gotten used to living with the cancer-teacher. I don't think I'm going to.

"Oh, I know, isn't it horrible? But she said her response to the treatment's been really good." Savannah looks at me for a minute with a helpless kind of smile, then shrugs. "So…you see where you have to multiply?"

I'm spending a lot of time at Savannah's again. Maybe that's the new routine, I don't know. It's kind of a choice between coming home from school to find Lorraine gliding around in our kitchen, or going straight to my best friend's, where her attitude is pretty much guaranteed to bug me after about fifteen minutes. Today it's Mrs. Mac that does it. Yesterday it was Nate.

I knew it would be, after what happened in class.

Yesterday, October 15, was my third day back at school. Dad—still feeling guilty, yay—lets Michael and me skip Monday to "get our sea legs," so I get a big head-start on writing this story, holed up in my room. But Tuesday he insists, so off we go, and guess what: I'm like a movie star. We both are. *Return of the Burgowskis.* Everyone wants to talk to us, ask us questions about the Mainland, because just about everyone we know has only ever lived on Dalby, except Tyler, and who cares. Michael tells me later that Cindy Deutsch, who's ignored him for three years, pulls her stool next to his during Art and whispers, "So, is it true that kids are really having sex in the bathrooms and stuff at those big high schools?"

I swear.

Of course Nate doesn't ask me about sex in the bathrooms, but he does want to know about school uniforms. Do the guys have to wear those little jackets, like in England? And the food: is it true we could have burgers and pizza every single day if we wanted to?

Mr. Evans actually gets so annoyed with Nate's whispering that he finally says, "You know what, Nate? Just pass notes. Okay? Don't bother learning any new vocabulary today. Knock yourself out."

So Nate does. We pass notes the whole period—although I do manage to learn some new words, thank you very much: Enigma. Crucial. Condescending.

Savannah's going nuts in the corner. She finally passes me a note, all the way across the room: "What are you guys TALKING about?" I pass it back: "Tell you later."

So of course she grabs me during P.E., and I tell her everything I've just told Nate, but that's not really what she wants to know about. Or what she wants me to know. She saves that for her room, after her mom carpools us home from school.

"The first week back? In September? At Tyler's birthday party?" Savannah's whole voice, not just her laugh, seems to slide upward these days. "Oh, Joss, you should *so* have been there. Tyler got, like, pretty much drunk on Rocky Mountains, and..."

Stupid Joss has to ask what those are. Mountain Dew and rum, turns out. "Sounds gross."

"Yeah, well, it's good. But...when we were helping him? When Tyler was throwing up? Nate put his hand on my boob." She tries to be wide-eyed, but I can see the triumph in her mouth.

What boob? I feel like snorting, but hey, I am trying to be a good friend here. So I ask a few more questions like, "On purpose?" "Has he done it again since then?"

This is what Savannah wants to talk about. Did I say fifteen minutes? I'm bugged in five. Tomorrow I'm definitely going to Louis's.

Mom's fine, by the way. At least that's what she told me on the phone a few minutes ago. "I'm fine, babe. Now tell me some more about school."

So I do. Then she wants to know how things are with Lorraine, so I tell her they're okay, and then there's this awkward pause where I can practically feel her eyes looking at me through the phone, so I know I have to go on. "She's really pretty nice," I say, "But sometimes, the way she looks at me, it feels like x-rays."

Mom says, "Uh-huh."

"Well, you know, that can get pretty annoying," I add, because it can.

"Mm," Mom says.

Okay, I've done my best with this topic, right? "So, Mom," I say, "how soon until you get to go home?"

And she says, "Pretty soon. But don't worry, babe. I'm fine."

Guess what??? I CAN FLY OTHER PEOPLE!!! Or rather, they can fly me—like you'd fly a winged horse or a Harry Potter thestral. Fly *on* me, really. Piggyback! That's it. All I have to do is get Louis on my back, and up we go, doubles! Yeah, the takeoff's pretty tricky; I kind of stagger, and the push-off is *way* harder. My thighs are really sore now, and my knees hurt worse than ever. But, oh wow. You should see Louis's face.

"Ohhhhhhh," he gasps, as I scramble into the air, and he doesn't stop ohhh-ing until we plop back down a couple of minutes later. I could've stayed up longer; once I'm in the air I don't feel his weight at all, but he is kind of choking me. So we just do a little test flight in circles above the Toad.

"Ohhh," Louis sighs one more time when I make my second landing, dumping him into a bramble patch. Doubles landings are going to take some practice, I can tell. But he bounces back up like off a trampoline. "Oh, wow. Oh, wow. Can we do that every day? Can we try it tonight when it's dark and we can really go somewhere? Can we fly to another island?"

"Jeez, Louis." I'm trying to catch my breath, but I'm smiling as big as he is. It feels so good to finally be able to make someone really and truly happy, not just *Don't-worry,-babe,-I'm-fine* happy. Rays of late-afternoon sun are warming my back, but Louis's expression feels even better.

It shifts suddenly, though. "Oh, shoot. It's too hard for you, huh? I'm too heavy, aren't I? That's okay, Joss, I don't need to fly every—"

"Louis, shut up, okay? It's fine. I just have to get used to it, but it's fine."

"Really? 'Cause…"

"Really. It's just…I can't figure out why we didn't think of this before. Way back last June, when I first told you."

"Oh, I thought of piggyback," Louis shrugs. "I just figured it wouldn't work, or you would've said something."

That kind of loyalty jolts me—like, *are you kidding? You really think I know what I'm doing?* But suddenly I do.

"Michael!"

Louis whirls around like he expects to see my brother sneering over his shoulder.

"No, no," I explain, waving my hands. "You just made me think of something. Michael wanted to fly with me too. I told him I couldn't, 'cause, you know, I thought I couldn't. But now that I can…"

Louis looks doubtful. "You think? Won't he just make fun of you, Joss?"

"He's seen me fly. Twice. He thinks it's cool. He even asked if I was gonna fly after school today, if he could come watch." It's true. Michael did.

Louis is awestruck. "And you said no? How come, Joss?"

That same feeling from this morning slides through me, a funny mix of pride and embarrassment. "Well, I'd already asked you, right? And I didn't want you to feel…"

Louis nods. He doesn't need me to tell him how Michael— and every other kid on Dalby—makes him feel. But now that Louis has single-handedly solved the problem of doubles flying, he'll be Michael's hero! I can't wait to try!

Problem is, I hardly ever get to talk to Michael alone anymore. All those months cooped up together in McClenton, and now that I really have something to share with him, there's all these other people in the way. Well, Dad and Lorraine. Guess I can't blame them for wanting to Keep An Eye on Michael after last summer, but still, do they have to be so obvious?

"You promised," Dad reminds us, when we object that Supervised Homework Time after school is a little-kid thing. Then he shows us our withdrawal grades from McClenton.

Michael and I are pretty embarrassed about all those Fs. We do our homework at opposite sides of the kitchen table, not looking at each other. Only Tion's happy. She flops onto our notebooks and purrs, like this new arrangement is all for her.

The worst part is, Lorraine's the supervisor half the time. Probably they worked it out that way, so she can get some Parenting Practice.

If receiving one-word answers to long, sensitive questions about our homework is practice, Lorraine's getting plenty.

"So, Ron tells me you guys both need a Free Choice Reading book," she says today. We're in Week Two of the new homework-jail plan; a whole weekend has come and gone and I still haven't had the chance to take my brother flying. Dad took him fishing with a buddy on Saturday, and Sunday Lorraine took me over to the big island to shop for new jeans. Oh, wow, was that a long day. I'm trying to be polite and all, but I just can't get over the fact that she's not some visiting guest. She really *lives* with us, but I can't tell her to quit staring at me when she doesn't think I'm looking. Or that annoying sniffing thing she does. And all that politeness in your own house feels weird, like wearing dress-up clothes at breakfast.

Michael ignores her. "Mm-hm," I say, because total silence feels too rude.

Lorraine starts chopping onions. "D'you want to stop by the library and look at the young adult shelves?" she says after a few moments. "Or maybe I could bring some books home for you?"

I glare at Michael to let him know it's his turn to answer, but he keeps his eyes stuck to his Physics book. So I have to say it for him. "Mm-kay."

Soft fizzling sound, onion-butter smell. It's hard to concentrate on *The Secret Life of Bees*; I'm pretty sure I already read that paragraph.

Then Lorraine's whispy voice is wafting with the onion-fumes: "Sorry…but was that Okay, bring books home, or Okay, I'll stop by the library? I'm just—"

"Whichever," I kind of snap, because Michael's not helping me out, because I know it's my own stupid fault I'm in Homework Jail, because the way things are going I'll never have the chance to take my brother flying, and who knows if I even can anymore? *Remember what happened last time I didn't use my power?* "But thank you," I add, politely.

"Oh, you're welcome," my stepmother says. "I'll just bring some home, then." And she stirs away at the onions, and I re-read my paragraph, both of us in our stiff, Sunday best.

Finally! It's Thursday afternoon, and, miracle of miracles, neither Michael nor I has any homework, which we've proven to Dad by showing him the signed notes from our teachers.

So now we're free from jail, and we're out on the Toad with Louis, demonstrating the principle of Piggyback Flight. And Michael's frowning, but he says, "Okay, Joss. What the hell. I'll probably kill us both, but…"

"I'm sure it'll work," I say firmly, because, well, it has to. *I've been such a good girl!* For two weeks I've been coming straight home, doing my homework, then racing over to Louis's until it's time to set the table. I haven't been sneaking out; I haven't done anything to mess up my magic or the happy-happy, polite family we've all become. Louis and I have been practicing, taking longer, higher flights out here where we feel pretty safe, except yesterday when we spotted Savannah heading this direction with Nate and Tyler. But even that was cool, because I found out how to do a perfect doubles-landing: turns out you do it *fast*, and bend your knees a lot.

Point is, I'm past ready to try this. And Michael needs it even more than me. Yeah, he's all good with Dad now, no more pot, no more potty-mouth. But I can see it in his face every afternoon when I head over to Louis's: *This is so not fair.*

"Get on fast," I tell him, because I'm worried about takeoff the most. He shuffles over, looking suddenly enormous.

"No way," he mutters, but his hair can't quite hide the glint of wild hopefulness. "Like this?" He moves behind me and puts his hands on my shoulders. They feel like cinderblocks. *Oh, wow, what was I thinking? This is never gonna work.*

"Hold up." Louis pushes forward, glowing proudly from our demonstration of twosies-flight. "I'll boost you."

Both Michael and I stare at him. Louis is the absolute definition of "shrimp." But he gives us this macho nod, so we look at each other and shrug, and Michael takes a big leap onto my back and I guess Louis kind of boosts his butt and I take my stagger-steps and what do you know...

"WHOOO-HOOO!!!!" my brother whoops, right in my ear. And keeps whooping. Oh, wow. I can still kind of hear it ringing around in there. But it's okay. He hasn't had anything to whoop about for a long time.

"Whoa, do that again!" Michael gasps when I bank sharply for the return. My brother's long arms are actually stabilizing our flight—we're a jumbo jet! It feels so cool I keep rotating in one giant, smooth, spiral. "Sweet," he mumbles, but I know he's talking to himself.

I think we would've stayed up there till dark, rising dreamily like hawks, if some bright movement at the edge of the forest hadn't caught my eye. Then a second glance shows me it's time to land.

"Aw, no way! Stay up, stay up!" Michael urges, but then he sees them too, and swears.

"What?" Louis asks when we scramble up from our landing a minute later. It's not too bad; Michael's only bleeding a little.

"We got company," I say, panting, just like a movie-hero, and that's how I feel: grim. Protective. Of what, I'm not sure yet.

"Let 'em come," Michael says, but his face is all hard now. Louis asks, "Who is it?" sounding scared.

But now we all hear the Mozart-laugh and the low reply, and we both look at Michael, like, *Okay, now what?*

A fire-red blob pops over the crest of the Toad: Savannah's wearing her hat with the pom-poms. Must've been what I saw from the air. "Oh, hey, you guys!" she shrieks when she sees us. "Fancy meeting you here!"

"Dude," Tyler nods at Michael, ignoring the rest of us. It's just the two of them—no Nate. *That's something, anyway.* But here they are, in Louis's and my special place, like it's theirs now. *Well, I've been gone a long time. Maybe it is.*

Or not. A bright spark of anger shoots through my nervous stomach. "Hey, *dude.* You guys come up here to smoke your stupid weed? Better not set the trees on fire."

Four faces jerk my way, but Savannah's is the brightest. She turns red as her hat when she's pissed. "What-*ever*, Joss. What makes you think I'm gonna smoke anything? And who made you the boss of this place?"

"Yeah, run along, little girl," Tyler adds, even though he's only nine months older than me.

The spark flames up. *Don't tell me to run along. I'm the Flying Burgowski, and this is my domain. If I can't fly around the Toad, where can I fly?*

"Don't be an idiot, Joss," Michael says behind me. But I don't care if my best friend hates me forever. I want them off of here.

"You know what, you guys?" I start, but suddenly I realize I have absolutely no point to make; all they've done is climb up here, and nobody's smoking anything, so what can I say? But that's when Tyler helps me out.

"Hey, yo, Michael, what's the deal? You gettin' paid to babysit, man?"

"Shut up, Tyler," says Louis's voice. A little quavery, but definitely Louis.

"Oh, no you *didn't* just tell me to shut up," Tyler says, and he sounds like such a perfect imitation of Crystal from McClenton that I want to laugh. But then he's snarling, "You little fag," and starting for Louis, and the laugh dies.

Savannah grabs at his arm. "C'mon, Ty, he's not worth it," she says, trying to sound superior, but the look she shoots me, oh wow. *We're done*, it says.

"Think you're so hard, don't you," "Ty" continues, ignoring her. "Thought I taught you to keep your mouth shut, but here you are with your ugly-ass girlfriend and suddenly you're a big hero. Okay, guess I'll have to—hey!"

All of this nastiness is aimed at Louis like a careful sighting through a gun, until Michael steps in front of Louis and clamps down on Tyler's arm.

"Dude, what the frick!" (Or words to that effect).

"Cut the crap," my brother responds—again, my translation. "You know what? I'm gettin' tired of you."

"Please let go of my arm," is what Tyler does not say, but I'm sure that's what he means. "Who do you think you are? I thought we were friends." (Hey, I'm getting pretty good at this translation business. Maybe I should re-think the being a cop idea.)

"Yeah, right. Like I'm gonna hang around someone who beats up on perfectly decent human beings just 'cause…" Michael goes on for a while about the various things that are wrong with Tyler's psychology and, for that matter, his anatomy too. We're all just staring at him, and I guess my mouth must be as open as Savannah's and Tyler's. Not Louis, though. His face is white and closed.

"…so here's what I want you to do," Michael finishes. "I want you to apologize to Louis, then I want you to get your sorry ass off this rock and make sure you don't come back here for, I don't know, as long as it takes you to grow up."

And here's the amazing thing—I mean, even more amazing than my brother turning his former smoking-buddy into a bad-guy getting a scolding from Spider-Man: Tyler's actually way tougher than Michael, and both of them know it. If they had really fought, Tyler could've thrown my brother right off the Toad. But something about Michael's face, and his grip, must've told Tyler he was already beaten.

"Sorry," mutters Tyler, and Michael drops his arm like it's something gross, then stands there with his hair falling back over his eyes while Tyler turns and struts back down the slope of the Toad.

And Savannah? *What just happened?* her face says, and I realize I'm thinking the same thing.

"You don't have to go," I tell her. It's even more awkward than it sounds. Savannah looks at me, totally blank, then turns around and walks away, where Tyler has already disappeared down the curve of blotchy granite.

A weird, shuddery noise turns my head: it's Louis, and he's sighing out what looks like about ten years' worth of bad, bad days in one, long sigh.

"Aw, man, don't *cry*," Michael says, frowning. "He totally asked for that, okay? Just don't expect more help any time soon." But he sounds more fake-disgusted than real, like he's pretty proud of himself.

Louis just nods a whole lot.

"Wanna fly again?" I ask; it seems like the best thing right now. Louis nods some more. "Let's just give 'em a couple more minutes to get out of here."

"You kids do that," Michael says—no, this time I'm not translating, he really says that. And smiles. "I don't guess your legs can take any more of me right now, huh, Joss." He turns, my noble white-knight brother, and then totally ruins that image by adding, "But we can go up again later, right? How 'bout if I set the table for you?"

"Deal!" Wow. For that kind of respect, I'll sneak out anytime.

Louis and I wait a few more minutes to make sure Tyler and Savannah are really gone. I don't want to embarrass him by staring, but I've never seen anyone's face flicker through so many emotions in a row. "C'mon," I say finally, stretching out my arms. "Air Joss, Flight Two-Oh-Two, ready for takeoff."

Louis's face settles into a nice, relaxed smile. He clambers onto my back—*oh jeez, my* knees.

But I am the Flying Burgowski, and in a half-second we're airborne and flying like a single creature, like a centaur with wings.

I think it's me who whoops this time.

It's already dark by the time we're done looping around the Toad, so I fly Louis right back to his house! No one can see us. And when I get home, sure enough: Michael's set the table for me.

"Wow," Lorraine says as I breeze into the kitchen. "Did your brother lose a bet or something?"

A wave of irritation sloshes at me, but I brush it back: she's making lasagna, after all. "Yeah, kind of." I'm starving. Doubles-flying uses up double energy, turns out.

"Whatever it was, did it involve that scrape on his hand? Or was that something else?" Lorraine goes on, grating mozzarella.

"Oh. I guess that was something else." It's not technically a lie, and anyway, it's none of her business. "Can I have a piece of noodle?"

She cuts off the end of one and proffers it. "By the way," she says, "I brought some books home for you. They're on the counter. And we'll eat in about an hour, okay?"

"Sounds good," I say, glancing at the pile of books. I really wasn't planning to look at them any time soon; it's not like I don't have other homework, right? But the title of the top book catches my eye: in bright orange, shaky-type letters, it screams, *Which Witch?*

It's a picture book! *Are you kidding me? How old does she think I am, six?*

"Oh, that." Lorraine sees me looking. "I know, it's dumb, but I couldn't help it. I was getting all these books out for our Halloween display, and that one kind of waved at me. D'you remember it? It's one of my old Storytime favorites, so I'll bet I read it to you and your mom once upon a time."

I shake my head, but start leafing through the book in spite of myself. It's about a sassy little witch-girl; the facial expressions are pretty funny.

"Of course you can't use that for your Outside Reading requirement," Lorraine says. "But there are a couple in there…"

Yes, there are. One about the science behind the magic of Harry Potter looks faintly interesting. Then there's a skinny one that looks to be about a girl who doesn't fit in…one about a guy who…let's see…doesn't fit in…*Oh, gimme a break.* I shoot my stepmother a look, but she's busily stirring sauce.

Well, great. Not reading one of these books will just lead to drama; I can see her talking to Dad behind my back: "I try so hard, but she just keeps rejecting me…" *Fine. I'll pick one.* The bottom book is fat and hard-covered: *A History of Witches.*

"Another Halloween book?" I ask, holding it up. It looks as old and leathery as you'd want a book on witches to look.

Lorraine looks over. "Oh, yeah." She sounds sheepish. "I figured the little kids wouldn't go for it, 'cause it doesn't have pictures—well, some old illustrations, but really, it's pretty mature reading." She shrugs. "Honestly, it's just an old book I liked when I was your age. In fact, it used to be mine. In no way will my feelings be hurt if you don't read it, Jocelyn. You'll have to bear with me; I'm still learning what your tastes are. Speaking of which, tell me if this needs more salt." She's holding out a spoonful of sauce.

Here's what I would've thought yesterday: *Jeez, what a suck-up.*

Here's what I think now: *Oh. Thanks. It's great.* So that's what I say out loud.

"I guess I'll give this big fatty a try," I add, hefting *A History of Witches*. I swear, it's not just the homemade food that's making the difference; if it was, I'd have been in love with Lorraine since day one. I think it's the way she told me it was her book, like she was embarrassed but couldn't help herself. And the way she put it on the bottom of the pile.

I have to say, that lasagna was fantastic. I plan on sneaking back to the kitchen before bed for another little bite.

Hey, looks like I'm pretty much done telling my story, huh. This Journal thing is kind of cool, so I might check in now and then if anything new happens with Savannah, or, like, I learn some new flying technique. But things are working so good these days, I don't think I'll need to assign myself any more Reflections for a while, okay?

Cool. Now I'm gonna have a look at that book.

CHAPTER SEVENTEEN

NEVER ASSUME

"Never assume," Mrs. Mac always told us. You'd think I'd re-member.

I thought I was done writing. Oh, I was gonna describe some of the new aerial moves I've learned flying jumbo-jet style, or say what it's like flying in the rain. Maybe mention how Nate passes notes with me almost every day now. And how Savannah and Tyler are officially Dating, even though Dating means pretty much sneaking out to the woods to do whatever. But really, for the first time since I became a Flyer, I was feeling so normal I thought I could give the writing a rest.

Never assume. It makes an ass out of u and me.

Mom tried to kill herself yesterday.

So...now I'm not sure what else to say.

I'll write some more later.

This is going to be one weird Thanksgiving. Lorraine's making sandwiches.

Dad's gone over to McClenton to "be there" for Mom now that she's woken back up. Arnie was the one who found her and called 9-1-1. Good ol' Arnie. I wondered how Mom could've got her pill collection saved up again so fast, after being home for only a week, but Michael said that kind of thing is easy if you really want to. Guess she wanted to.

Or maybe not. Maybe not enough to make sure Arnie would've been too late. I mean, she does live on the fourth floor. She could've just jumped off the balcony, right?

I can't believe I'm even thinking this stuff. Jeez, Mom. I'm *fourteen.*

"You don't want to go flying, do you?" Louis pokes his head into my room. I'm lying on my bed, staring up at my poster of Harry Potter with his wand raised to ward off evil.

"Not today," I mumble. It takes effort to move my lips.

"Yeah, it's raining pretty hard, I guess." Harry Potter's face is streaked with dirty sweat. He's fighting the basilisk. "Yeah."

"Well…see ya, then."

I do hear the rain now. It's really coming down.

"Happy Thanksgiving," Louis adds, leaving.

"Yeah."

A soft but persistent knocking drags me back awake, out of the familiar, McClenton-grey fog of daytime sleep. Then Lorraine's voice: "Joss? Dinner's ready, such as it is."

"I'm not hungry," I croak.

"I know, sweetie. But I really, really think you should eat something. It'll make you feel…"

Huh. Even Lorraine can't make herself say the cheerful lie, *"better."*

"Well, come on out when you're ready," she adds after a pause. "Michael's having a sandwich, so am I. So, if you're up to it… come join us, okay?"

I say, "Okay." Maybe I am a little hungry.

Michael's gone by the time I drag myself off my bed and into the kitchen, but Lorraine's still there; she seems to be re-organizing the silverware drawer. She motions me to the sandwiches without saying a word.

They're turkey. Happy Thanksgiving.

I chew and Lorraine rattles and clinks. I'm almost to the end of my Thanksgiving feast when Lorraine says, "Joss, honey—"

The phone rings. We look at each other.

"You go ahead," I say with my mouth full. I know it's Dad, I know I should want to talk to him. Pump him with questions. I'm just so *tired*.

"H'lo? Hi, dear. Where are you? Oh, thank goodness."

The scene is so clear in my mind: my mother, small and dingy in the bright hospital sheets, her dark eyes huge like a Disney character. She wouldn't be back in the same room, of course, and...oh yeah. Her eyes are probably not open at the moment. Now I see a different picture, a sleeping doll in the light of a streetlamp.

"Well, sure," Lorraine is saying. "We could almost see that coming, couldn't we?...I mean," she adds, "being released all alone? Going home to that empty little apartment, after what she'd just been through?...Oh, no, no, I'm not blaming anybody, who is there to blame? I'm just saying I understand...Yeah. Poor Beth, how's she supposed to feel good about life right now? And at Thanksgiving, of all times..."

Michael was right, I feel like saying. I could grab the phone and yell that to Dad. *He said this would happen. We should have stayed with her.*

"I know. I know." Lorraine repeats this, softer each time. *She's feeling guilty. She's going to apologize for convincing Dad to exile us in the first place.* I'm too tired to revel in the moment.

"It's okay, Ron," my stepmother says, so low I can barely hear. She glances over at me and I see the glitter of tears in her eyes before I look down again. "Don't beat yourself up. You did what you thought was the right thing at the time, you know that..."

What? I look back at Lorraine; her face is blotching a little, but her voice is steady. "Michael did need settling down, you were right. And he has, hasn't he? And if Joss hadn't gone with him, well, who knows how things would have turned out? Your instincts were wonderful, sweetie. You're a wonderful dad."

"D'you mean it was *Dad's* idea to send us to McClenton? But we thought…"

Lorraine's face whips toward me; I must have said it out loud. "I know it seems like everything's crashed and burned, but Ron: this is not your fault," she says to the phone. "It's no one's fault. You tried one way of making things better, and yes, it hasn't worked out so well yet, but sweetie: you did *not* make it worse. Beth is who she is."

Dad sent us to McClenton. He just let us think it was Lorraine. All those phone calls home. All those heavy sighs, all that, *"Well, I wasn't so sure about this idea, guys, but if you're happy…"* And letting us talk him into staying there. No wonder! He must have wanted it all along.

"Joss?" Lorraine is waggling the phone toward me, her hand over the receiver.

No way. No. Way. I shake my head violently and dash for my room, crashing my thigh against the edge of the table. Behind me I hear Lorraine say, "…not up for talking right now, let me get Michael," and then I slam my door, and all I can hear is the rain.

So.
Dad's a liar.
Mom's in trouble.
Michael was right.
That's all I have to go on.

It's after midnight. 12:12, actually. How stupid is this: I can't sleep anymore. Guess I've used it all up. Don't feel like writing either. My stomach hurts, like that sandwich just turned into gravel inside me. Tion came to my door a while back, I could hear her mewing, and I didn't even get up to let her in. How can your mind be so jumpy when your body's a lump of lead?

Is that how Mom's feeling now? I hope she's asleep. I wish I was. Maybe I'll look at that big fat witch book.

Witches get burned at the stake whenever too much bad stuff is happening in the village and people need somebody to blame. They go for whatever woman seems the most different. That's what I'm getting from Lorraine's book, pretty much. Crop failure? Witchcraft. Little babies dying in their cradles? Gotta be witchcraft. Plague? Hey, what else could it be? But nobody ever checks to see whether the bad stuff stops after they've killed the witch.

Turns out people were always keeping their eyes out for witches back then, like those Neighborhood Watch signs they had in McClenton. I just read about this one guy who catches his village witch after staking out her house "bye Sun and bye Moone thirty Dayes." He finally sees her out gathering herbs, and that's all it takes: he testifies in court, she gets hung. Hanged. Whatever. He doesn't even need a video camera!

Huh. Haven't thought about that video for, like, ever. Wonder if that guy was on a stakeout too. Wonder what happened to him and his flying Dalby Ghost. Wonder why we've never heard of it. Maybe people today aren't as nosy as they were back in the 1600s. Whatever.

Great. Now I'm really not going to sleep, ever again. I just read about this one girl who was supposedly seen flying over her village in broad daylight, in 1609. You can probably guess what happened to her. Fourteen years old—or "yeares", as the book says.

So…good thing I wasn't born four hundred years ago. But. Maybe that doesn't matter.

What I mean is…I don't know. I'm so tired, and my head

hurts. But maybe I am, like, you know. Bad luck. I mean, I start flying, and everything falls apart.

I know, I know. Mom was a mess before I became a Flyer. Michael was a jerk. But everyone was puttering along, weren't they? No one was in the hospital. No one was trying to get rid of their kids.

That's stupid. I used my flying to save Mom. Remember? And Air Joss is the best thing that ever happened to Louis. And Michael's not a jerk anymore. He flies with me. He does my chores.

Yeah, and what happens when everything's going so great? When I get all caught up in being a Flyer? Mom tries to kill herself, that's what, and this time I'm not around to save her. It takes Arnie. What are the chances Arnie's gonna be there next time?

Oh, wow, my head aches. But I feel like I'm getting closer to an answer. Whatever the question was.

3:24, the clock says. Maybe I slept a little. My thigh feels tender where I crashed into the table, but my head feels better. Clearer. Like I think I know what I have to do.

Listen: it makes sense. When I fly, it's so cool, and wonderful stuff happens. But that's just a trap. The Flying Burgowski is all about herself. Yeah, she saves her mom, gives her friend rides, makes up with her brother. But the more she gets caught up in her magic, the more she forgets about all the needs around her. Look what happened to Mrs. Mac when I went away. Look how I forgot about Louis. And look at Mom. Most of all, when she needed me, where was I? Zooming around the Toad without a care in the world.

That's what I've figured out. The flying: it's a test. Like Spider-Man: "With great power comes great responsibility." I'm supposed to take care of people. Why else should I get to be so special? But if I just keep on flying around Dalby, like all that magic is nothing but a big old piece of frosted cake for me to stuff myself on, well, then, I flunk the test. And look what happens.

It's time to dump the cake and brush my teeth. I have to go back to McClenton.

Okay, it's thirty minutes later and I haven't changed my mind. The more I think about it, the less my head hurts. That's gotta mean something. If I go back to McClenton High, get the grades I can get if I halfway feel like it, if I quit flying and just focus all my power and all my magic on taking care of Mom—then she really will be fine. And I really will be a superhero.

And if not—not.

Doesn't that suck?

I'll get Lorraine to take me in the morning. Wait, I guess it already is morning. Whatever. If I say I have to see Mom, she'll take me. Me alone, not Michael. And I'll bring all my stuff and hide it in the back of her car, and maybe get someone at the dock to pretend one of my bags is theirs, so Lorraine won't know... I'll take the bus to McClenton like we used to, and when I'm there I'll tell Dad I'm staying. I'll tell him I know that's what he wanted all along, and I'll tell him I can take better care of Mom than anybody. We don't need him. We don't need Lorraine. We don't even need Michael. She's my *mom*, right? They can't make me leave.

Louis will be okay. He's under Michael's protection now, right? And Mrs. Mac is getting better on her own, she doesn't need me like Mom does. And it's not like Nate will really care if I'm gone, it's not like he kept in touch before. I'm pretty sure he's starting to like Greta anyway.

And maybe I can fly, you know, every now and then, in Mc-Clenton. Right off the balcony maybe...

Or not. Remember. Great power, blah blah blah. You said you were going to take care of Mom. Remember what happens when you get all stuck up there in the sky.

Tion wakes me, batting my nose like she does when she's bored. Lorraine must have let her in, not wanting to wake me herself. It's ten thirty, and the morning light in the kitchen is pale and weak as I feel. Good thing it's not a school day. A little wobble of excitement wavers through me—Thanksgiving weekend!—before I remember it all. Oh yeah. Mom. Dad. McClenton.

My decision.

Ferry schedule: that's what I need. When's the afternoon boat? I have to give Lorraine a little notice, after all. Two-thirty? Fine. I'm not letting myself think about it. What I should do next is eat breakfast, but I feel too hard and tight for food. Gonna go pack.

I get all the way to the ferry before Lorraine figures out my plan.

"Goodness, Joss," she says, opening the back of her old Volvo in the drop-off lot, and I realize I'm busted. Damn! I covered my suitcase with a blanket so she wouldn't notice, but as we parked I got distracted. There were these two eagles sailing over the headland by the dock, right over our car, and one of 'em landed in that madrona tree that leans out over the water like a farewell wave, but the other one kept swooping, and it made me think about the feel of the wind on my skin, and the lily-smell, and I forgot, I *forgot* to scramble back there and grab my stuff before Lorraine could see what-all I'm taking to McClenton for what's supposed to be a weekend visit. I was planning to find another passenger to help me with my escape, but that's all shot now.

"Are you bringing Beth some things...?" she goes on when I don't answer.

"Yeah," I say eagerly, but then we both realize what a rotten liar I am. Lorraine looks at me.

"Jocelyn..."

"It's none of your business," I say roughly. "She's going through a really crappy time. Who else is s'posed to take care of her? Dad?"

"Honey." The rest of what Lorraine's planning to say is cut off by a rude horn blast: the boat's here, swinging wide around the headland to aim its fat front at the dock.

I push on. "I can go to school there just fine, okay? I can ride the bus and come home and make dinner for me and Mom. And don't worry about my grades, I'm not gonna skip anymore, I promised, remember?" All the arguments I've worked on through my sleep-free night come pouring out. "And Michael will get all of your attention without me around, and Mom will be super proud of me and she'll want to get better and stay better 'cause she knows I'm really there for *her*, and not just 'cause Dad sent me."

Lorraine winces. "Joss, don't be too hard on your dad for that. It was my idea too."

"Like that even matters now!" I yell. "Like I care which one of you was trying to get rid of us last summer. You're getting what you want, ok? You can all be one big happy family, and I'll go take care of Mom since no one else wants to." I grab my bags and cross the ferry lane to stand beneath the shelter with the other walk-on people. I clench my jaw and watch the boat churning the water white. One of the eagles twitters loudly but I don't look up. The rain starts again.

Lorraine follows. "Joss, I'm not going to stop you. You...may be doing the right thing." The people around us are staring; she drops her voice even lower. "I just want you to be with Beth for the right reasons. That's all I ever wanted."

"Are you kidding me?" I shriek. "'The right reasons?' What— so you can make sure Mom never ever comes back here?"

"No," she gasps. The other walk-ons shrink away from our drama but I don't care.

"So you can make Dad forget he still likes her? So no one will even talk about her anymore?"

"No, no."

"So she'll disappear from—"

"No, Joss! So you can fly together."

"Wh…"

Lorraine clamps her hands over her mouth. Her face is white and her eyes are huge.

CHAPTER EIGHTEEN

AIN'T NO SPIDER-MAN

"*Fly together'?*"

Lorraine nods once, hands still tight across her mouth as if to trap any further secrets. But it's too late.

"My mom? Like me?" She nods again, her face blotching.

"You know. You *knew*. About me. And Mom?" Still the nodding, eyes closed now. The ferry roars and straightens at the dock. The woman in the orange vest starts lowering the ramp. "Why didn't you tell me?" I whisper.

Tears are running down my stepmother's cheeks. She wipes at them. "I thought…the books all say you can destroy a Flyer's power by calling it out in the open. I didn't want to take that chance. And now—oh!" Now it's her eyes she's covering.

"What. What?!"

"What if I have? Messed up your power? Oh Joss, maybe we shouldn't speak of it…"

"Oh, hell yeah, we'll speak of it," I mutter. A whirlwind starts spinning in my chest. Shock and rage and disbelief and wild, wild hope. I grab the edge of the passenger shelter to keep myself grounded. And that's when I see this lady's phone. It's pink, and she's folding it shut while her golden retriever tries to pull them both back into the rain.

"Hey, can I borrow that?" She turns to me in surprise and I

quickly add, "Please? I have to talk to someone, it's an emergency. I don't have a phone."

"Jocelyn," Lorraine bleats, but the lady's saying, "Well, sure you can, just make it quick, we're loading soon, okay?" and I'm grabbing it like a lifeline while the tornado roars inside me.

"What's her number? Mom's? At the hospital? You have it, right?"

"Joss…"

"I swear," I growl, "if you don't give me the number I'm flying to McClenton right now."

Lorraine wipes her eyes again and digs a paper from her purse. I turn my back on her and the dog-lady and huddle in the corner of the shelter. The number goes straight to my mom's hospital room.

"Hello?" So frail. *How could she possibly share my power?*

"Mom. Lorraine says you can fly. Is it true?"

I hear the grind of suitcase wheels on pavement as the arriving passengers walk past. "Oh, babe," my mother sighs.

"IS IT?"

"Yes." Mom's voice sounds as small and skinny as the lady's phone, but there's something else there, some note I've never heard before. "My turn," she says. "Can you?"

Can't talk. Can hardly breathe.

"I knew it," Mom says, and I hear it again. Triumph. "You're a Flyer, Jocelyn. Aren't you." She waits, but I can't answer, even if it were a question. "I knew, dammit. I knew it and I never said…"

I clench the phone like it's an oxygen mask.

"Joss? Where are you, babe? You're not at home, are you?"

"I'm—" My flight-engines are still doing their best to lift me. "I'm at the ferry. Mom. I'm coming out to be with you."

"Oh, babe, that is so—"

"Just to be with you, Mom," I push on. "Not to fly. Not to get all closey-close and share our secret powers together because, huh, no one TOLD me you had 'em too. No one who KNEW all along. And I'm not flying anymore, Mom. I'm done. Everything's totally screwed, and I just want us to be normal again."

"Joss. Listen." The scratches are back in her voice. "Don't get on that boat, babe. Do you hear me? Don't come here yet."

My heart is slowing from its crazy race. Now it's going numb. Cars are snorting their way off the ferry and up the ramp.

"Joss, I know we have to talk, okay? There's so much. Just give me a little time, babe. Give me a day or two to get my sh—to get my stuff together, okay? Then you can come on out here. We'll talk all night if we have to."

It's almost time to board. And still I can't seem to move my mouth.

"Joss? You there, babe?"

I force a croak: "How did you know about me? How did Lorraine know?"

"Oh, Jocelyn," my mom sighs, and that's when the golden-retriever lady clears her throat politely.

"Ah...do you mind, darlin'?"

"Jocelyn," Lorraine and Mom say at the same time. It feels like being lassoed by two different ropes. "Stay there for now," Mom says, and Lorraine, more urgently: "Sweetie—she needs her phone back."

"I'm coming anyway." I snap the phone shut and hold it out blindly. With a kind, troubled face, the lady takes it, and down the ramp she goes, calling "You're so welcome, take care," to Lorraine's thanks.

The rest of the walk-ons shuffle after her, umbrellas bumping. I stand there and watch the rings of the raindrops on the bay.

"What do you want to do?" Lorraine asks.

I swallow for what feels like the first time in a month. "She said stay here."

From the edge of my vision I see Lorraine nod. The rain intensifies, making a layer of grey velvet above the sea. Behind me, the line of cars begins to load. There would still be time to walk on after the last car…but Mom said stay here.

She said a lot of things.

But not enough. She knew the whole time, and she never said anything. She let me go through all that craziness by myself, and she knew. *I flew and I stopped flying and I flew again, and the whole time she could have…we could have…*

"You knew too." I turn to face my stepmother. Lorraine takes a half-step back, shrinking from the curtain of rain at the shelter's edge. "How'd you know? HOW'D YOU KNOW?" I'm roaring now, above the rain and the clank of the loading cars. Lorraine looks stricken. "What's the matter with everybody? Are you guys, like, the secret guardians of some stupid secret cult or something? Am I s'posed to feel so special 'cause I joined your special secret club of magic that you already know everything about?" An even more ferocious thought strikes me: "You've been reading my journal!"

"No, Joss, no." She is horrified, or is that only guilt on her face? "I promise, I never…Look, I'm sorry, I didn't mean to blurt it out like that. I just wanted you to know what the two of you share—"

"We don't share anything!" I scream. "My mother's crazy, haven't you noticed? I'm not like that! I have a plan! Or I did till you screwed it up! You think you're so great and all-knowing, probably been spying on me from the start, just watching all quiet and never saying anything, saving it all up to make me think I'm some sort of screwed-up freak like my mom, like you're gonna make it all better by keeping me here, feeding me stupid books about what happens to girls who can fly…"

It doesn't make any sense and I know it. I might as well be howling random vowel sounds. The tornado's a firestorm now, fueled by fury. *Yes. I'll fly to McClenton. She can't keep me here. I'll have it out with her.* Mom and Lorraine have blended into a tight web of infuriating adults who want to lock me down, and I have to blast out of here.

I dash out of the shelter, but I'm running, not flying, and my feet are carrying me across the ramp of loading cars, not down into the boat. A pickup lurches to avoid me, and then I am racing through the parking lot. Behind me Lorraine shrieks something—*what, she thinks I'm gonna hurl myself into the ocean?* I have no idea where I'm going—away, away, that's all, into the woods where no one's telling me they've always known about my secret powers.

Too bad there's a fence. So instead of a dramatic getaway into the dripping trees, here I am mashed up against a giant chain-link barrier, forced to turn around and face the pale, wet woman who has run across the parking lot behind me.

"Joss," Lorraine pants, and puts her hands out—in apology or appeal, and the hood of her raincoat slides back so the rain starts plastering her frizzy bangs to her forehead.

That kills me, that bright hair so dark and wet and helpless. *The magic's just* there, it says. *It's always been there, and things are still a mess.* My flight-tornado dies, and I sink down against the fence, ready to cry my heart out.

But I don't.

"I can't fix her," I say to the loops of metal in front of my face.

Lorraine doesn't try to raise me off the pavement, she just kind of leans over me like a human shelter, letting the rain drip off her elbows onto my feet.

"It doesn't matter if I sacrifice my power or not, huh. Magic can't fix anything by itself. Magic just *is*. If things're screwed…" I look up at Lorraine. "I gotta just deal with 'em."

"Jocelyn, if I've ruined your power by bringing it out in the open," she closes her eyes, "how will you ever forgive me? I won't forgive myself."

"No, see—it doesn't matter," I say. "If I can fly or not."

"Of course it matters!" Lorraine straightens up and the raindrops hit me in the face. "Look what happened to Beth!"

"I mean," I struggle, "it matters to *me*. If I can't fly anymore, I'll probably explode."

"Joss, that's—"

"But!" I stand up. We are face to face, drenched. "Me flying or not-flying, that doesn't matter to anyone else because I will DEAL with…stuff. Whatever I have to deal with. Me, Jocelyn. Not The Flying Burgowski."

Lorraine wipes away raindrops, or maybe tears. "The Flying Burgowski," she repeats. It's weird to hear someone else say it. "That's you."

"Yeah. But she ain't Spider-Man." Lorraine looks confused, so I mumble, "You know, that whole great-power, great-responsibility thing…" I hug myself, and my sweatshirt feels like a sponge. "Let's go home."

"But aren't you worried about whether you can still…? Do you want to go somewhere and try?"

I can still feel the leftover warmth of that fire-tornado. "I'm not worried," I say. "Just frickin' wet."

The ferry's gone; so is everyone else. We cross the lot and bundle our sopping selves into the Volvo before I remember my bags. Of course they're still sitting there all lonely in the shelter. No one messes with stuff on Dalby.

Off to McClenton to save my mom? And I call her crazy.

As I climb back into the car, a loud twitter filters down. The eagles are still there, right above us. I never heard one call out like that in the rain before.

"Look, let's get ourselves dry," Lorraine says. She pulls the old blanket from the back seat and we towel our heads with it. "We'll talk to Ron, let him know you want to go back to McClenton, at least for a while. He won't be thrilled," she goes on, smoothing her wet hair with a wetter sleeve, "but if Bethany wants you, he won't say no. She'll be able to pick you up in a day or two. So you can get your teachers to give you a couple weeks of home-work. See how things—"

"It's okay," I interrupt. "I'm staying here. Mom will come talk to me when she's ready."

"Come back to Dalby? But what if she doesn't?"

"She will. She just needs time, like she said. I'll wait."

"My goodness," Lorraine breathes, starting the car. "I can't be-lieve how mature you're being about—"

"Yeah, well, good for you," I say, wrapping my freezing hands in the blanket. "Now tell me what the hell you know about flying."

CHAPTER NINETEEN

THE GIFT

So Lorraine starts the car, and her story.

"I'm a librarian, you know. I read, Joss. I read everything. Always have. So, yeah, you could say I've known about Flyers, about flying women, since forever, at least since I was your age." We pull out of the ferry lot and head up the tree-lined hill. "There are so many books, once you know what you're looking for, so many stories…And oh, how I did wish I were one of them. I didn't really believe they existed, of course, not anymore; maybe back in the time of dragons and unicorns, but not today…All the stories were so ancient. I told myself, well, once upon a time, maybe there were these women with special powers, but they got burned as witches, or they drowned themselves, afraid of damnation…"

I hug the blanket around myself and let her words drip into me like a new, warm kind of rain.

"…alive and well in India, I found, and Nepal, and a couple of other places I wandered around, after my first marriage broke up…there were still stories, you know? Not written in any language I could read, but local stories about women with these powers, enough to give me hope that maybe the Flyers hadn't died out so completely after all. I was willing to believe; it made me feel better about going back to Indiana to start my life over. And then I saw one. A real live Flyer. She flew right over my head one night outside this little village in Punjab, and she saw me see her, and she smiled at me…Next day I smelled that sweet scent on her, just like the books said. She wouldn't talk to me, she just nodded and smiled, and I kept her secret, and that was enough! I pulled together what was left of my money and I went on home and became a librarian and moved to Dalby, always knowing I lived in a world where women could still fly, and I kept reading everything I could get my hands on, and I kept my eyes open. I never saw another one. But then I met Bethany."

We round a field full of soggy cows. Back in those dark trees, the Toad crouches, waiting for me.

"When I met Beth she had just moved to the island," Lorraine continues. "She was living with your dad, but she was still pretty wild. Not in a bad way; I mean wary, like a wild animal, you know?" She looks at me, so I nod.

"She had dropped out of college, and she got a couple of part-time jobs in the village, so I saw her around. There was something about her that made me think about that woman in India. The way she smiled, kind of shy and secret…"

"But that's ridiculous!" I burst out. "If you can tell someone can fly just by looking at them, why doesn't everyone know? I didn't even know it about myself, so how could *you* know?"

Lorraine smiles. "Librarian, remember? I've made a study of this, Joss. My whole life, almost. So, yeah, you bet I know the signs, I look for them in every woman I see. A special kind of light in the eyes…and the smell, of course. But I never got very close to Beth, so I wasn't sure enough to, you know…ask. Because, like I said, you don't want to spook Flyers. They're already pretty freaked out about their power; if someone challenges them, it can just… dry up. That's what the books say. And I couldn't do that to Beth, could I?" She bites her lip. "Oh, I wish I knew that I haven't done it to you."

"Michael challenged me, and I still flew," I say firmly.

Lorraine shifts gears, looking relieved. "Maybe you're tougher than Beth. But I'll bet you've had…" she glances at me, "disruptions, haven't you?"

Behind the 7-Eleven…that oily puddle. *Can't fly, won't cry.* My classroom window. *"Disruptions."* "Well, yeah."

"That's what I worried about, for Beth. So I just kept an eye out. Seemed like she and Ron were really happy together. They were such a beautiful couple—oh, you should have seen them at this one community dance. Your mom wore this orangey-gold dress…"

"What about the flying?" I urge, as she seems to be drifting into memory.

"Well. I liked to think she was getting out regularly, probably in the evenings when Ron was out fishing with his dad. I couldn't wait to talk with her about it, someday when she was ready. I could see that Flyer's grace in the way she walked, always glancing up like the sky was pulling her, and she had that lily smell—"

"She *what?*"

Lorraine laughs, the first laughter I've heard in days, feels like. "Oh, of course! You know that smell. The sky, isn't it? That's what the old stories all say. Some just say it smells like flowers, but some are quite specific: lilies. I'm surprised you didn't read about it in that witchy-book. It's what I smelled on you, Joss, the night of your birthday. And when you came in late to Movie Night. The scent lingers…and then you kept getting all those scrapes and bruises."

I'm speechless. At least until we've parked and carried my bags into our kitchen. Then I'm starving. I haven't eaten anything since that stupid turkey sandwich last night.

Lorraine starts making cocoa immediately, like it's a kind of first aid. I bumble into my room, change into dry clothes while she clinks around. Michael is off somewhere, thank goodness. When I come out, the kitchen smells like cinnamon toast. I wolf down three slices while she goes to change, and when she returns, I dive back into my own history.

"So you knew then? About me?"

She nods.

"Why'n't you say anything? Oh. Yeah. It might've…the magic might've…"

She nods again.

"Okay, so I got it from Mom? If that always happens, why aren't there more of us?"

This time she shakes her head. "It doesn't. You're actually pretty rare. I've only read about one other case, in France, of mother-daughter Flyers, and…it's not pretty, what happened to them."

She's right, I saw a picture of it in the "witchy-book." It was gross. "So what happened to Mom? Why'd she quit flying? Why couldn't she tell me? That wouldn't have messed up the magic, would it, one Flyer to another? Why couldn't she have, like, initiated me or whatever?"

Yup, that's the question, all right. I grip my mug hard, concentrating on the warmth.

It takes Lorraine so long to answer that I have myself under control again before she says, "Mmm."

I look at her, really look at her, seeing lines around her eyes I never noticed before. She seems to be making up her mind. I force myself into patience with a sip of cocoa.

"I want to be careful," she says finally. "I don't want to put my ideas into your head before you've had a chance to talk to Beth. You have to remember, Joss, I've never shared what I knew about her. If I had, if I'd let her confide her secret in me, I might have saved her…an awful lot of pain. But I didn't, so…"

She drifts again, and her eyes well up.

"But you couldn't!" I jump in. "You said yourself Flyers are, what—spooky, right? Anything you said to her, you might've screwed up her magic, and that would've been even worse, right?"

"I don't know what would have been worse," Lorraine says miserably. "All I know is, I kept my mouth shut. Your mom tried desperately to be a normal woman, flying when she could and staying in touch with her sky self. And then she got pregnant with Michael, and it all fell apart. And I just sat there and watched."

"What fell apart? The flying? You mean she couldn't fly anymore?" A crazy picture pops into my head: my skinny little mom with a gigantic belly, flailing helplessly a foot above the Toad.

"Oh, she could fly. I still smelled it on her, in those early months. But then I guess she and your dad started having some issues—probably the usual stuff about who's going to do what in the marriage. And that's when your grandfather suddenly died, and all those debts came out, and the bank took the boat and Ron had to start working at the store…"

"But that wasn't Mom's fault!" I kind of yell. "What's all that got to do with it, why couldn't she keep flying even if times were kinda bad? Jeez, seems like that would make her want to fly more than ever!"

Lorraine looks down into her cup, but she's smiling.

"What?" I demand. "What's funny?"

She looks up, eyebrows raised. "Giving up flying in order to fix the ills of the world? I don't know, Joss. I thought you might find that impulse…kind of familiar."

I gape at her. *"I just wanted the two of you to know what you share."*

"So—so…she didn't just lose the power to fly, when she had Michael? She…"

"She gave it up, Joss. On purpose. I watched it happen. I even smelled it, for goodness' sake—that lily smell turned sour on her skin, like, I don't know—like scum on a puddle. She gave up flying, to support your Dad, to try to fix things, to try to be a normal wife and mother. And it almost killed her. It's still killing her."

My hands have strayed, on their own, to the opposite shoulders. I am a statue of a girl hugging herself.

"Why didn't you talk to her?" I whisper.

Lorraine sighs. "I wanted to. Oh, believe me, I wish I had. But when things got bad for them, I saw Beth less and less in town, and when I did she had this tightness about her, like she was barely keeping herself inside her skin, and if I probed even the tiniest bit, she would just fall apart. So I was afraid to say anything. I realized much later that was the medication I was seeing; she was holding herself together with prescriptions, probably, and then, later on, with alcohol, and…well, with whatever worked. And it did work, obviously. She had baby Michael, she carried him everywhere in a little pouch thing, and I convinced myself she'd made her peace and all was well."

"But then…if she was happy again, why couldn't she let herself fly?"

Lorraine shakes her head. "I don't know. I've wondered. Maybe life was going adequately, so she was afraid to mess with it. Beth's never been one to assume the sun will come out tomorrow, you know? Or maybe…"

"She tried," I interrupted. "She must have tried to fly again and she couldn't. She gave it up so long, her power went away." *Of course.* I remember that devastating feeling of loss outside the 7-Eleven, no one to blame but myself.

"Well, perhaps," Lorraine breaks into my confident nodding. "Except—there was one time when she did fly, when Michael was already a toddler. Beth brought him in for his first Storytime at the library, and I smelled the lilies, like before." She smiles again, a sad little flicker. "She must have thought I was nuts, the way I stared at her, but all I could think was, 'Good for you, girl, you found a way!' But that was it. She never flew again after that. I'm sure of it."

"Why?" I wail. I've been there myself, I lost the power and

I got it back, and it's the most precious thing in the world, and I would never, never, never give it up again, not for… *Oh. Yeah.* What did Lorraine say? "*Giving up flying in order to fix the ills of the world.*" My McClenton plan. My packed bags.

"*It almost killed her. It's still killing her.*"

"She found a way to survive," Lorraine says simply. "That's all most of us adults do, you know."

I'm still digesting this ultra-depressing piece of information when my stepmom smiles again. This time it's a real one, all the way through her face.

"But you know what, Joss? That last flight of Beth's, when she brought Michael in to Storytime that morning, it was in September. The Autumnal Equinox, as a matter of fact: September twenty-first, when the sun is halfway—"

"I know what the Autumnal Equinox is," I interrupt. *What's that got to do with flying or not flying or becoming a messed-up, addicted adult?*

"Of 1991," Lorraine says firmly. "Exactly nine months, to the day, before June twenty-first, 1992, otherwise known as Summer Solstice, otherwise known as…"

"My birthday," I breathe. My mom's last flight, before she gave up flying forever.

We look at each other.

"So I think," Lorraine goes on, "that's what did it. Conceiving you and then taking that last, joyous, self-sacrificing flight, well— it's like a sacred thing. In that moment, she made you a Flyer, Joss, I'd bet my life on it. She passed up her gift, but the way she did it, it passed itself right along to you."

I can't think of anything to say. When I finally do, it's the dumbest detail. "How do you know she flew on that exact date?"

"I've *seen* it," Lorraine says.

Was not expecting that. "Huh?"

"The date. And that flight of hers. On film. Someone managed to catch her on camera, and the date was right there…"

"Oh my god, you mean that ghost video? That's real? That's my *mom*?"

Lorraine looks confused. "Wait, you saw it too? But that was about four years ago, it aired on TV, one of those silly local stories around Halloween time. You would only have been about ten… but you remember that?"

"No, it's on the internet! Now, I mean. Michael showed it to me last summer. This guy goes, 'Did you see that? Did you see that?' I watched it a bunch. That was Mom???"

Lorraine says, "Show me."

So we watch it together, the grainy, shaky picture, the whispering, the *step step boom* takeoff. *That's* Mom. *It was Mom the whole time.*

We watch her pale, fuzzy figure over and over as our cocoa gets cold. Finally I ask the obvious question. "If this was filmed back in 1991, how come it didn't get on TV until four years ago? And how come it didn't get on the internet before now?"

Lorraine is quiet, thinking. She's not one of those grown-ups who has to have all the answers. "Well, when they showed it, I remember they said it was sent in anonymously, and they don't usually air that sort of thing, but since it was Halloween…So whoever did it must have waited ten years for some reason."

"And," I pick up where she leaves off, "they didn't have You-Tube back when I was ten, right? So somebody must've just uploaded it this year, like, 'Hey, cool idea, this is better than a TV station.' But who—"

"But why—" Lorraine says at the same time. We laugh. I can't remember the last time I even felt like laughing.

"It was so strange back then," she goes on, "seeing it on TV and realizing nobody but me knew what it meant. I was dying to find out: who could have filmed Beth? Was somebody stalking her? I had a theory, but there was no one to talk to about it. Beth was off the island by then, and I couldn't exactly call her up and ask… Everybody joked about it for a day or two, and then it just went away."

A thought hits me. "Do you think she knew? About being stalked? So maybe that's why she gave up flying, so she wouldn't be, like, exposed. To the media and stuff."

Lorraine gives me a sympathetic look, like she knows what I'm getting at: if Mom gave up flying to protect herself, instead of just to be a better mother, then I don't have anything to feel guilty about.

"You could be right," she nods. "And pretty soon, you can ask her yourself." Lorraine rubs her neck, then heads back to the kitchen to gather our dishes. "I'm not your mother, Joss, so I'm not going to give you any advice on all this. Just—just one small piece, I guess. Whatever her reasons, she gave you her power as a gift. Remember that, okay? Because it turned out to be a pretty precious one. Don't waste it."

CHAPTER TWENTY

ALL I WANT FOR CHRISTMAS

Who knew a cat made such a great housewarming gift?

Okay, let me explain: Mom moved back to Dalby two weeks ago. Yup—all on her own. She and Dad and Lorraine talked, and decided she could move into Lorraine's old place. The Human Bean Café was advertising for help, and a real job with benefits would open up eventually.

Mom was kind of— what's that new vocab. word Mr. Evans just gave us?—"apprehensive" about moving into Lorraine's hand-me-down house, although in my opinion that's no weirder than a hand-me-down husband. But when Michael and I brought Tion over and she curled up on the couch like she owned it, purring like crazy, that was it. Tion lives with Mom now, which gives us an excuse to stop by after school.

"How's my girl?" Michael sings as he walks in. The first time he did it I saw Mom's eyes narrow dangerously, like she believed her son was saying that to *her*, and I thought, *Uh-oh*. But then she saw Michael kissing noses with our cat, and her face pinked up for a second. "Hey, Tion, ask him how he did on his Physics test, why doncha?" she said, and I guess that set the pattern. People talk about what they can talk about.

But yeah, Mom and I talked for real the first day she came home.

The morning after that crazy, rainy day when Lorraine pulled my magic out from its hiding place, I woke up from the world's heaviest sleep. Something was different.

Mom's a Flyer! The thought sat me straight up in bed. I didn't dream it!

"We have to talk."

It about killed me to wait. It took TWO DAYS for Mom to check out of the hospital and get everything squared away with her employer. I wanted to call every second, but I remembered what Lorraine said about her being "wary, like a wild animal." I took myself for my longest flight ever, around the whole island, solo, just to distract myself. And to let my power vibrate freely through every inch of my lily-scented body. *How could I ever give this up? How could anyone?*

And when Dad and Mom finally arrived from the ferry late at night, there was no time or place to talk anyway.

I almost gasped when Mom took off her coat, she was so thin. I kept my mouth shut, though, and she hugged me hard enough I felt a little reassured.

And shy. This was, after all, a whole new person I was hugging. The Flying Burgowski Mother.

Wow. That's the first time I've written that.

I guess she felt a little shy too. Except for, "Hey, kiddo," she didn't say anything to me. Then we were all unloading her boxes and chatting about neutral stuff: Wasn't it nice that the rain had stopped? Didn't the wood stove feel cozy? I felt her eyes on me every time we passed each other going in or out of the house, but our glances bounced apart like wrong-way magnets.

"Okay, troops, time to let this poor woman get some rest," Dad said when the last box had been carried in, and this is how weirded out I was: I turned to go without a backward look.

It took my pale, peeled-down mom to say, "Wait." Everyone looked at her.

"Ron, Michael, Lorraine—you guys go ahead. You guys are awesome, thanks for moving me. But I gotta talk to this kid here." She meant me.

Finally, finally, my mom and I were going to talk: Flyer to Flyer.

"I let him think I was a nut case," were the first words out of Mom's mouth as the door shut on the rest of my family.

I must have looked as stupid as I felt.

"Ron," Mom explained. "Your father. My ex. That's what you want to know, isn't it? How I handled the flying thing with him? Easy. I just became emotionally fragile. *That* he understood."

"Wh…" Out of all the possible questions, my brain chose: "Why?"

"Oh, babe." Mom put her hand on my shoulder and sort of scooped me toward the couch, plunking us both in a pool of warmth and light. "Where to start. Ohhh-kay. I was about your age when I learned about flying, and I had to keep it a secret, of course—"

"How'd you find out?" I asked eagerly. "Did you dream about it first? I did, tons of times! And it wasn't until I actually flew that I figured out how long I'd been kinda preparing myself by dreaming…"

I petered out like you always do when someone just looks at you with their eyebrows up. "Sorry for interrupting," I muttered.

"Oh!" Mom gave a startled little laugh. "I'm not offended, Joss. I'm just realizing how much—." She stopped so abruptly I had only time to think, *Huh?* before I saw how she had clamped her mouth into a tight line. And clenched her fist underneath her chin like a chair against a door. And squeezed her eyes shut. My mom was struggling not to cry.

That might not sound like much, but listen: she never has. Not that I've ever seen. Snarl, barf, pass out—yeah. Not cry. My own stomach fluttered, in fear or sympathy, and I looked politely at my lap.

But Mom won the struggle. "Sorry," she sighed after a moment. "It just hit me all of a sudden how much make-up work I have to do. *Get* to do," she added, and a real smile blazed out. "So okay. Where was I?"

"Starting to fly," I murmured.

"Yep. Thirteen, a little earlier than you. Just getting my period, for whatever that's worth. Don't know if there's some kind of connection there, between flying and maturity—"

"Oh, there is," I put in. "In that book Lorraine gave me, it talked about it, how the witches always needed to fly when their 'Wymen's Sycknesse Came Upon Them.' But it wasn't like that for me; I think maybe the stress just brought the magic out. It tends to do that."

"Witches, huh?" Mom smiled. "So Lorraine gave you a book? Figures. That is one smart woman, Joss. I think she must've always known about me."

"Yeah, she...yeah." Lorraine could fill Mom in about that later, I decided, and motioned Mom to keep going.

"Anyhow, I kept it to myself. My mom would've freaked out and sent me to military school if I'd said I could fly. Oh, I can tell you some stories—and I will, babe. There'll be time. But it's late now, so I just wanted you to know the basics. I was a happy little secret Flyer, all through middle school and high school. There's plenty of places to fly where I grew up: up and down the river, over all that forest, right? I even flew around the sawmill where Dad used to work—later, after it closed down."

The old story popped into my head: Mom's dad, killed in a sawmill accident when she was twelve and a half. So maybe stress caused her magic to come out too.

"Did..." *So many questions!* "Didn't you tell *anybody*?"

"Of course not!" She frowned. "You can't tell, especially at the beginning. It might make you...Well, hell, Joss, you should know about this."

I felt myself teetering. *I have to tell her, she has to find out she was wrong.* But how would that feel, twenty-three years later, to learn that your twenty-three years of silence were stupid and unnecessary?

"How do you know you're not allowed to tell?" I said it real quietly.

"You just know," Mom said defiantly, but her eyes were getting jumpy. "Plus, you've read Lorraine's stuff, right, I'll bet the books all say it's secret magic, can't be shared or dire things happen... right?"

I nodded, because that's exactly what the book says: "Ye Witches' power do fleete before those who do Stande and wytness it." Lucky for me I read it too late. So what if I broke some kind of ancient rule by telling? I was still a "happy little Flyer," and Mom was a wreck.

She had to know. I stopped nodding and looked right in her big, sad eyes. "I told, Mom."

"Who, Lorraine? That doesn't count. She knew anyway."

"No. I told Louis. Well, first I told Michael, I told him right away..." *Oh, shoot.* She was staring a hole in me. "He—he didn't believe me," I added. "He was a real jerk about it, and everything got awful for a while after that, so maybe I did, you know, mess things up for myself, but I didn't stop flying, at least not right away, and then Michael did finally believe me because I...because on the night that you..."

Shoot, shoot, shoot. Why am I such an idiot? Here I am bringing up the worst night of her life... Keep going, Joss, I thought bitterly, *and you'll send her right back to McClenton.*

Mom kept staring. I swear I could see the thoughts scurrying around behind the curtain of her expression. I concentrated on a stain in the rug by my foot. Maybe coffee.

I have no idea how long we sat there like that.

What she finally said was, "Ohhh-kay."

Then she said: "Michael, huh? So that time when we were having chicken, when he was yanking your chain…you'd already told him."

I nodded.

"And Louis? Two boys. You told two boys."

This was it. Her own history was sinking in. I didn't dare look up.

"And you kept flying."

I nodded again.

"You can still fly."

That one sounded a little like a question. She had to know. I took a deep breath. "We fly doubles," I said faintly. She made a little sound in her throat like she was trapping something, so I kept going. "Really, Mom. It's so cool. Louis figured out how, and it's the coolest thing, take-offs are the worst, but then you get up there and it's like twice the power when you bank the turns, y'know? And it's a whole extra set of eyes too, like last time Michael spotted this fox that I totally would've missed if it'd been just me alone…"

I finally peeled my eyes off that stain and looked up, because Mom was laughing, so I laughed too, out of pure relief. And then I stopped, because she seemed to be choking.

What an idiot. This time she was crying for real.

And she kept talking right through the tears, like a person who's forgotten their umbrella, but figures, *Oh well.*

"Sorry, babe," she smiled all crookedy. "I've been doing this a lot lately and you know what, I think I'm starting to like it, so you might as well get used to it, okay? I just…I never thought about it that way, Joss. You do miss stuff when it's just you alone. I've been doing it my whole life."

"You couldn't help it," I said desperately. I wanted to put my arms around her but I was afraid. *What if she pushes me away now?*

"No, I couldn't," she sighed. "I never could. Talk about irony, huh? Here I am trying to play by the rules, be a good girl and wife and mother and keep the crazy magic to myself, and all it does is send me to the loony bin…when all along I could've just done what you did without even thinking about it. Share. Share the magic. That's all you did, and it hasn't gone away from you. You're stronger than ever."

She cried for a while, and I sat there, slowly unclenching. I was just thinking of maybe patting her arm when she took a deep breath that wasn't the least bit shivery, in spite of all the crying.

"Ohhh-kay," she finally said again, wiping her eyes with her sleeve. "Well. Joke's on me, huh?"

"Mmm," I said. *Which Mom will emerge from the tears?* This was new territory.

"So. Like daughter, like mother, maybe. If sharing worked for you, then…I'll try it. With Michael, and—with Ron. Wow. You have no idea," she gulped and sighed, sounding a little more like a more normal crying-person, "how good that sounds."

Suddenly Tion hopped into Mom's lap and reached to put her paws on Mom's shoulder.

"She likes to lie on your neck when you cry," I explained. "I call it Cat Therapy. But, Mom… about Dad? I haven't actually told him yet."

"Well, good," Mom said, leaning back to make a stairway for Tion. "We'll give him one big shock instead of two. Then maybe he won't need as much Cat Therapy."

Seeing Tion take charge like that must have made me bolder, because I hadn't planned to bring this up right away, but…*what the heck. Time to ask about that video.* "So, Mom? Wasn't part of giving up flying because, like, you knew someone was onto you?"

"What're you talking about?" she asked sleepily.

"You know, that flying video. The one we emailed to you last summer? That was you, right?"

"Oh. That." She opened her eyes, closed them again. "I'm

sorry, babe. I don't remember too well. I think it hit me pretty hard, seeing that out of the blue. All those memories. Guess I didn't react too well." She reached up to rub Tion's ear.

"No, I don't mean that." *Not a good time to bring up that drunken phone call.* "I'm sorry too; we were dumb to send it. But what I meant was: did you know? That someone filmed you? Did you quit because you didn't want them to expose you?" *Wouldn't that be a good reason, one neither of us has to feel bad about?*

"Nope, had no idea," Mom said, busting my bubble. "But I wasn't surprised someone got me on film. I was pretty reckless, even when I told myself I was being careful. There was this one time when I was about Michael's age…"

So we spent the night on her couch, two of us yawning our heads off, one purring. Trading flight stories, near misses, amazing sights captured from above. Mom was almost struck by lightning once; another time she'd caught her math teacher making out with the principal. Her stories were way better than mine, and of course she had a lot more of them. But she laughed like crazy about Nate calling me a frickin' condor.

As the night wore on, I got sleepier and fuzzier. About the last thing I remember asking is, "Hey, Mom? When you cry, how do you keep from getting all hiccuppy?"

She laughed so long Tion finally got tired of the vibration and climbed off her neck. "Wha's so funny?" I mumbled.

"You are," my mom said. "It's nice to know I have *some* wisdom to pass on to my daughter, instead of all the other way around."

So why didn't I ask her if she'd tried to fly since I was born? That's easy. You don't ask what you don't want to know.

But I can't help it. I'm turning into a ridiculous optimist. Mom came home, didn't she? She's off pills now, lets herself cry, does Cat Therapy and laughs about it. She even signed up for classes in Accounting over at Islands Community College. No matter what devastating flight failures she might have suffered, no matter how shriveled-up her unused powers, I *know* the magic is still in her. It has to be. She *has* to try again. With her flying daughter at her side.

Or not. This is my mom we're talking about.

Oh, she told Dad and Michael, just like she said. Two days after moving here, she dropped it casually on the table with the salad she'd brought over for our shared dinner.

"So you guys probably know by now that you have two flying witches in this family, right?"

When he got it, Michael said, "Whoa, how cool is that? I'm a son of a witch!"

When Dad got it, he said nothing. He said it for a long time. Can you blame the guy?

It took Lorraine to lay it all out for him. Mom wasn't much help. I guess since she'd decided to Share the Magic, she figured Dad would leap right in there with her and go, "Okay, sure, I get it, I was married to a magic lady for nine years, hmm, no wonder we had some problems, and now my daughter's magic too. Cool. Pass the salt, please." Mom's never been real patient.

Lorraine started at the beginning—after she got Dad to quit interrupting with things like, "So that time when you…" She explained about Flyers, how they float through the generations like dandelion seeds, occasionally sprouting and growing up in perfectly normal families and towns and freaking everybody out if they get discovered. How they're always female, though nobody knows why, but then nobody really *knows* anything about any of it, since no Flyer's crazy enough to offer herself to a science lab for experiments. She told her own story, about the Flyer in India, and all her research, and she reminded Dad about how hard his young wife had worked, after he settled her on Dalby, to fit in, to care for her new husband and baby Michael and still find time to steal into the sky sometimes when everyone was asleep.

"You said it was insomnia, Beth," Dad mumbled, in the funny, subdued voice he'd been using ever since Mom set her salad and our history down in front of him.

"Well, what was I supposed to say?"

"You could have told me."

"No, she couldn't, Ron," Lorraine said earnestly. "At least she thought she couldn't. Beth was right to think so; no one ever did, apparently, not for centuries, not without paying some terrible consequences."

"Until me!" Kind of immature, I know, but I was feeling pretty damn triumphant. Who wouldn't, with her dad looking stupefied, her brother bragging about her landing skills, and her stepmom providing historical commentary that makes her sound like the star of a documentary?

It was a long dinner. The enchiladas got cold. But by the end of it, when everyone was hoarse from remembering and exclaiming and asking questions and exclaiming again, three amazing things happened.

Number One: Mom apologized to me and Michael, for "trying so hard not to be a nut case, I became a nut case."

Number Two: Dad apologized to me for "not being the kind of guy you could talk to... apparently."

Number Three: Mom and Dad apologized to each other. That came awfully close to being mushy.

But still. Mom won't try to fly with me.

We got everybody out to the Toad for a little demonstration a few days after the big Explanation Dinner. You'd think any parent of a kid that can fly would want to rush right out there and see it, right? But Dad dragged his feet, and Lorraine didn't push him. "Part of him still doesn't want to believe it," she explained to me. "That's a lot of years he has to re-think."

Mom cried again when she saw me fly doubles with Michael. But that's nothing compared to Dad. He turned white and sat down on the wet moss so fast I think he kind of fainted there for a minute. Lorraine held onto his shoulders, but she kept looking up as we wheeled above them, and her face just shone. I saw her mouth move, but whether she was talking to Dad or herself, I couldn't tell, because Michael was whooping in my ear.

When we all watched the Dalby Ghost video together, Dad said, "Jesus Christ." Over and over. Poor old Dad—I guess it is pretty freaky for him. Lorraine and Michael and I got into a great discussion about whether the video-guy still lived on the island, and what we'd do if a picture of *me* turned up on the internet. That woke Dad up: he said in his best Dad-voice, "That is NOT going to happen," and made me promise to be careful about where I fly.

I was a good girl and promised sincerely. And later that night, when I saw Dad playing that video over and over by himself in the living room, I was glad I had. He still looked kind of pale.

"Give it a rest, babe," Mom finally said last week, as we lugged a little Christmas tree two whole miles from the tree farm to her house. I'd wondered out loud if maybe we could use our awesome flying powers to carry the tree between us in the air and save ourselves a lot of time. "I'm all done with that. Don't you think I'd know if I still had the power? It's been fifteen years!"

"It can always come back," I muttered, but she looked away and announced firmly she was thinking of cooking lamb for Christmas Eve. So I let myself be distracted by the idea of Mom really cooking. I like this new happy Mom so much, I don't want to mess things up by making her mad.

Or, if she truly can't fly anymore, making her something much worse.

"So, you gonna tell Savannah?" Louis asks in my ear. We're on our longest doubles flight yet, way out over Whittier's Bluff, where a gentle slope of trees drops suddenly off this crazy cliff, down to a miniature bay. It's so fun to swoop over the edge, pretending you don't know what's coming—Louis and I are on our third swoop.

"Hell no."

Behind my head I can feel Louis smiling. The sun's out for the first time in weeks, feels like, and we're taking advantage. One more day till Christmas Break!

He has to give me a little test, though. "Thought she was your best friend."

"Maybe she is," I say cautiously. Who ever knows anything about anybody? I mean, look at Dad! He still goes around these days shaking his head like it's one of those little plastic puzzles where you try to make the tiny balls fit in the holes. "I mean, yeah, she probably will be. But these days she's kind of..."

"Yeah," Louis says, politely not bringing up how Savannah walked past us both after school today like we weren't there, whispering something into Tyler the Gangsta Jerk's ear.

Whoosh! Over the edge. Some of the rocks are streaked white from bird poop, and from up here, in the sun, it looks like silver. That makes me smile, because it reminds me of something Mom said yesterday when I was helping her chop up nuts for this cake she'd decided to make—yeah, cake! My mom!—"Yup, guess it's true that poop makes good fertilizer," except she didn't say "poop." She was talking about her life.

"Yaaahhh!" Louis and I yell, kind of quietly, because even though the beach is deserted, there is a boat not far out in the bay—but you have to yell for swoops like that. Then a fast, jumbo-jet turn, skimming the giant rocks at the bottom. I could do this all day.

"Mrs. Mac took her hat off today," Louis chirps in my ear.

"She made it kind of a ceremony, like, look how far I've come, you know?"

"What did her head look like?"

"Kinda patchy. But nobody laughed. Erin goes, 'That rocks, Mrs. Mac, I'm gettin' mine like that.' It was pretty cool." It must have been. I'll bet Mrs. Mac gave Erin one of her eyebrow-smiles. Boy, I wish she taught ninth grade. Mr. Evans's eyebrows don't smile.

Back up we go, past a tough little madrona that's planted itself ridiculously halfway up the cliff. It still has some red berries on it, like a Christmas tree.

Louis says, "Hey, Nate calls me 'Red' now."

"Really? How come?"

"Duh, Joss, 'cause of my hair."

"No, I mean—that's kind of a nice nickname, right? I mean it's better than…"

"Yeah," Louis says. "I guess he thinks I'm cool now, or some-thing. 'Cause you are," he adds, simply. I wonder if he can feel me blushing.

For some reason I feel like changing the subject. "Whaddya want for Christmas?" I ask as we go rocketing back over the firs at the top.

"Oh, I already know, my mom told me she's getting me this astrology book," Louis goes, and I'm thinking, *Oh, boy,* till he adds, "so I can, like, tell everybody's fortune and stuff. Pretty cool, huh?" Talk about making fertilizer from poop! "She's giving it to me tomorrow, though," he goes on, "not for Christmas. For Solstice."

"Solstice?" We bank into another turn.

"Yeah, you know. Winter."

"Oh, yeah!" I forgot there was a winter one. "To celebrate… what does it celebrate? Same as the one in June? Same as my birthday?"

"Hope, I think," Louis says. "You know…light in the middle of darkness. Things getting better. You know."

I do know. Here goes Swoop Number Four.

"Happy half-birthday," Mom says when I stop by after school next day. She never used to remember stuff like that. It's a half-day release for Winter Break, so we're going to have lunch together, and celebrate her news: she got the job at The Human Bean, so she can drink mocha lattes all day long and still make money.

"Thanks," I say around the humongous meatloaf sandwich she's made me. Homemade meatloaf from Mom! "Four more dave till Christmush!"

"True," Mom nods. "S'pose it's a little late for me to ask you what you want, huh. Not that I think you're expecting much… trained you pretty well that way, haven't I?" She smiles sadly.

I shrug and use my sandwich as a way not to have to answer. Then I realize she actually wants to know something.

"A prev—" I swallow an enormous chunk, "a present?"

"It's what people usually do at Christmas."

"Duh, Mom. I'm just thinking…" and I am. Usually I have a long list of stuff in my head. But now I can't think of anything, at least until J.K. Rowling gets off her butt and finishes the last Harry Potter book.

"How about a cape?" Mom asks. "You know, made of satin or something, with a big FB on it—"

"Mommm!" But I don't really mind her teasing me about my Name, which I told her about last week. She kept saying it randomly all afternoon, and smiling.

I watch her chewing on her own sandwich. She's gained a bunch of weight in the past month. *Happy, healthy, confident Mom…*

"Actually, I do know what I want."

She looks at me expectantly. I look back.

"Ohhh…" She gets it. She shakes her head. But she's smiling.

"Please, Mom? Just a try? It's Solstice, you know. That's when I got my power. It *has* to work on Solstice."

Mom glances out the window. "It's raining, Joss."

"It's funner in the rain! Really! It feels like tickles!" She laughs.

"The sky and the ocean kind of blend together, it's the coolest feeling, you know, like you're swimming in the air…"

"Yes," Mom says quietly. "I do know."

"And the seagulls are *so* surprised when you zoom by, like they think no one else is crazy enough to be out in the rain, and if you swoop real low you can hear it hissing off the—"

"Okay," she says.

"Okay?" What an idiot. I'm actually confused for a second. "Oh! Really?"

"Really. Right now. Before I lose my nerve. Let's go." She's up and bustling through the little kitchen before I can close my mouth. "Now where did I put my raincoat…? Oh. Hah! Who cares! The Flying Burgowski Mother scorns raincoats. Come on, girl. Let's go greet the elements."

As she charges out the door ahead of me, I have to say she looks pretty terrified. For all I know she's going to back out when we get up to the Toad, my special, magic launch pad. She might freeze up. She might cry. She might even try to fly and fall flat on her butt in the soggy moss.

But she's going to try. And I'm going to be there to help, no matter how many tries it takes. She'll get back in the sky, I know she will. It's our habitat.

The door slams behind me, and I go racing after her into the rain.

THE END

ABOUT THE AUTHOR

Gretchen K. Wing always wished to fly unaided, but since the magic never visited her, she learned to fly on paper instead. After twenty years of teaching teenagers, she now devotes her time to writing and professional baking. She misses the kids, but grading essays…not so much. *The Flying Burgowski*, Book One of the Flying Burgowski trilogy, is her first novel.

Made in the USA
San Bernardino, CA
11 February 2015